GEORGES SIMENON

THE HANGED MAN OF SAINT-PHOLIEN

&

THE CARTER OF *LA PROVIDENCE*

Complete and Unabridged

ULVERSCROFT
Leicester

The Hanged Man of Saint-Pholien first published in French as le Pendu de Saint-Pholien by Fayard in 1931

This translation first published in Great Britain in 2014

The Carter of La Providence first published in French as Le Charretier de la Providence by Fayard in 1931

This translation first published in Great Britain in 2014

This Ulverscroft Edition published 2019
by arrangement with
Penguin Random House UK
London

A catalogue record for this book is available
from the British Library.

ISBN 978–1–4448–4298–2

Published by
F. A. Thorpe (Publishing)
Anstey, Leicestershire

Set by Words & Graphics Ltd.
Anstey, Leicestershire
Printed and bound in Great Britain by
T. J. International Ltd., Padstow, Cornwall

This book is printed on acid-free paper

Contents

The Hanged Man
of Saint-Pholien

Translated by
LINDA COVERDALE

1

The Crime of Inspector Maigret

No one noticed what was happening. No one suspected that something serious was taking place in the small station's waiting room, where only six passengers sat dejectedly among odours of coffee, beer and lemonade.

It was five in the afternoon, and night was falling. The lamps had been lighted, but through the windows one could still see both German and Dutch railway and customs officials pacing along the platform, stamping their feet for warmth in the grey dusk.

For Gare de Neuschanz is at the northern tip of Holland, on the German border.

A railway station of no importance. Neuschanz is barely a village. It isn't on any main railway line. A few trains come through mostly in the morning and evening, carrying German workers attracted by the high wages paid in Dutch factories.

And the same ceremony is performed every time: the German train stops at one end of the platform; the Dutch train waits at the other end. The train staff in orange caps and the ones wearing the dull green or Prussian blue uniforms get together to pass the time during the hour allotted for customs formalities.

As there are only twenty or so passengers per

train, mostly regular commuters on a first-name basis with the customs men, such formalities do not take long.

The passengers go and sit in the station restaurant, which resembles all those found at international borders. The prices are marked in *cents* and *Pfennige*. A display case contains Dutch chocolate and German cigarettes. Gin and schnapps are served.

That evening, the place felt stuffy. A woman dozed at the cash register. Steam was shooting from the coffee percolator. Through the open kitchen door came the whistling of a wireless as a boy fiddled with its knobs.

A cosy scene, and yet a few small things were enough to insinuate an uneasy sense of mystery and adventure into the atmosphere: the two different national uniforms, for example, and the posters, some advertising German winter sports, others a trade fair in Utrecht.

Off in a corner was a man of about thirty, his face wan and stubbled, in threadbare clothing and a soft felt hat of some vague grey, someone who might well have drifted all around Europe.

He had arrived on the Holland train. When he had produced a ticket for Bremen, the conductor had explained in German that he had chosen a roundabout route without any express trains.

The man had indicated that he did not understand. He had ordered coffee, in French, and everyone had considered him with curiosity.

His eyes were feverish, too deeply sunk in their orbits. He smoked with his cigarette stuck to his lower lip, a small detail that spoke volumes about

4

his weariness or indifference.

At his feet was a small suitcase of the kind sold in any cheap store, made of cardboard treated to look like leather. It was new.

When his coffee arrived, he pulled a handful of loose change from his pocket: French and Belgian tokens, some tiny silver Dutch coins.

The waitress had to select the correct amount herself.

People paid less attention to a traveller sitting at the neighbouring table, a tall, heavy fellow, broad in the shoulders. He wore a thick black overcoat with a velvet collar and a celluloid protector cradled the knot of his necktie.

The first man kept anxiously watching the railway employees through the glass door, as if he feared missing a train.

The second man studied him, calmly, almost implacably, puffing on his pipe.

The nervous traveller left his seat for two minutes to go to the toilet. Without even leaning down, simply by moving a foot, the other man then drew the small suitcase towards him and replaced it with one exactly like it.

Thirty minutes later, the train left. The two men took seats in the same third-class compartment, but without speaking to each other.

At Leer, the other passengers left the train, which still continued along its way for the two remaining travellers.

At ten o'clock it pulled in beneath the monumental glass roof of Bremen Station, where the arc-lamps made everyone's face look deathly pale.

The first traveller must not have known a word of German, because he headed several times in the wrong direction, went into the first-class restaurant and managed only after much coming and going to find the third-class buffet, where he did not sit down. Pointing at some sausages in bread rolls, he gestured to explain that he wished to take them with him and once again paid by holding out a handful of coins.

Carrying his small suitcase, he wandered for more than half an hour through the wide streets near the station, as if he were looking for something.

And when the man with the velvet collar, who was following him patiently, saw him finally turn left and walk quickly into a poorer neighbourhood, he understood that the fellow had simply been seeking an inexpensive hotel.

The younger man's pace was slowing down, and he examined several such establishments suspiciously before choosing a seedy-looking one with a large white globe of frosted glass over the front door.

He was still carrying his suitcase in one hand and his little sausages in bread rolls wrapped in tissue paper in the other.

The street was bustling. Fog began to drift in, dimming the light from the shop windows.

The man with the heavy overcoat finally managed to obtain the room next to that of the first traveller.

A poor room, like all the other poor rooms in

the world, except, perhaps, that poverty is nowhere more dispiriting than in northern Germany.

But there was a communicating door between the two rooms, a door with a keyhole.

The second man was thus able to witness the opening of the suitcase, which turned out to contain only old newspapers.

He saw the other fellow turn so white that it was painful to witness, saw him turn the suitcase over and over in his trembling hands, scattering the newspapers around the room.

The rolls and sausages sat on the table, still in their wrapping, but the young man, who had not eaten since four that afternoon, never even gave them a glance.

He rushed back to the station, losing his way, asking for directions ten times, blurting out over and over in such a strong accent that he could barely be understood: '*Bahnhof?*'

He was so upset that, to make himself better understood, he imitated the sound of a train!

He reached the station. He wandered in the vast hall, spotted a pile of luggage somewhere and stole up to it like a thief to make sure that his suitcase wasn't there.

And he gave a start whenever someone went by with the same kind of suitcase.

The second man followed him everywhere, keeping a sombre eye on him.

Not until midnight, one following the other, did they return to the hotel.

The keyhole framed the scene: the young man collapsed in a chair, his head in his hands. When he stood up, he snapped his fingers as if both enraged and overcome by his fate.

And that was the end. He pulled a revolver from his pocket, opened his mouth as wide as he could and pressed the trigger.

A moment later there were ten people in the room, although Detective Chief Inspector Maigret, still in his overcoat with its velvet collar, was attempting to keep them out. *Polizei*, they kept saying, and *Mörder*.

The young man was even more pitiful dead than alive. The soles of his shoes had holes in them, and one leg of his trousers had been pushed up by his fall, revealing an incongruously red sock on a pale, hairy shin.

A policeman arrived and with a few imperious words sent the crowd out on to the landing, except for Maigret, who produced his detective chief inspector's badge of the Police Judiciaire in Paris.

The officer did not speak French. Maigret could venture only a few words of German.

Within ten minutes, a car pulled up outside the hotel, and some officials in civilian clothes rushed in.

Out on the landing, the onlookers now discussed the *Franzose* instead of the *Polizei* and watched the inspector with interest. As if snapping off a light, however, a few orders put an end to their excited speculation, and they returned to their rooms. Down in the street, a silent group of bystanders kept a respectful distance.

Inspector Maigret still clenched his pipe

between his teeth, but it had gone out. And his fleshy face, which seemed punched out of dense clay by strong thumbs, bore an expression bordering on fear or disaster.

'I would like permission to conduct my own inquiry while you are conducting yours,' he announced. 'One thing is certain: this man committed suicide. He is a Frenchman.'

'You were following him?'

'It would take too long to explain. I would like your technicians to photograph him from all angles and with as much clarity of detail as possible.'

Commotion had given way to silence in the hotel room; only Maigret and two policemen were left.

One of the Germans, a fresh-faced young man with a shaved head, wore a morning coat and striped trousers. His official title was something like 'doctor of forensic science', and every now and then he wiped the lenses of his gold-rimmed spectacles.

The other man, equally rosy but less formal in his attire, was rummaging around everywhere and making an effort to speak French.

They found nothing except a passport in the name of Louis Jeunet, mechanic, born in Aubervilliers. As for the revolver, it carried the mark of a firearms manufacturer in Herstal, Belgium.

That night, back at the headquarters of the Police Judiciaire on Quai des Orfèvres, no one would have pictured Maigret, silent and seemingly crushed by the turn of events,

9

watching his German colleagues work, keeping out of the way of the photographers and forensic pathologists, waiting with stubborn concern, his pipe still out, for the pathetic harvest handed over to him at around three in the morning: the dead man's clothes, his passport and a dozen photos taken by magnesium flashlights to hallucinatory effect.

Maigret was not far from — indeed quite close to — thinking that he had just killed a man.

A man he didn't know! He knew nothing about him! There was no proof whatsoever that he was wanted by the law!

★   ★   ★

It had all begun the previous day in Brussels, in the most unexpected way. Maigret happened to have been sent there to confer with the Belgian police about some Italian refugees who had been expelled from France and whose activities were now cause for concern.

An assignment that had seemed like a pleasure trip! The meetings had taken less time than anticipated, leaving the inspector a few hours to himself.

And simple curiosity had led him to step inside a small café in Rue Montagne aux Herbes Potagères.

It was ten in the morning; the café was practically deserted. While the jovial proprietor was talking his ear off in a friendly way, however, Maigret had noticed a customer at the far end of the room, where the light was dim, who was

10

absorbed in a strange task.

The man was shabby and looked for all the world like one of the chronically unemployed found in every big city, always on the lookout for an opportunity.

Except that he was pulling thousand-franc notes from his pocket and counting them, after which he wrapped them in grey paper, tied the package with string and addressed it. At least thirty notes, 30,000 Belgian francs! Maigret had frowned at that, and when the unknown man left after paying for his coffee, the inspector had followed him to the nearest post office.

There he had managed to read the address over the man's shoulder, an address written in a handwriting much more sophisticated than a simple schoolboy scrawl:

Monsieur Louis Jeunet
18, Rue de la Roquette, Paris

But what struck Maigret the most was the description: *Printed matter.*

Thirty thousand francs travelling as simple newsprint, as ordinary brochures — because the parcel hadn't even been sent via registered mail!

A postal clerk weighed it: 'Seventy centimes . . . '

The sender paid and left. Maigret had noted down the name and address. He then followed his man and had been amused — for a moment — at the thought of making a present of him to the Belgian police. Later on he would go to find the chief commissioner of the Brussels police and casually remark, 'Oh, by the way, while I was having a glass of your delicious gueuze beer, I spotted a crook . . . All you'll have to do is pick him up at such-and-such a place . . . '

Maigret was feeling positively cheerful. A gentle play of autumn sunshine sent warm air wafting through the city.

At eleven o'clock, the unknown man spent thirty-two francs on a suitcase of imitation leather — perhaps even imitation canvas — in a shop in Rue Neuve. And Maigret, playing along, bought the same one, with no thought of what might come next.

At half past eleven, the man turned into a little alley and entered a hotel, the name of which Maigret couldn't manage to see. The man shortly reappeared and at Gare du Nord took the train to Amsterdam.

This time, the inspector hesitated. Was his decision influenced, perhaps, by the feeling that he had already seen that face somewhere?

'It probably isn't anything important. But — what if it is?'

No urgent business awaited him in Paris. At the Dutch border, he had been intrigued by the way the man, with what was clearly practised skill, heaved his suitcase up on to the roof of the train before it stopped at the customs station.

'We'll see what happens when he gets off somewhere . . . '

Except that he did not stay in Amsterdam, where he simply purchased a third-class ticket for Bremen. Then the train set off across the Dutch plain, with its canals dotted with sailboats that seemed to be gliding along right out in the fields.

Neuschanz . . . Bremen . . .

Just on the off chance, Maigret had managed to switch the suitcases. For hours on end, he had tried without success to classify this fellow with one of the familiar police labels.

'Too nervous for a real international criminal. Or else he's the kind of underling who gets his bosses nabbed . . . A conspirator? Anarchist? He speaks only French, and we've hardly any conspirators in France these days, or even any militant anarchists! Some petty crook off on his own?'

Would a crook have lived so cheaply after mailing off 30,000-franc notes in plain grey paper?

In the stations where there was a long wait, the man drank no alcohol, consuming simply coffee and the occasional roll or brioche.

He was not familiar with the line, because at every station he would ask nervously — even anxiously — if he was going in the right direction.

Although he was not a strong, burly man, his hands bore the signs of manual labour. His nails were black, and too long as well, which suggested that he had not worked for a while.

His complexion indicated anaemia, perhaps destitution.

And Maigret gradually forgot the clever joke he'd thought of playing on the Belgian police by jauntily presenting them with a trussed-up crook.

This conundrum fascinated him. He kept finding excuses for his behaviour.

'Amsterdam isn't that far from Paris . . . '

And then . . .

'So what! I can take an express from Bremen and be back in thirteen hours.'

★   ★   ★

The man was dead. There was no compromising paper on him, nothing to reveal what he had been doing except an ordinary revolver of the most popular make in Europe.

He seemed to have killed himself only because someone had stolen his suitcase! Otherwise, why would he have bought rolls from the station buffet but never eaten them? And why spend a day travelling, when he might have stayed in Brussels and blown his brains out just as easily as in a German hotel?

Still, there was the suitcase, which might hold the solution to this puzzle. And that's why — after the naked body had been photographed and examined from head to toe, carried out wrapped in a sheet, hoisted into a police van and driven away — the inspector shut himself up in his hotel room.

He looked haggard. Although he filled his pipe as always, tapping gently with his thumb, he was only trying to persuade himself that he felt calm.

The dead man's thin, drawn face was haunting him. He kept seeing him snapping his fingers, then immediately opening his mouth wide for the gunshot.

14

Maigret felt so troubled — indeed, almost remorseful — that only after painful hesitation did he reach for the suitcase.

And yet that suitcase would supposedly prove him right! Wasn't he going to find there evidence that the man he was weak enough to pity was a crook, a dangerous criminal, perhaps a murderer?

The keys still hung from a string tied to the handle, as they had in the shop in Rue Neuve. Maigret opened the suitcase and first took out a dark-grey suit, less threadbare than the one the dead man had been wearing. Beneath the suit were two dirty shirts frayed at the collar and cuffs, rolled into a ball, and a detachable collar with thin pink stripes that had been worn for at least two weeks, because it was quite soiled wherever it had touched the wearer's neck . . . Soiled and shoddy . . .

That was all. Except for the bottom of the suitcase: green paper lining, two brand-new straps with buckles and swiveling tabs that hadn't been used.

Maigret shook out the clothing, checked the pockets. Empty! Seized with a choking sense of anguish, he kept looking, driven by his desire — his need — to find something.

Hadn't a man killed himself because someone had stolen this suitcase? And there was nothing in it but an old suit and some dirty laundry!

Not even a piece of paper. Nothing in the way of documents. No sign of any clue to the dead man's past.

The hotel room was decorated with new,

15

inexpensive and aggressively floral wallpaper in garish colours. The furniture, however, was old and rickety, broken-down, and the printed calico draped over the table was too filthy to touch.

The street was deserted, the shutters of the shops were closed, but a hundred metres away there was the reassuring thrum of steady traffic at a crossroads.

Maigret looked at the communicating door, at the keyhole he no longer dared to peek through. He remembered that the technicians had chalked the outline of the body on the floor of the neighbouring room for future study.

Carrying the dead man's suit, still wrinkled from the suitcase, he went next door on tiptoe so as not to awaken other guests, and perhaps because he felt burdened by this mystery.

The outline on the floor was contorted, but accurately drawn.

When Maigret tried to fit the jacket, waistcoat and trousers into the outline, his eyes lit up, and he bit down hard on his pipe-stem. The clothing was at least three sizes too large: it did not belong to the dead man.

What the tramp had been keeping so protectively in his suitcase, a thing so precious to him that he'd killed himself when it was lost, was someone else's suit!

2

Monsieur Van Damme

The Bremen newspapers simply announced in a few lines that a Frenchman named Louis Jeunet, a mechanic, had committed suicide in a hotel in the city and that poverty seemed to have been the motive for his act.

But by the time those lines appeared the following morning, that information was no longer correct. In fact, while leafing through Jeunet's passport, Maigret had noticed an interesting detail: on the sixth page, in the column listing *age*, *height*, *hair*, *forehead*, *eyebrows* and so on for the bearer's description, the word *forehead* appeared before *hair* instead of after it.

It so happened that six months earlier, the Paris Sûreté had discovered in Saint-Ouen a veritable factory for fake passports, military records, foreign residence permits and other official documents, a certain number of which they had seized. The counterfeiters themselves had admitted, however, that hundreds of their forgeries had been in circulation for several years and that, because they had kept no records, they could not provide a list of their customers.

The passport proved that Louis Jeunet had been one of them, which meant that his name was not Louis Jeunet.

And so, the single more or less solid fact in this inquiry had melted away. The man who had killed himself that night was now a complete unknown.

* * *

Having been granted all the authorization he needed, at nine o'clock the next morning Maigret arrived at the morgue, which the general public was free to visit after it opened its doors for the day.

He searched in vain for a dark corner from which to keep watch, although he really didn't expect much in the way of results. The morgue was a modern building, like most of the city and all its public buildings, and it was even more sinister than the ancient morgue in Quai de l'Horloge, in Paris. More sinister precisely because of its sharp, clean lines and perspectives, the uniform white of the walls, which reflected a harsh light, and the refrigeration units as shiny as machines in a power station. The place looked like a model factory: one where the raw material was human bodies.

The man who had called himself Louis Jeunet was there, less disfigured than might have been expected, because specialists had partially reconstructed his face. There were also a young woman and a drowned fellow who'd been fished from the harbour.

Brimming with health and tightly buttoned into his spotless uniform, the guard looked like a museum attendant.

18

In the space of an hour, surprisingly enough, some thirty people passed through the viewing hall. When one woman asked to see a body that was not on display, electric bells rang and numbers were barked into a telephone.

In an area on the first floor, one of the drawers in a vast cabinet filling an entire wall glided out into a freight lift, and a few moments later a steel box emerged on the ground floor just as books in some libraries are delivered to reading rooms.

It was the body that had been requested. The woman bent over it — and was led away, sobbing, to an office at the far end of the hall, where a young clerk took down her statement.

Few people took any interest in Louis Jeunet. Shortly after ten o'clock, however, a smartly attired man arrived in a private car, entered the hall, looked around for the suicide and examined him carefully.

Maigret was not far away. He drew closer and, after studying the visitor, decided that he didn't look German.

As soon as this visitor noticed Maigret approaching, moreover, he started uneasily, and must have come to the same conclusion as Maigret had about him.

'Are you French?' he asked bluntly.

'Yes. You, too?'

'Actually, I'm Belgian, but I've been living in Bremen for a few years now.'

'And you knew a man named Jeunet?'

'No! I . . . I read in this morning's paper that a Frenchman had committed suicide in Bremen . . . I lived in Paris for a long time . . . and I felt

19

curious enough to come and take a look.'

Maigret was completely calm, as he always was in such moments, when his face would settle into an expression of such stubborn density that he seemed even a touch bovine.

'Are you with the police?'

'Yes! The Police Judiciaire.'

'So you've come up here because of this case? Oh, wait: that's impossible, the suicide only happened last night . . . Tell me, do you have any French acquaintances in Bremen? No? In that case, if I can assist you in any way . . . May I offer you an aperitif?'

Shortly afterwards, Maigret followed the other man outside and joined him in his car, which the Belgian drove himself.

And as he drove he chattered away, a perfect example of the enthusiastic, energetic business-man. He seemed to know everyone, greeted passers-by, pointed out buildings, provided a running commentary.

'Here you have Norddeutscher Lloyd . . . Have you heard about the new liner they've launched? They're clients of mine . . . '

He waved towards a building in which almost every window displayed the name of a different firm.

'On the fifth floor, to the left, you can see my office.'

Porcelain sign letters on the window spelled out: *Joseph Van Damme, Import-Export Commission Agent.*

'Would you believe that sometimes I go a month without having a chance to speak French?

My employees and even my secretary are German. That's business for you!'

It would have been hard to divine a single one of Maigret's thoughts from his expression; he seemed a man devoid of subtlety. He agreed; he approved. He admired what he was asked to admire, including the car and its patented suspension system, proudly praised by Van Damme.

The inspector followed his host into a large brasserie teeming with businessmen talking loudly over the tireless efforts of a Viennese orchestra and the clinking of beer mugs.

'You'd never guess how much this clientele is worth in millions!' crowed the Belgian. 'Listen! You don't understand German? Well, our neighbour here is busy selling a cargo of wool currently on its way to Europe from Australia; he has thirty or forty ships in his fleet, and I could show you others like him. So, what'll you have? Personally, I recommend the Pilsner. By the way . . . '

Maigret's face showed no trace of a smile at the transition.

'By the way, what do you think about this suicide? A poor man down on his luck, as the papers here are saying?'

'It's possible.'

'Are you looking into it?'

'No: that's a matter for the German police. And as it's a clear case of suicide . . . '

'Oh, obviously! Of course, the thing that struck me was only that he was French, because we get so few of them up in the North!'

21

He rose to go and shake the hand of a man who was on his way out, then hurried back.

'Please excuse me — he runs a big insurance company, he's worth a hundred million . . . But listen, inspector: it's almost noon, you must come and have lunch with me! I'm not married, so I can only invite you to a restaurant, and you won't eat as you would in Paris, but I'll do my best to see that you don't do too badly. So, that's settled, right?'

He summoned the waiter, paid the bill. And when he pulled his wallet from his pocket, he did something that Maigret had often seen when businessmen like him had their aperitifs in bars around the Paris stock exchange, for they had that inimitable way of leaning backwards, throwing out their chests while tucking in their chins and opening with careless satisfaction that sacred object: the leather *portefeuille* plump with money.

'Let's go!'

*   *   *

Van Damme hung on to the inspector until almost five o'clock, after sweeping him along to his office — three clerks and a typist — but by then he'd made him promise that if he did not leave Bremen that evening, they would spend it together at a well-known cabaret.

Maigret found himself back in the crowd, alone with his thoughts, although they were in considerable disarray. Strictly speaking, were they even really thoughts?

22

His mind was comparing two figures, two men, and trying to establish a relationship between them.

Because there was one! Van Damme hadn't gone to the trouble of driving to the morgue simply to look at the dead body of a stranger. And the pleasure of speaking French was not the only reason he had invited Maigret to lunch. Besides, he had gradually revealed his true personality only after becoming increasingly persuaded that his companion had no interest in the case. And perhaps not much in the way of brains, either!

That morning, Van Damme had been worried. His smile had seemed forced. By the end of the afternoon, on the other hand, he had resurfaced as a sharp little operator, always on the go, busy, chatty, enthusiastic, mixing with financial big shots, driving his car, on the phone, rattling off instructions to his typist and hosting expensive dinners, proud and happy to be what he was.

And the second man was an anaemic tramp with grubby clothes and worn-out shoes, who had bought some sausages in rolls without the faintest idea that he would never get to eat them!

Van Damme must have already found himself another companion for the evening aperitif, in the same atmosphere of Viennese music and beer.

At six o'clock, a cover would close quietly on a metal bin, shutting away the naked body of the false Louis Jeunet, and the lift would deliver it to the freezer to spend the night in a numbered compartment.

23

Maigret went along to the Polizeipräsidium. Some officers were exercising, stripped to the waist in spite of the chill, in a courtyard with vivid red walls.

In the laboratory, a young man with a faraway look in his eye was waiting for him near a table on which all the dead man's possessions had been laid out and neatly labelled.

The man spoke perfect textbook French and took pride in coming up with *le mot juste.*

Beginning with the nondescript grey suit Jeunet had been wearing when he died, he explained that all the linings had been unpicked, every seam examined, and that nothing had been found.

'The suit comes from La Belle Jardinière in Paris. The material is fifty per cent cotton, so it is a cheap garment. We noticed some grease spots, including stains of mineral jelly, which suggest that the man worked in or was often inside a factory, workshop or garage. There are no labels or laundry marks in his linen. The shoes were purchased in Rheims. Same as the clothing: mass-produced, of mediocre quality. The socks are of cotton, the kind peddled in the street at four or five francs a pair. They have holes in them but have never been mended.

'All these clothes have been placed in a strong paper bag and shaken, and the dust obtained was analysed.

'We were thus able to confirm the provenance of those grease stains. The clothes are in fact impregnated with a fine metallic powder found only on the belongings of fitters, metal-workers,

24

and, in general, those who labour in machine shops.

'These elements are absent from the items I will call clothing B, items which have not been worn for at least six years.

'One more difference: in the pockets of suit A we found traces of French government-issue tobacco, what you call shag tobacco. In the pockets of clothing B, however, there were particles of yellowish imitation Egyptian tobacco.

'But now I come to the most important point. The spots found on clothing B are not grease spots. They are old human bloodstains, probably from arterial blood.

'The material has not been washed for years. The man who wore this suit must have been literally drenched in blood. And finally, certain tears suggest that there may have been a struggle, because in various places, for example on the lapels, the weave of the cloth has been torn as if it had been clawed by fingernails.

'The items of clothing B have labels from the tailor Roger Morcel, Rue Haute-Sauvenière, in Liège.

'As for the revolver, it's a model that was discontinued two years ago.

'If you wish to leave me your address, I will send you a copy of the report I'll be drawing up for my superiors.'

* * *

By eight that evening, Maigret had finished with the formalities. The German police had handed the dead man's clothes over to him along with the ones in the suitcase, which the technician had referred to as clothing B. And it had been decided that, until further notice, the body would be kept at the disposition of the French authorities in the mortuary refrigerator unit.

Maigret had a copy of Joseph Van Damme's public record: born in Liège of Flemish parents; travelling salesman, then director of a commission agency bearing his name.

He was thirty-two. A bachelor. He had lived in Bremen for only three years and, after some initial difficulties, now seemed to be doing nicely.

The inspector returned to his hotel room, where he sat for a long time on the edge of his bed with the two cheap suitcases in front of him. He had opened the communicating door to the neighbouring room, where nothing had been touched since the previous day, and he was struck by how little disorder the tragedy had left behind. In one place on the wallpaper, beneath a pink flower, was a very small brown spot, the only bloodstain. On the table lay the two sausage bread rolls, still wrapped in paper. A fly was sitting on them.

That morning, Maigret had sent two photos of the dead man to Paris and asked that the Police Judiciaire publish them in as many newspapers as possible.

Should the search begin there? In Paris, where the police at least had an address, the one where Jeunet had sent himself the thirty thousand-franc notes from Brussels?

Or in Liège, where clothing B had been bought a few years before? In Rheims, where the dead man's shoes had come from? In Brussels, where Jeunet had wrapped up his package of 30,000 francs? Bremen, where he had died and where a certain Joseph Van Damme had come to take a look at his corpse, denying all the while that he had ever known him?

The hotel manager appeared, made a long speech in German and, as far as the inspector could tell, asked him if the room where the tragedy had taken place could be cleaned and rented out.

Maigret grunted his assent, washed his hands, paid and went off with his two suitcases, their obviously poor quality in stark contrast with his comfortably bourgeois appearance.

There was no clear reason to tackle his investigation from one angle or another. And if he chose Paris, it was above all because of the strikingly foreign atmosphere all around him that constantly disturbed his habits, his way of thinking and, in the end, depressed him.

The local tobacco — rather yellow and too mild — had even killed his desire to smoke!

He slept in the express, waking at the Belgian border as day was breaking, and passed through Liège thirty minutes later. He stood at the door of the carriage to stare half-heartedly out at the station, where the train halted for only thirty minutes, not enough time for a visit to Rue Haute-Sauvenière.

At two that afternoon he arrived at Gare du Nord and plunged into the Parisian crowds,

27

where his first concern was to visit a tobacconist.

He was groping around in his pockets for some French coins when someone jostled him. The two suitcases were sitting at his feet. When he bent to retrieve them, he could find only one, and looking around in vain for the other, he realized that there was no point in alerting the police.

One detail, in any case, reassured him. The remaining suitcase had its two keys tied to the handle with a small string. That was the suitcase containing the clothing.

The thief had carried off the one full of old newspapers.

Had he been simply a thief, the kind that prowl through stations? In which case, wasn't it odd that he'd stolen such a crummy-looking piece of luggage?

Maigret settled into a taxi, savouring both his pipe and the familiar hubbub of the streets. Passing a kiosk, he caught a glimpse of a front-page photograph and even at a distance recognized one of the pictures of Louis Jeunet he had sent from Bremen.

He considered stopping by his home on Boulevard Richard-Lenoir to kiss his wife and change his clothes, but the incident at the station was bothering him.

'If the thief really was after the second suit of clothes, then how was he informed in Paris that I was carrying them and would arrive precisely when I did?'

It was as if fresh mysteries now hovered around the pale face and thin form of the tramp of Neuschanz and Bremen: shadowy forms were shifting, as on a photographic plate plunged into a developing bath.

And they would have to become clearer, revealing faces, names, thoughts and feelings, entire lives.

For the moment, in the centre of that plate lay only a naked body, and a harsh light shone on the face German doctors had done their fumbling best to make look human again.

The shadows? First, a man in Paris who was making off with the suitcase at that very moment. Plus another man who — from Bremen or elsewhere — had sent him instructions. The convivial Joseph Van Damme, perhaps? Or perhaps not! And then there was the person who, years ago, had worn clothing B . . . and the one who, during the struggle, had bled all over him. And the person who had supplied the 30,000 francs to 'Louis Jeunet' — or the person from whom they had been stolen!

It was sunny; the café terraces, heated by braziers, were thronged with people. Drivers were hailing one another. Swarms of people were pushing their way on to buses and trams.

From among all this seething humanity, here and in Bremen, Brussels, Rheims and still other places, the hunt would have to track down two, three, four, five individuals . . .

Fewer, perhaps? Or maybe more . . .

Maigret looked up fondly at the austere façade of police headquarters as he crossed the front courtyard carrying the small suitcase. He greeted the office boy by his first name.

29

'Did you get my telegram? Did you light a stove?'

'There's a lady here, about the picture! She's in the waiting room, been there for two hours now.'

Maigret did not stop to take off his hat and coat. He didn't even set down the suitcase.

The waiting room, at the end of the corridor lined with the chief inspectors' offices, is almost completely glassed-in and furnished with a few chairs upholstered in green velvet; its sole brick wall displays the list of policemen killed while on special duty.

On one of the chairs sat a woman who was still young, dressed with the humble care that bespeaks long hours of sewing by lamplight, making do with the best one has.

Her black cloth coat had a very thin fur collar. Her hands, in their grey cotton gloves, clutched a handbag made, like Maigret's suitcase, of imitation leather.

Did the inspector notice a vague resemblance between his visitor and the dead man?

Not a facial resemblance, no, but a similarity of expression, of social *class*, so to speak.

She, too, had the washed-out, weary eyes of those whose courage has abandoned them. Her nostrils were pinched and her complexion unhealthily dull.

She had been waiting for two hours and naturally hadn't dared change seats or even move at all. She looked at Maigret through the glass with no hope that he might at last be the person she needed to see.

He opened the door.

'If you would care to follow me to my office, madame.'

When he ushered her in ahead of him she appeared astonished at his courtesy and hesitated, as if confused, in the middle of the room. Along with her handbag she carried a rumpled newspaper showing part of Jeunet's photograph.

'I'm told you know the man who — '

But before he could finish she bit her lips and buried her face in her hands. Almost overcome by a sob she could not control, she moaned, 'He's my husband, monsieur.'

Hiding his feeling, Maigret turned away, then rolled a heavy armchair over for her.

3

The Herbalist's Shop in Rue Picpus

'Did he suffer much?' she asked, as soon as she could speak again.

'No, madame. I can assure you that death was instantaneous.'

She looked at the newspaper in her hand. The words were hard to say.

'In the mouth?'

When the inspector simply nodded, she stared down at the floor, suddenly calm, and as if speaking about a mischievous child she said solemnly, 'He always had to be different from everyone else . . . '

She spoke not as a lover, or even a wife. Although she was not yet thirty, she had a maternal tenderness about her, and the gentle resignation of a nun.

The poor are used to stifling any expression of their despair, because they must get on with life, with work, with the demands made of them day after day, hour after hour. She wiped her eyes with her handkerchief, and her slightly reddened nose erased any prettiness she possessed.

The corners of her mouth kept drooping sadly though she tried to smile as she looked at Maigret.

'Would you mind if I asked you a few questions?' he said, sitting down at his desk. 'Was

your husband's name indeed Louis Jeunet? And
. . . when did he leave you for the last time?'

Tears sprang to her eyes; she almost began
weeping again. Her fingers had balled the
handkerchief into a hard little wad.

'Two years ago . . . But I saw him again, once,
peering in at the shop window. If my mother
hadn't been there . . . '

Maigret realized that he need simply let her
talk. Because she would, as much for herself as
for him.

'You want to know all about our life, isn't that
right? It's the only way to understand why Louis
did that . . . My father was a male nurse in
Beaujon. He had set up a small herbalist's shop
in Rue Picpus, which my mother managed.

'My father died six years ago, and Mama and I
have kept up the business.

'I met Louis . . . '

'That was six years ago, did you say?' Maigret
asked her. 'Was he already calling himself
Jeunet?'

'Yes!' she replied, in some astonishment. 'He
was a milling machine operator in a workshop in
Belleville . . . He earned a good living . . . I don't
know why things happened so quickly, you can't
imagine — he was in a hurry about everything,
as if some fever were eating at him.

'I'd been seeing him for barely a month when
we got married, and he came to live with us. The
living quarters behind the shop are too small for
three people; we rented a room for Mama over in
Rue du Chemin-Vert. She let me have the shop,
but as she hadn't saved enough to live on, we

gave her 200 francs every month.

'We were happy, I swear to you! Louis would go off to work in the morning; my mother would come to keep me company. He stayed home in the evenings.

'I don't know how to explain this to you, but — I always felt that something was wrong!

'I mean, for example . . . it was as if Louis didn't belong to our world, as if the way we lived was sometimes too much for him.

'He was very sweet to me . . . '

Her expression became wistful; she was almost beautiful when she confessed, 'I don't think many men are like this: he would take me suddenly in his arms, looking so deeply into my eyes that it hurt. Then sometimes, out of the blue, he would push me away — I've never seen such a thing from anyone else — and he'd sigh to himself, 'Yet I really am fond of you, my little Jeanne . . . '

'Then it was over. He'd keep busy with this or that without giving me another glance, spend hours repairing a piece of furniture, making me something handy for housework, or fixing a clock.

'My mother didn't much care for him, precisely because she understood that he wasn't like other people.'

'Among his belongings, weren't there some items he guarded with particular care?'

'How did you know?'

She started, a touch frightened, and blurted out, 'An old suit! Once he came home when I'd taken it from a cardboard box on top of the

34

wardrobe and was brushing it. The suit would have been still good enough to wear around the house. I was even going to mend the tears. Louis grabbed it from me, he was furious, shouting cruel things, and that evening — you'd have sworn he hated me!

'We'd been married for a month. After that . . .'

She sighed and looked at Maigret as if in apology for having nothing more for him than this poor story.

'He became more and more strange?'

'It isn't his fault, I'm sure of that! I think he was ill, he worried so . . . We were often in the kitchen, and whenever we'd been happy for a little while, I used to see him change suddenly: he'd stop speaking, look at things — and me — with a nasty smile, and go and throw himself down on his bed without saying goodnight to me.'

'He had no friends?'

'No! No one ever came to see him.'

'He never travelled, received any letters?'

'No. And he didn't like having people in our home. Once in a while, a neighbour who had no sewing machine would come over to use mine, and that was guaranteed to enrage Louis. But he didn't become angry like everyone else, it was something shut up inside . . . and he was the one who seemed to suffer!

'When I told him we were going to have a child, he stared at me like a madman . . .

'That was when he started to drink, fits of it, binges, especially after the baby was born. And

35

yet I know that he loved that child! Sometimes he used to gaze at him in adoration, the way he did with me at first . . .

'The next day, he'd come home drunk, lie down, lock the bedroom door and spend hours in there, whole days.

'The first few times, he'd cry and beg me to forgive him. Maybe if Mama hadn't interfered I might have managed to keep him, but my mother tried to lecture him, and there were awful arguments. Especially when Louis went two or three days without going to work!

'Towards the end, we were desperately unhappy. You know what it's like, don't you? His temper got worse and worse. My mother threw him out twice, to remind him that he wasn't the lord and master there.

'But I just know that it wasn't his fault! Something was pushing him, driving him! He would still look at me, or our son, in that old way I told you about . . .

'Only now not so often, and it didn't last long. The final quarrel was dreadful. Mama was there. Louis had helped himself to some money from the shop, and she called him a thief. He went so pale, his eyes all red, as on his bad days, and a crazed look in those eyes . . .

'I can still see him coming closer as if to strangle me! I was terrified and screamed, 'Louis!'

'He left, slamming the door so hard the glass shattered.

'That was two years ago. Some neighbourhood women saw him around now and again . . . I

36

went to that factory in Belleville, but they told me he didn't work there any more.

'Someone saw him, though, in a small workshop in Rue de la Roquette where they make beer pumps.

'Me, I saw him once more, maybe six months ago now, through the shop window. Mama is living with me and the child again, and she was in the shop . . . she kept me from running to the door.

'You swear to me that he didn't suffer? That he died instantly? He was an unhappy, unfortunate man, don't you see? You must have understood that by now . . . '

She had relived her story with such intensity, and her husband had had such a strong hold on her, that, without realizing it, she had been reflecting all the feelings she was describing on her own face.

As in his first impression, Maigret was struck by an unnerving resemblance between this woman and the man in Bremen who had snapped his fingers before shooting a bullet into his mouth.

What's more, that raging fever she had just evoked seemed to have infected her. She fell silent, but all her nerves remained on edge, and she almost gasped for breath. She was waiting for something, she didn't know what.

'He never spoke to you about his past, his childhood?'

'No. He didn't talk much. I only know that he was born in Aubervilliers. And I've always thought he was educated beyond his station in life; he had lovely handwriting, and he knew the Latin names of all the plants. When the woman from the haberdashery next door had a difficult letter to write, he was the one she came to.'

'And you never saw his family?'

'Before we were married, he told me he was an orphan. Chief inspector, there's one more thing I'd like to ask you. Will he be brought back to France?'

When Maigret hesitated to reply, she turned her face away to hide her embarrassment.

'Now the shop belongs to my mother. And the money, too. I know she won't want to pay anything to bring the body home — or give me enough to go and see him! Would it be possible, in this case . . . '

The words died in her throat, and she quickly bent down to retrieve her handkerchief, which had fallen to the floor.

'I will see to it that your husband is brought home, madame.'

She gave him a touching smile, then wiped a tear from her cheek.

'You've understood, I can tell! You feel the same way I do, chief inspector! It wasn't his fault . . . He was an unhappy man . . . '

'Did he ever have any large sums of money?'

'Only his wages. In the beginning, he gave everything to me. Later on, when he began drinking . . . '

Another faint smile, very sad, and yet full of pity.

She left somewhat calmer, gathering the skimpy fur collar tightly round her neck with her right hand, still clutching the handbag and the tightly folded newspaper in the other.

★   ★   ★

Maigret found a seedy-looking hotel at 18, Rue de la Roquette, right where it joins Rue de Lappe, with its accordion-band dance halls and squalid housing. That stretch of Roquette is a good fifty metres from Place de la Bastille. Every ground floor hosts a bistro, every house a hotel frequented by drifters, immigrants, tarts and the chronically unemployed.

Tucked away within these vaguely sinister haunts of the underclass, however, are a few workshops, their doors wide open to the street, where men wield hammers and blowtorches amid a constant traffic of heavy trucks.

The contrast is striking: these steady workers, busy employees with waybills in hand, and the sordid or insolent creatures who hang around everywhere.

'Jeunet!' rumbled the inspector, pushing open the door of the hotel office on the ground floor.

'Not here!'

'He's still got his room?'

He'd been spotted for a policeman, and got a reluctant reply.

'Yes, room 19!'

'By the week? The month?'

'The month!'

'You have any mail for him?'

The manager turned evasive, but in the end handed over to Maigret the package Jeunet had sent himself from Brussels.

'Did he receive many like this?'

'A few times . . . '

'Never any letters?'

'No! Maybe he got three packages, in all. A quiet man. I don't see why the police should want to come bothering him.'

'He worked?'

'At number 65, down the street.'

'Regularly?'

'Depended. Some weeks yes, others, no.'

Maigret demanded the key to the room. He found nothing there, however, except a ruined pair of shoes with flapping soles, an empty tube of aspirin and some mechanic's overalls tossed into a corner.

Back downstairs, he questioned the manager again, learning that Louis Jeunet saw no one, did not go out with women and basically led a humdrum life, aside from a few trips lasting three or four days.

But no one stays in one of these hotels, in this neighbourhood, unless there's something wrong somewhere, and the manager knew that as well as Maigret.

'It's not what you think,' he admitted grudgingly. 'With him, it's the bottle! And how — in binges. Novenas, my wife and I call them. Buckle down for three weeks, go off to work every day, then . . . for a while he'd drink until he passed out on his bed.'

'You never saw anything suspicious about his behaviour?'

But the man shrugged, as if to say that in his

hotel everyone who walked through the door looked suspicious.

At number 65, in a huge workshop open to the street, they made machines to draw off beer. Maigret was met by a foreman, who had already seen Jeunet's picture in the paper.

'I was just going to write to the police!' he exclaimed. 'He was still working here last week. A fellow who earned eight francs fifty an hour!'

'When he was working.'

'Ah, you already know? When he was working, true! There are lots of them like that, but in general those others regularly take one drink too many, or they splurge on a champion hangover every Saturday. Him, it was sudden-like, no warning: he'd drink for a solid week. Once, when we had a rush job, I went to his hotel room. Well! There he was, all alone, drinking right out of a bottle set on the floor by his bed. A sorry sight, I swear.'

★   ★   ★

In Aubervilliers, nothing. The registry office held a single record of one Louis Jeunet, son of Gaston Jeunet, day labourer, and Berthe Marie Dufoin, domestic servant. Gaston Jeunet had died ten years earlier; his wife had moved away.

As for Louis Jeunet, no one knew anything about him, except that six years before he had written from Paris to request a copy of his birth certificate.

But the passport was still a forgery, which meant that the man who had killed himself in

Bremen — after marrying the herbalist woman in Rue Picpus and having a son — was not the real Jeunet.

The criminal records in the Préfecture were another dead end: nothing indexed under the name of Jeunet, no fingerprints matching the ones of the dead man, taken in Germany. Evidently this desperate soul had never run afoul of the law in France or abroad, because headquarters kept tabs on the police records of most European nations.

The records went back only six years. At which point, there was a Louis Jeunet, a drilling machine operator, who had a job and lived the life of a decent working man.

He married. He already owned clothing B, which had provoked the first scene with his wife and years later would prove the cause of his death.

He had no friends, received no mail. He appeared to know Latin and therefore to have received an above-average education.

Back in his office, Maigret drew up a request for the German police to release the body, disposed of a few current matters and, with a sullen, sour face, once again opened the yellow suitcase, the contents of which had been so carefully labelled by the technician in Bremen.

To this he added the package of thirty Belgian thousand-franc notes — but abruptly decided to snap the string and copy down the serial numbers on the bills, a list he sent off to the police in Brussels, asking that they be traced.

He did all this with studied concentration, as if

he were trying to convince himself that he was doing something useful.

From time to time, however, he would glance with a kind of bitterness at the crime-scene photos spread out on his desk, and his pen would hover in mid-air as he chewed on the stem of his pipe.

Regretfully, he was about to set the investigation aside and leave for home when he learned that he had a telephone call from Rheims.

It was about the picture published in the papers. The proprietor of the Café de Paris, in Rue Carnot, claimed to have seen the man in question in his establishment six days earlier — and had remembered this because the man got so drunk that he had finally stopped serving him.

Maigret hesitated. The dead man's shoes had come from Rheims — which had now cropped up again.

Moreover, these worn-out shoes had been bought months earlier, so Louis Jeunet had not just happened to be in Rheims by accident.

One hour later, the inspector took his seat on the Rheims express, arriving there at ten o'clock. A fashionable establishment favoured by the bourgeoisie, the Café de Paris was crowded that evening; three games of billiards were in full swing, and people at a few tables were playing cards.

It was a traditional café of the French provinces, where customers shake hands with the cashier and waiters know all the regulars by name: local notables, commercial travellers and so forth. It even had the traditional round nickel-plated receptacles for the café dishcloths.

'I am the inspector whom you telephoned earlier this evening.'

Standing by the counter, the proprietor was keeping an eye on his staff while he dispensed advice to the billiard players.

'Ah, yes! Well, I've already told you all I know.'

Somewhat embarrassed, he spoke in a low voice.

'Let me think . . . He was sitting over in that corner, near the third billiard table, and he ordered a brandy, then another, and a third . . . It was at about this same time of night. People were giving him funny looks because — how shall I put this? — he wasn't exactly our usual class of customer.'

'Did he have any luggage?'

'An old suitcase with a broken lock. I remember that when he left, the suitcase fell open and some old clothes spilled out. He even asked me for some string to tie it closed.'

'Did he speak to anyone?'

The proprietor glanced over at one of the billiard players, a tall, thin young man, a snappy dresser, the very picture of a sharp player whose every bank shot would be studied with respect.

'Not exactly . . . Won't you have something, inspector? We could sit over here, look!'

He chose a table with trays stacked on it, off to one side.

'By about midnight, he was as white as this marble tabletop. He'd had maybe eight or nine brandies. And I didn't like that stare he had — it takes some people that way, the alcohol. They don't get agitated or start rambling on, but at some point they simply pass out cold. Everyone had noticed him. I went over to tell him that I couldn't serve him any more, and he didn't protest in any way.'

'Was anyone still playing billiards?'

'The fellows you see over at that third table. Regulars, here every evening: they have a club, organize competitions. Well, the man left — and that's when there was that business with the suitcase falling open. The state he was in, I don't know how he managed to tie the string. I closed up a half-hour later. These gentlemen here shook my hand leaving, and I remember one of them said, 'We'll find him off somewhere in the gutter!'

The proprietor glanced again at the smartly dressed player with the white, well-manicured hands, the impeccable tie, the polished shoes that creaked each time he moved around the billiard table.

'I might as well tell you everything, especially since it's probably some fluke or a misunderstanding . . . The next day, a travelling salesman who drops by every month and who was here that night, well, he told me that at about one in the morning he'd seen the drunk and Monsieur Belloir walking along together. He even saw them both go into Monsieur Belloir's house!'

'That's the tall blond fellow?'

'Yes. He lives five minutes from here, in a handsome house in Rue de Vesle. He's the deputy director of the Banque de Crédit.'

45

'Is the salesman here tonight?'

'No, he's off on his regular tour through his eastern territories, won't be back until mid-November or so. I told him he must have been mistaken, but he stuck to his story. I almost mentioned it to Monsieur Belloir, as a little joke, but thought, better not. He might have been offended, right? In fact, I'd appreciate it if you wouldn't make a big deal out of what I just told you — or at least don't make it look as if it came from me. In my profession . . . '

Having just scored a break of forty-eight points, the player in question was looking around to gauge everyone's reaction while he rubbed the tip of his cue with green chalk. He frowned almost imperceptibly when he noticed Maigret sitting with the proprietor.

For, like most people trying to appear relaxed, the café owner looked worried, as if he were up to something.

Belloir called out to him from across the room.

'It's your turn, Monsieur Émile!'

4

The Unexpected Visitor

The house was new, and there was something in the studied refinement of its design and building materials that created a feeling of comfort, of crisp, confident modernism and a well-established fortune.

Red bricks, freshly repointed; natural stone; a front door of varnished oak, with brass fittings.

It was only 8.30 in the morning when Maigret turned up at that door, half hoping to catch a candid glimpse of the Belloir family's private life.

The façade, in any case, seemed suitable for a bank deputy director, an impression increased by the immaculately turned-out maid who opened the door. The entrance hall was quite large, with a door of bevelled glass panes at the end. The walls were of faux marble, and geometric patterns in two colours embellished the granite floor.

To the left, two sets of double doors of pale oak, leading to the drawing room and dining room.

Among the clothes hanging from a portman-teau was a coat for a child of four or five. A big-bellied umbrella stand held a Malacca cane with a gold pommel.

Maigret had only a moment to absorb this atmosphere of flawless domesticity, for he had barely mentioned Monsieur Belloir when the maid replied, 'If you'd be so good as to follow me, *the gentlemen* are expecting you.'

She walked towards the glass-paned door. Passing another, half-open door, the inspector caught a glimpse of the dining room, cosy and neat, where a young woman in a peignoir and a little boy of four were having their breakfast at a nicely laid table.

Beyond the last door was a staircase of pale wooden panelling with a red floral carpet runner fixed to each step by a brass rod.

A large green plant sat on the landing. The maid was already turning the knob of another door, to a study, where three men turned as one towards their visitor.

There was a reaction of shock, deep unease, even real distress that froze the looks in their eyes, which only the maid never noticed as she asked in a perfectly natural voice, 'Would you like me to take your coat?'

One of the three gentlemen was Belloir, perfectly dressed, with not a blond hair out of place. The man next to him was a little more casually attired, and a stranger to Maigret. The third man, however, was none other than Joseph Van Damme, the businessman from Bremen.

Two of the men spoke simultaneously.

With a dry hauteur in keeping with the décor and frowning as he stepped forwards, Belloir inquired, 'Monsieur?' — while at the same time Van Damme, in an effort to summon up his usual bonhomie, held out his hand to Maigret and exclaimed, 'What a surprise! Imagine seeing you here!'

The third man silently took in the scene in what looked like complete bafflement.

'Please excuse me for disturbing you,' began the inspector. 'I did not expect to be interrupting a meeting this early in the morning . . . '

'Not at all! Not at all!' replied Van Damme. 'Do sit down! Cigar?'

There was a box on the mahogany desk. He hurried to open it and select a Havana, talking all the while.

'Hold on, I'm looking for my lighter . . . You're not going to write me a ticket because these are missing their tobacco tax stamp, are you? But why didn't you tell me in Bremen that you knew Belloir! When I think that we might have made the trip together! I left a few hours after you did: a telegram, some business requiring my presence in Paris. And I've taken advantage of it to come and say hello to Belloir . . . '

The latter, having lost none of his starchy manner, kept looking from one to the other of the two men as if waiting for an explanation, and it was towards him that Maigret turned and spoke.

'I'll make my visit as short as possible, given that you're expecting someone . . . '

'I am? How do you know?'

'Simple! Your maid told me that I was expected. And as I cannot be the person in question, then clearly . . . '

His eyes were laughing in spite of himself, but his face stayed perfectly blank.

'Inspector Maigret, of the Police Judiciaire. Perhaps you noticed me yesterday evening at the Café de Paris, where I was seeking information relevant to an ongoing investigation.'

'It can't be that incident in Bremen, surely?' remarked Van Damme, with feigned indifference.

'The very one! Would you be so kind, Monsieur Belloir, as to look at this photograph and tell me if this is indeed the man you invited into your home one night last week?'

He held out a picture of the dead man. The deputy bank director looked at it, but vacantly, without seeing it.

'I don't know this person!' he stated, returning the photo to Maigret.

'You're certain this isn't the man who spoke to you when you were returning home from the Café de Paris?'

'What are you talking about?'

'Forgive me if I seem to labour the point, but I need some information that is, after all, of only minor importance, and I took the liberty of disturbing you at home because I assumed you would not mind helping us in our inquiries. On that evening, a drunk was sitting near the third billiard table, where you were playing. All the customers noticed him. He left shortly before you did, and later on, after you'd left your friends, he approached you.'

'I have a vague recollection . . . He asked me for a light.'

'And you came back here with him, isn't that right?'

Belloir smiled rather nastily.

50

'I've no idea who told you such nonsense. I'm hardly the sort of person to bring home tramps.'

'You might have recognized him — as an old friend, or . . . '

'I have better taste in friends!'

'You're saying that you went home alone?'

'Absolutely.'

'Was that man the same one in the photo I just showed you?'

'I have no idea. I never even looked at him.'

Listening with obvious impatience, Van Damme had been on the verge of interrupting several times. As for the third man, who had a short brown beard and was dressed all in black in a bygone but 'artistic' fashion, he was looking out of the window, occasionally wiping away the fog his breath left on the pane.

'In which case, I must now simply thank you and apologize once again, Monsieur Belloir.'

'Just a minute, inspector!' exclaimed Joseph Van Damme. 'You're not going to leave just like that? Please, do stay here with us for a moment, and Belloir will offer us some of that fine brandy he always keeps on hand . . . Do you realize that I'm rather put out with you for not coming to dinner with me, in Bremen? I waited for you all evening!'

'Did you travel here by train?'

'By plane! I almost always fly, like most businessmen, in fact! Then, in Paris, I felt like dropping in on my old friend Belloir. We were at university together.'

'In Liège?'

'Yes. And it's almost ten years now since we

last saw each other. I didn't even know that he'd got married! It's odd to find him again — with a fine young son! But . . . are you really still working on that suicide of yours?'

Belloir had rung for the maid, whom he told to bring brandy and some glasses. His every move was made slowly and carefully, but with each move he betrayed the gnawing uncertainty he felt.

'The investigation has only just begun,' said Maigret quietly. 'It's impossible to tell if it will be a long one or if the case will be all wrapped up in a day or two.'

When the front doorbell rang, the other three men exchanged furtive glances. Voices were heard; then someone with a strong Belgian accent asked, 'Are they all upstairs? Don't bother, I know the way.'

From the doorway he called out, 'Hello, fellows!'

And met with dead silence. When he saw Maigret, he looked questioningly at the others.

'Weren't you . . . expecting me?'

Belloir's expression tightened. Walking over to the inspector, he said, as if through clenched teeth, 'Jef Lombard, a friend.'

Then, pronouncing every syllable distinctly: 'Inspector Maigret, of the Police Judiciaire.'

The new arrival gave a little start, and stammered in a flat voice that squeaked in the most peculiar way, 'Aha! . . . I see . . . Well, fine . . . '

After which, in his bewilderment, he gave his overcoat to the maid, only to chase after her to retrieve the cigarettes he had left in a pocket.

52

'Another Belgian, inspector,' observed Van Damme. 'Yes, you're witnessing a real Belgian reunion! You must think this all looks like a conspiracy . . . What about that brandy, Belloir? Inspector, a cigar? Jef Lombard is the only one who still lives in Liège. It just so happens that business affairs have brought us all to the same place at the same moment, so we've decided to celebrate, and have a grand old time! And I wonder if . . . '

He hesitated for a moment, looking around at the others.

'You skipped that dinner I wanted to treat you to in Bremen. Why not have lunch with us later today?'

'Unfortunately, I have other engagements,' replied Maigret. 'Besides, I've already taken enough of your time.'

Jef Lombard had gone over to a table. He was pale, with irregular features, so tall and thin that his limbs seemed too long for his body.

'Ah! Here's the picture I was looking for,' muttered Maigret, as if to himself. 'I won't ask you, Monsieur Lombard, if you know this man, because that would be one chance in a million . . . '

But he contrived to show him the photo anyway — and saw the man's Adam's apple seem to swell, bobbing weirdly up and down.

'Don't know him,' Lombard managed to croak.

Belloir's manicured fingers were drumming on

his desk, while Van Damme cast about for something to say.

'So, inspector, I won't have the pleasure of seeing you again? You're going straight back to Paris?'

'I'm not sure yet. My apologies, gentlemen.'

Van Damme shook hands with him, so the others had to as well. Belloir's hand was hard and dry. The bearded man's handshake was more hesitant, and Jef Lombard was off in a corner of the study lighting a cigarette, so he simply nodded towards Maigret and grunted.

Maigret brushed past the green plant in its enormous porcelain pot and went back down the stairs with their brass carpet rods. In the front hall, over the shrill scraping of a violin lesson, he heard a woman's voice saying, 'Slow down . . . Keep your elbow level with your chin . . . Gently!'

It was Madame Belloir and her son. He caught sight of them from the street, through the drawing-room curtains.

★   ★   ★

It was 2 p.m., and Maigret had just finished lunch at the Café de Paris when he noticed Van Damme come in and look around as if searching for someone. Spotting Maigret, he smiled and came over with his hand outstretched.

'So this is what you call having other engagements! Eating alone in a restaurant! I understand: you wanted to leave us in peace.'

He was clearly one of those people who latch on to you without any invitation, ignoring any suggestion that their attentions might be unwelcome.

Maigret took selfish pleasure in his chilly response, but Van Damme sat down at his table anyway.

'You've finished? In that case, allow me to offer you a *digestif* . . . Waiter! Well, what will you have, inspector? An old Armagnac?'

He called for the drinks list, and after consultation with the proprietor, chose an 1867 Armagnac, to be served in snifters.

'I was wondering: when are you returning to Paris? I'm going there this afternoon, and since I cannot bear trains, I'll be hiring a car . . . If you like, I'll take you along. Well, what do you think of my friends?'

He inhaled the aroma of his brandy with a critical air, then pulled a cigar case from his pocket.

'Please, have one, they're quite good. There's only one place in Bremen where you can get them, and they're straight from Havana!'

Maigret had emptied his eyes of all thought and made his face a blank.

'It's funny, meeting again years later,' remarked Van Damme, who seemed unable to cope with silence. 'At the age of twenty, starting out, we're all on the same footing, so to speak. Time passes, and when we get together again, it's astonishing how far away from one another we seem . . . I'm not saying anything against them, mind you, it's just that, back at Belloir's

55

house, I felt . . . uncomfortable. That stifling provincial atmosphere! And Belloir himself, quite the clothes horse! Although he hasn't done badly for himself, seeing as he married the daughter of Morvandeau, the one who's in sprung mattresses. All Belloir's brothers-in-law are in industry. And him? He's sitting pretty in the bank, where he'll wind up director one of these days.'

'And the short man with the beard?' asked Maigret.

'That one . . . He may yet find his way and make good. Meanwhile, I think he's feeling the pinch, poor devil. He's a sculptor, in Paris. And talented, it seems — but what do you expect? You saw him, in that get-up from another century . . . Nothing modern about him! And no business sense.'

'Jef Lombard?'

'They don't make them any better! In his younger days, he was a real joker, could keep you laughing yourself silly for hours on end. He was going to be a painter . . . He earned a living as a newspaper artist, then worked as a photoen-graver in Liège. He's married. I believe they're expecting their third child.

'What I'm saying is, when I was with them I felt as if I couldn't breathe! Those petty lives, with their petty preoccupations and worries . . . It isn't their fault, but I can't wait to get back to the business world.'

He drained his glass and considered the almost deserted room, where a waiter at a table in the back was reading a newspaper.

'It's settled, then? You're returning to Paris with me?'

'But aren't you travelling with the short bearded fellow who came with you?'

'Janin? No, by this time he has already taken the train back.'

'Married?'

'Not exactly. But he always has some girlfriend or other who lives with him for a week, a year — and then he gets a new one! Whom he always introduces as 'Madame Janin''. Oh, waiter! The same again, here!'

Maigret had to be careful, at times, not to let his eyes give away how keenly he was listening. He had left the address of the Café de Paris back at headquarters, and the proprietor now came over to tell him personally that he was wanted on the phone.

News had been wired from Brussels to the Police Judiciaire: *The 30,000-franc notes were handed over by the Banque Générale de Belgique to one Louis Jeunet in payment of a cheque signed by Maurice Belloir.*

Opening the door to leave the telephone booth, Maigret saw that Van Damme, unaware that he was being observed, had allowed himself to drop his mask — and now seemed deflated and, above all, less glowing with health and optimism.

He must have felt those watchful eyes on him, however, for he shuddered, automatically becoming the jovial businessman once again.

'We're set, then?' he called out. 'You're coming with me? *Patron!* Would you arrange for us to be picked up here by car and driven to Paris? A comfortable car! See to it, will you? And in the meantime, let's have another.'

He chewed on the end of his cigar and just for an instant, as he stared down at the marble table, his eyes lost their lustre, while the corners of his mouth drooped as if the tobacco had left a bitter taste in his mouth.

'It's when you live abroad that you really appreciate the wines and liqueurs of France!'

His words rang hollow, echoing in the abyss lying between them and the man's troubled mind.

Jef Lombard went by in the street, his silhouette slightly blurred by the tulle curtains. He was alone. He walked with long strides, slowly and sadly, seeing nothing of the city all around him.

He was carrying an overnight bag, and Maigret found himself thinking about those two yellow suitcases . . . Lombard's was of better quality, though, with two straps and a sleeve for a calling card. The man's shoe heels were starting to wear down on one side, and his clothes did not look as if anyone brushed them regularly. Jef Lombard was walking all the way to the station.

Van Damme, sporting a large platinum signet ring on one finger, was wreathing himself in a fragrant cloud of cigar smoke heightened by the alcohol's sharp bouquet. Off in the background, the proprietor could be heard on the phone, arranging for the car.

Belloir was probably setting out from his new house for the marble portal of the bank, while his wife took their son for a walk along the avenues. Everyone would wish Belloir a good afternoon. His father-in-law was the biggest businessman around. His brothers-in-law were 'in industry'. A bright future lay ahead of him.

As for Janin, with his black goatee and his artistic *laval-lière* bow tie, he was on his way to Paris — in third class, Maigret would have bet on it.

And down at the bottom of the heap was the pale traveller of Neuschanz and Bremen, the husband of the herbalist in Rue Picpus, the milling machine operator from Rue de la Roquette, the solitary drinker who went to gaze at his wife through the shop window, sent himself banknotes as if they were a package of old newspapers, bought sausages in rolls at a station buffet and shot himself in the mouth because he'd been robbed of an old suit that wasn't even his.

'Ready, inspector?'

Maigret flinched and stared in confusion at Van Damme, his gaze so vacant that the other man tried uneasily to laugh and botched it, stammering, 'Were you daydreaming? Wherever you were, it was far away . . . I suspect it's that suicide of yours you're still worried about.'

Not entirely. When startled from his reverie, Maigret — and even he did not know why — had been concentrating on an unusual list, counting up the children involved in this case: one in Rue Picpus, a small figure between his mother and grandmother in a shop smelling of mint and rubber; one in Rheims, who was learning to hold his elbow up by his chin while drawing his bow across the strings of a violin; two in Liège, in the home of Jef Lombard, where a third was on the way . . .

'One last Armagnac, what do you say?'

'Thank you: I've had enough.'

'Come on! We'll have a stirrup cup, or in our case one for the road!'

Only Joseph Van Damme laughed, as he constantly felt he must, like a little boy so afraid to go down into the cellar that he tries to whistle up some courage.

5

Breakdown at Luzancy

As they drove at a fast clip through the gathering dusk, there was hardly a moment's silence. Joseph Van Damme was never at a loss for words and, fuelled by the Armagnac, he managed to keep up a stream of convivial patter. The vehicle was an old sedan, a saloon car with worn cushions, flower holders and marquetry side pockets. The driver was wearing a trench coat, with a knitted scarf around his neck.

They had been driving for about two hours when the driver pulled over to the side of the road and stopped at least a kilometre from a village, a few lights of which gleamed in the misty evening.

After inspecting the rear wheels, the driver informed his passengers that he had found a flat tyre, which it would take him fifteen minutes or so to repair.

The two men got out. The driver was already settling a jack under the rear axle and assured them that he did not need any help.

Was it Maigret or Van Damme who suggested a short walk? Neither of them, actually; it seemed only natural for them to walk a little way along the road, where they noticed a path leading down to the rushing waters of a river.

'Look! The Marne!' said Van Damme. 'It's in

spate . . . ' As they strolled slowly along the little path, smoking their cigars, they heard a noise that puzzled them until they reached the riverbank.

A hundred metres away, across the water, they saw the lock at Luzancy: its gates were closed, and there was no one around. Right at their feet was a dam, with its milky overspill, churning waters and powerful current. The Marne was running high.

In the darkness they could just make out branches, perhaps entire trees, smashing repeatedly into the barrier until swept at last over its edge.

The only light came from the lock, on the far side of the river.

Joseph Van Damme kept talking away.

'Every year the Germans make tremendous efforts to harness the energy of rivers, and the Russians are right behind them: in the Ukraine they're constructing a dam that'll cost 120 million dollars but will provide electricity to three provinces.'

It was almost unnoticeable, the way his voice faltered — briefly — at the word *electricity*. And then, coughing, Van Damme had to take out his handkerchief to blow his nose.

They were on the very brink of the river. Shoved suddenly from behind, Maigret lost his balance, turning as he fell forwards, and grabbed the edge of the grassy riverbank with both hands, his feet now in the water, while his hat was already plunging over the dam.

The rest happened quickly, for he had been

expecting that push. Clods of earth were giving way under his right hand, but he had spotted a branch sturdy enough for him to cling to with his other hand.

Only seconds later, he was on his knees on the towpath and then on his feet, shouting at a figure fading away.

'Stop!'

It was strange: Van Damme didn't dare run. He was heading towards the car in only a modest hurry and kept looking back, his legs wobbly with shock.

And he allowed himself to be overtaken. With his head down and pulled like a turtle's into the collar of his overcoat, he simply swung his fist once through the air, in rage, as if he were pounding on an imaginary table and growled through clenched teeth, 'Idiot!'

Just to be safe, Maigret had brought out his revolver. Gun in hand, without taking his eyes off the other man, he shook the legs of his trousers, soaked to the knees, while water spurted from his shoes.

Back at the road, the driver was tapping on the horn to let them know that the car was roadworthy again.

'Let's go!' said the inspector.

And they took their same seats in the car, in silence. Van Damme still had his cigar between his teeth but he would not meet Maigret's eyes.

Ten kilometres. Twenty kilometres. They slowed down to go through a town, where people were going about their business in the lighted streets. Then it was back to the highway.

'You still can't arrest me, though,' said Van Damme abruptly, and Maigret started with surprise. And yet these words — so unexpected, spoken so slowly, even stubbornly — had echoed his own misgivings . . .

They reached Meaux. Countryside gave way to the outer suburbs. A light rain began to fall, and whenever the car passed a streetlamp, each drop became a star. Then the inspector leaned forwards to speak into the voice-pipe.

'You're to take us to the Police Judiciaire, Quai des Orfèvres.'

He filled a pipe he could not smoke because his matches were now wet. Van Damme's face was almost completely turned away from him and further obscured in the dim light, but he could sense the man's fury.

There was now a hard edge to the atmosphere, something rancorous and intense.

Maigret himself had his chin thrust out belligerently.

This tension led to a ridiculous incident after the car pulled up in front of the Préfecture and the men got out, the inspector first.

'Come along!'

The driver was waiting to be paid, but Van Damme was ignoring him. There was a moment of hesitation, indecision.

'Well?' said Maigret, not unaware of the absurdity of the situation. 'You're the one who hired the car.'

'Pardon me: if I travelled as your prisoner, it's up to you to pay.'

A small matter, but didn't it show how much

had happened since Rheims and, most importantly, how much the Belgian businessman had changed?

Maigret paid and silently showed Van Damme to his office. After closing the door behind him, the first thing he did was to stir up the fire in the stove.

Next he took some clothing from a cupboard and, without a glance at the other man, changed his trousers, shoes and socks and placed his damp things near the stove to dry.

Van Damme had sat down without waiting to be asked. In the bright light, the change in him was even more striking: he'd left his bogus bonhomie, his open manner and somewhat strained smile back at Luzancy and now, with a grim and cunning look, he was waiting.

Pretending to pay him no attention, Maigret kept busy for a little while around his office, organizing dossiers, telephoning his boss for some information that had nothing to do with the current case.

Finally, he went over to confront Van Damme.

'When, where and how did you first meet the man who committed suicide in Bremen and who was travelling with a passport in the name of Louis Jeunet?'

The other man flinched almost imperceptibly but faced his challenger with bold composure.

'Why am I here?'

'You refuse to answer my question?'

Van Damme laughed, but now his laughter was cold and sarcastic.

'I know the law as well as you do, inspector.

65

Either you charge me and must show me the arrest warrant, or you don't charge me and I don't have to answer you. And in the first case, the law allows me to wait for the assistance of a lawyer before speaking to you.'

Maigret did not seem angry or even annoyed by the man's attitude. On the contrary! He studied him with curiosity and perhaps a certain satisfaction.

Thanks to the incident at Luzancy, Joseph Van Damme had been forced to abandon his play-acting and the pretence he had kept up not only with Maigret, but with everyone else and even, in the end, with himself.

There was almost nothing left of the jolly, shallow businessman from Bremen, constantly on the go between his modern office and the finest taverns and restaurants. Gone was the happy-go-lucky operator raking in money with zestful energy and a taste for the good life. All that remained was a haggard face drained of colour, and it was uncanny how quickly dark, puffy circles seemed to have appeared under his eyes.

Only an hour earlier, hadn't Van Damme still been a free man who, although he did have something on his conscience, yet enjoyed the self-assurance guaranteed by his broker's licence, his reputation, his money and his shrewdness?

And he himself had emphasized this change.

In Rheims, he was used to standing round after round of drinks. He offered his guests the finest cigars. He had only to give an order, and a café proprietor would hasten to curry favour, phoning a garage to hire their most comfortable car.

He was somebody!

In Paris? He had refused to pay for the trip. He invoked the law. He appeared ready to argue, to defend himself at every turn, fiercely, like a man fighting for his life.

And he was furious with himself! His angry exclamation after what had happened on the bank of the Marne was proof of that. There had been no premeditation. He hadn't known the driver. Even when they had stopped for the flat tyre, he hadn't immediately realized how that might work to his advantage.

Only when they had reached the water . . . The swirling current, the trees swept by as if they were simply dead leaves . . . Like a fool, without thinking twice, he'd given that push with his shoulder.

Now he was beside himself. He was sure that the inspector had been waiting for that move! He probably even realized that he was done for — and was all the more determined to strike back with everything he had.

When he went to light a new cigar, Maigret snatched it from his mouth, tossed it into the coal scuttle — and for good measure removed the hat Van Damme hadn't bothered to take off.

★   ★   ★

'For your information,' said the Belgian, 'I have business to attend to. If you do not mean to officially arrest me in accordance with the regulations, I must ask you to be good enough to release me. If you don't, I'll be forced to file a complaint for false imprisonment.

'With regard to your little dip in the river, I might as well tell you that I'll deny everything: the towpath was soggy and you slipped in the mud. The driver will confirm that I never tried to run away, as I would have if I'd really tried to drown you.

'As for the rest, I still don't know what you might have against me. I came to Paris on business and I can prove that. Then I went to Rheims to see an old friend, an upstanding citizen like myself.

'After meeting you in Bremen, where we don't often see Frenchmen, I was trusting enough to consider you a friend, taking you out for dinner and drinks and then offering you a ride back to Paris.

'You showed me and my friends the photograph of a man we do not know. A man who killed himself! That's been materially proved. No one has lodged a complaint, so you have no grounds for taking action.

'And that's all I have to say to you.'

Maigret stuck a twist of paper into the stove, lit his pipe and remarked, almost as an afterthought, 'You're perfectly free to go.'

He could not help smiling to see Van Damme so dumb-founded by his suspiciously easy victory.

'What do you mean?'

'That you're free, that's all! May I add that

I'm quite ready to return your hospitality and invite you to dinner.'

Rarely had he felt so light-hearted. The other man gaped at him in amazement, almost in fear, as if the inspector's words had been heavy with hidden threats. Warily, Van Damme rose to his feet.

'I'm free to return to Bremen?'

'Why not? You just said yourself that you've committed no crime.'

For an instant, it seemed that Van Damme might recover his confidence and bluster, might even accept that dinner invitation and explain away the incident at Luzancy as clumsiness or a momentary aberration . . .

But the smile on Maigret's face snuffed out that flicker of optimism. Van Damme grabbed his hat and clapped it on to his head.

'How much do I owe you for the car?'

'Nothing at all. Only too happy to have been of service.'

Van Damme was at such a loss for words that his lips were trembling, and he had no idea how to leave gracefully. In the end he shrugged and walked out, muttering, 'Idiot!'

But it was impossible to tell what or whom he meant by that.

Out on the staircase, as Maigret leaned over the handrail to watch him go, he was still saying it over and over . . .

Sergeant Lucas happened along with some files, on his way to his boss's office.

'Quick! Get your hat and coat: follow that man to the ends of the earth if you have to . . . '

And Maigret plucked the files from his subordinate's hands.

* * *

The inspector had just finished filling out various requests for information, each headed by a different name. Sent out to the appropriate divisions, these forms would return to him with detailed reports on these persons of interest: Maurice Belloir, a native of Liège, deputy director of a bank, Rue de Vesle, Rheims; Jef Lombard, photoengraver in Liège; Gaston Janin, sculptor, Rue Lepic, Paris; and Joseph Van Damme, import-export commission agent in Bremen.

He was filling out the last form when the office boy announced that a man wanted to see him regarding the suicide of Louis Jeunet.

It was late. Headquarters was practically deserted, although an inspector was typing a report in the neighbouring office.

'Come!'

Ushered in, his visitor stopped at the door, looking awkward and ill at ease, as if he might already be sorry to have come.

'Sit down, why don't you!'

Maigret had taken his measure: tall, thin, with whitish-blond hair, poorly shaved, wearing shabby clothes rather like Louis Jeunet's. His overcoat was missing a button, the collar was soiled, and the lapels in need of a brushing.

From a few other tiny signs — a certain attitude, a way of sitting down and looking

70

around — the inspector recognized an ex-con, someone whose papers may all be in order but who still cannot help being nervous around the police.

'You're here because of the photo? Why didn't you come in right away? That picture appeared in the papers two days ago.'

'I don't read them,' the man explained. 'But my wife happened to bring some shopping home wrapped in a bit of newspaper.'

Maigret realized that he'd seen this somewhere before, this constantly shifting expression, this nervous twitching and most of all, the morbid anxiety in the man's eyes.

'Did you know Louis Jeunet?'

'I'm not sure. It isn't a good photo. But I think . . . I believe he's my brother.'

Maigret couldn't help it: he sighed with relief. He felt that this time the whole mystery would be cleared up at last. And he went to stand with his back to the stove, as he often did when in a good mood.

'In which case, your name would be Jeunet?'

'No, but that's it, that's why I hesitated to come here, and yet — he really is my brother! I'm sure of that, now that I see a better photo on the desk . . . That scar, for example! But I don't understand why he killed himself — or why in the world he would change his name.'

'And yours is . . . '

'Armand Lecocq d'Arneville. I brought my papers.'

And there again, that way he reached into his pocket for a grimy passport betrayed his status

71

on the margins of society, someone used to attracting suspicion and proving his identity.

'D'Arneville with a small *d* and an apostrophe?'

'Yes.'

'You were born in Liège,' continued the inspector, consulting the passport. 'You're thirty-five years old. Your profession?'

'At present, I'm an office messenger in a factory at Issy-les-Moulineaux. We live in Grenelle, my wife and I.'

'It says here you're a mechanic.'

'I was one. I've done this and that . . . '

'Even some prison time!' exclaimed Maigret, leafing through the passport. 'You're a deserter.'

'There was an amnesty! Just let me explain . . . My father had money, he ran a tyre business, but I was only six when he abandoned my mother, who'd just given birth to my brother Jean. That's where it all started!

'We moved to a little place in Rue de la Province, in Liège, and in the beginning my father sent us money to live on fairly regularly. He liked to live it up, had mistresses; once, when he came by to drop off our monthly envelope, there was a woman in the car waiting for him down in the street. There were scenes, arguments, and my father stopped paying, or maybe he began paying less and less. My mother worked as a cleaning woman and she gradually went half-mad, not crazy enough to be shut away, but she'd go up to people and pour out her troubles, and she used to roam the streets in tears . . .

72

'I hardly ever saw my brother. I was off running with the local kids. They must have hauled us in to the police station ten times. Then I was sent to work in a hardware store. My mother was always crying, so I stayed away from home as much as I could. She liked all the old neighbour women to come over so she could wail her heart out with them.

'I joined the army when I was sixteen and asked to be sent to the Congo, but I only lasted a month. For about a week I hid in Matadi, then I stowed away on a passenger steamer bound for Europe. I got caught, served some time, escaped and made it to France, where I worked at all sorts of jobs. I've gone starving hungry, slept in the market here at Les Halles.

'I haven't always been on the up and up, but I swear to you, I've buckled down and been clean for four years. I'm even married now! To a factory worker. She's had to keep her job because I don't earn much and sometimes there's nothing for me . . .

'I've never tried to go back to Belgium. Someone told me that my mother died in a lunatic asylum but that my father's still alive. He never wanted to bother with us, though. He has a second family.'

And the man gave a crooked smile, as if to apologize.

'What about your brother?'

'It was different with him: Jean was serious. He won a scholarship as a boy and went on to secondary school. When I left Belgium for the Congo he was only thirteen, and I haven't seen

73

him since. I heard news now and again, whenever I ran into anyone from Liège. Some people took an interest in him, and he went on to study at the university there. That was ten years ago . . . After that, any Belgians I saw told me they didn't know anything about him, that he must have gone abroad, because he'd dropped out of sight.

'It was a real shock to see the photograph, and especially to think that he'd died in Bremen, under a false name. You can't have any idea . . . Me, I got off to a bad start, I messed up, did stupid things, but when I remember Jean, at thirteen . . . He was like me, but steadier, more serious, already reading poetry. He used to study all by himself at night, reading by the light of candle ends he got from a sacristan. I was sure he'd make it. Listen, even when he was little, he would never have been a street kid, not at any price — and the neighbourhood bad boys even made fun of him!

'But me, I was always short of money, and I wasn't ashamed to hound my mother for it. She used to go without to give me some . . . She adored us. At sixteen, you don't understand! But now I can remember a time when I was mean to her simply because I'd promised some girl I'd take her to the movies . . . Well, my mother had no money. I cried, I threatened her! A charity had just got some medicines for her — and she went and sold them.

'Can you understand? And now it's Jean who's dead, like that, up there, with someone else's name! I don't know what he did. I cannot believe he went down the same wrong road I did. You wouldn't believe it either if you'd known him as a child . . .

'Please, can you tell me anything?'

But Maigret handed the man's passport back to him and asked, 'In Liège, do you know any Belloirs, Van Dammes, Janins, Lombards?'

'A Belloir, yes: the father was a doctor, in our neighbourhood. The son was a student. But they were well-to-do, respectable people, out of my league.'

'And the others?'

'I've heard the name Van Damme before. I think there was a big grocery store in Rue de la Cathédrale by that name. Oh, it's so long ago now . . . ' He seemed to hesitate.

And then Armand Lecocq d'Arneville asked, 'Could I see Jean's body? Has it been brought here?'

'It will arrive in Paris tomorrow.'

'Are you sure that he really did kill himself?'

Maigret looked away, disturbed by the thought that he was more than sure of it: he had witnessed the tragedy and been the unwitting cause of it.

The other man was twisting his cap in his hands, shifting from one foot to the other, awaiting his dismissal. Lost within pale lids, his deep-set eyes with their pupils flecked grey like confetti reminded Maigret so poignantly of the humble, anxious eyes of the traveller from Neuschanz that within his breast the inspector felt a sharp pang that was very like remorse.

6

The Hanged Men

It was nine o'clock in the evening. Maigret was at home in Boulevard Richard-Lenoir in his shirt-sleeves, his collar off, and his wife was sewing when Lucas came in soaked from the downpour outside, shrugging the rain from his shoulders.

'The man left town,' he said. 'Seeing as I wasn't sure if I was supposed to follow him abroad . . .'

'Liège?'

'That's it! You already knew? His luggage was at the Hôtel du Louvre. He had dinner there, changed and took the 6.19 Liège express. Single ticket, first class. He bought a whole slew of magazines at the station newsstand.'

'You'd think he was trying to get underfoot on purpose!' groused the inspector. 'In Bremen, when I've no idea he even exists, he's the one who shows up at the morgue, invites me to lunch and plain latches on to me. I get back to Paris: he's here a few hours before or after I arrive . . . Probably before, because he took a plane. I go to Rheims; he's already there. An hour ago, I decided to return to Liège tomorrow — and he'll be there by this evening! And the last straw? He's well aware that I'm coming and that his presence there almost amounts to an accusation against him.'

Lucas, who knew nothing about the case, ventured a suggestion.

'Maybe he wants to draw suspicion on himself to protect somebody else?'

'Are you talking about a crime?' asked Mme Maigret peaceably, without looking up from her sewing.

But her husband rose with a sigh and looked back at the armchair in which he'd been so comfortable just a moment before.

'How late do the trains run to Belgium?'

'Only the night train is left, at 9.30. It arrives in Liège at around 6 a.m.'

'Would you pack my bag?' Maigret asked his wife. 'Lucas, a little something? Help yourself, you know where everything is in the cabinet. My sister-in-law has just sent us some plum brandy, and she makes it herself, in Alsace. It's the bottle with the long neck . . . '

He dressed, removed clothing B from the yellow suitcase and placed it, well wrapped, in his travel bag. Half an hour later, he left with Lucas, and they waited outside for a taxi.

'What case is this?' Lucas asked. 'I haven't heard anything about it around the shop.'

'I hardly know myself!' the inspector exclaimed. 'A very strange fellow died, in a way that makes no sense, right in front of me — and *that* incident is all tied up in the most ungodly tangle of events, which I'm attempting to figure out. I'm charging blindly at it like a wild boar and wouldn't be surprised if I wound up getting my knuckles rapped . . . Here's a taxi. Shall I drop you off somewhere?'

It was eight in the morning when Maigret left the Hôtel du Chemin de Fer, across from Gare des Guillemins, in Liège. He'd taken a bath, shaved and was carrying a package containing not all of clothing B, just the suit jacket.

He found Rue Haute-Sauvenière, a steep and busy street, where he asked for directions to Morcel's. In the dim light of the tailor's shop, a man in shirt-sleeves examined the jacket, turning it over and over carefully while questioning the inspector.

'It's old,' he finally announced, 'and it's torn. That's about all I can tell you.'

'Nothing else comes to mind?'

'Not a thing. The collar's poorly cut. It's imitation English woollen cloth, made in Verviers.'

And then the man became more chatty.

'You're French? Does this jacket belong to someone you know?'

With a sigh, Maigret retrieved the suit jacket as the man nattered on and at last wound up where he ought to have started.

'You see, I've only been here for the past six months. If I'd made the suit in question, it wouldn't have had time to wear out like that.'

'And Monsieur Morcel?'

'In Robermont!'

'Is that far from here?'

The tailor laughed, tickled by the misunderstanding.

'Robermont, that's our cemetery. Monsieur

Morcel died at the beginning of this year, and I took over his business.'

Back out in the street with his package under his arm, Maigret headed for Rue Hors-Château, one of the oldest streets in the city, where, at the far end of a courtyard, he found a zinc plaque announcing: *Photogravure Centrale — Jef Lombard — Rapid results for work of all kinds.*

The windows had small panes, in the style of historic Liège, and in the centre of the courtyard of small, uneven paving stones was a fountain bearing the sculpted coat of arms of some great lord of long ago.

The inspector rang. He heard footsteps coming down from the first floor, and an old woman peeked out from the ancient-looking door.

'Just push it open,' she said, pointing to a glazed door. 'The workshop's all the way at the end of the passage.'

A long room, lit by a glass roof; two men in blue overalls working among zinc plates and tubs full of acids; a floor strewn with photographic proofs and paper smeared with thick, greasy ink.

The walls were crowded with posters, advertisements, magazine covers.

'Monsieur Lombard?'

'He's in the office, with a gentleman. Please come this way — and don't get any ink on you! Take a left turn, then it's the first door.'

The building must have been constructed piecemeal; stairs went up and down, and doors opened on to abandoned rooms.

The feeling was both antiquated and weirdly

cheerful, like the old woman who'd greeted him downstairs and the atmosphere in the workroom.

Coming to a shadowy corridor, the inspector heard voices and thought he recognized that of Joseph Van Damme. He tried in vain to make out the words, and when he took a few steps closer, the voices stopped. A man stuck his head out of the half-open door: it was Jef Lombard.

'Is it for me?' he called, not recognizing his visitor in the half-light.

The office was smaller than the other rooms and furnished with two chairs, shelves full of photographic negatives and a table cluttered with bills, prospectuses and business letters from various companies.

And perched on a corner of the table was Van Damme, who nodded vaguely in Maigret's direction and then sat perfectly still, scowling and staring straight ahead.

Jef Lombard was in his work clothes; his hands were dirty, and there were tiny blackish flecks on his face.

'May I help you?'

He cleared papers off a chair, which he pushed over to his visitor, and then he looked around for the cigarette butt he'd left balanced on the edge of a wooden shelf now beginning to char.

'Just some information,' replied the inspector, without sitting down. 'I'm sorry to bother you, but I'd like to know if, a few years ago, you ever knew a certain Jean Lecocq d'Arneville . . . '

There was a quick, distinct change. Van Damme shuddered, but resisted turning towards Maigret, while Lombard bent abruptly down to pick up a crumpled paper lying on the floor.

'I . . . may have heard that name before,' murmured the photoengraver. 'He . . . From Liège, isn't he?'

The colour had drained from his face. He moved a pile of plates from one spot to another.

'I don't know what became of him. I . . . It was so long ago . . . '

'Jef! Jef, hurry!'

It was a woman's voice, coming from the labyrinth of stairs and corridors, and she arrived at the open door breathless from running, so excited that her legs were shaky and she had to wipe her face with a corner of her apron. Maigret recognized the old lady he'd seen downstairs.

'Jef!'

And he, now even whiter from emotion, his eyes gleaming, gasped, 'Well?'

'A girl! Hurry!'

The man looked around, stammered something impossible to decipher and dashed out of the door.

★ ★ ★

Alone with Maigret, Van Damme pulled a cigar from his pocket, lit it slowly, crushed out the match with his shoe. He wore the same wooden expression as in Maigret's office: his mouth was set in the same hard line, and he ground his jaws in the same way.

But the inspector pretended not to notice him and, hands in his pockets, pipe between his teeth, he began to walk around the office, examining the walls.

Very little of the original wallpaper was still visible, however, because any space not taken up by shelves was covered with drawings, etchings, and paintings that were simply canvases on stretchers without frames, rather plodding landscapes in which the tree foliage and grass were of the same even, pasty green.

There were a few caricatures signed *Jef*, some of them touched up with watercolours, some cut from a local paper.

What struck Maigret, though, was how many of the drawings were all variations on one particular theme. The drawing paper had yellowed with age, and a few dates indicated that these sketches had been done about ten years earlier.

They were executed in a different style as well, with a more darkly Romantic sensibility, and seemed like the efforts of a young art student imitating the work of Gustave Doré.

A first ink drawing showed a hanged man swinging from a gallows on which perched an enormous crow. And there were at least twenty other etchings and pen or pencil sketches that had the same leitmotif of hanging.

On the edge of a forest: a man hanging from every branch.

A church steeple: beneath the weathercock, a human body dangling from each arm of the cross.

There were hanged men of all kinds. Some were dressed in the fashions of the sixteenth century and formed a kind of Court of Miracles, where everybody was swinging a few feet above the ground.

There was one crazy hanged man in a top hat and tails, cane in hand, whose gallows was a lamp post.

Below another sketch were written four lines from François Villon's *Ballad of the Hanged Men*.

There were dates, always from around the same time, and all these macabre pictures from ten years earlier were now displayed along with captioned sketches for comic papers, drawings for calendars and almanacs, landscapes of the surrounding Ardennes and advertising posters.

Another recurrent theme was the steeple — in fact, so was the whole church, depicted from the front, from the sides, from below. The church portal, on its own. The gargoyles. The parvis, with its six steps looming large in perspective . . .

Always the same church! And as Maigret moved from one wall to another, he could sense Van Damme's growing agitation, an uneasiness fuelled, perhaps, by the same temptation that had overwhelmed him by the dam at Luzancy.

A quarter of an hour passed like this, and then Jef Lombard returned, his eyes moist with emotion, wiping his hand across his forehead and brushing away a stray lock of hair.

'Please forgive me,' he said. 'My wife has just given birth. A girl!'

There was a hint of pride in his voice, but, as he spoke, he was looking anxiously back and forth between Maigret and Van Damme.

'Our third child. But I'm still as excited as I was the first time! You saw my mother-in-law, well — she had eleven and she's sobbing with joy, she's gone to give the workmen the good news and wants them to see our baby girl.'

His eyes followed Maigret's gaze, now fixed upon the two men hanging from the church-steeple cross, and he became even more nervous.

'The sins of my youth,' he murmured, clearly uncomfortable. 'Terrible stuff. But at the time I thought I was going to be a great artist . . . '

'It's a church in Liège?'

Jef didn't answer right away. And when he finally did, it was almost with regret.

'It's been gone for seven years. They tore it down to build a new church. The old one wasn't beautiful, it didn't even have any style to speak of, but it was very old, with a touch of mystery in all its lines and in the little streets and alleys around it . . . They've all been levelled now.'

'What was its name?'

'The Church of Saint-Pholien. The new one is in the same place and bears the same name.'

Still seated on the corner of Lombard's table, Joseph Van Damme was fidgeting as if his nerves were burning him inside, an inner turmoil betrayed only by the faintest of movements, uneven breathing, a trembling in his fingers, and the way one foot was jiggling against a table leg.

'Were you married at that time?' continued Maigret.

Lombard laughed.

'I was nineteen! I was studying at the Académie des Beaux-Arts. Look over there . . . '

84

And he pointed, with a look of fond nostalgia, to a clumsy portrait in gloomy colours that was nevertheless recognizable as him, thanks to the telling irregularity of his features. His hair was almost shoulder length; he wore a black tunic buttoned up to his neck and an ample *lavallière* bow tie.

The painting was flagrantly Romantic, even to the traditional death's-head in the background.

'If you'd told me back then that I'd wind up a photo-engraver!' he marvelled, with helpless irony.

Jef Lombard seemed equally unsettled by Van Damme and Maigret, but he clearly had no idea how to get them to leave.

A workman came for advice about a plate that wasn't ready.

'Have them come back this afternoon.'

'But they say that will be too late!'

'So what! Tell them I've just had a daughter . . .'

Lombard's eyes, his movements, the pallor of his complexion pocked with tiny acid marks — everything about him reflected a disturbing confusion of joy, anxiety, perhaps even anguish.

'If I may, I'd like to offer you something . . . We'll go down to the house.'

The three men walked back along the maze of corridors and through the door where the old woman had spoken to Maigret. There were blue tiles in the hall and a clean smell faintly scented, however, with a kind of staleness, perhaps from the stuffiness of the lying-in room.

'The two boys are at my brother-in-law's.

Come through here . . . '

He opened the door to the dining room, where the small panes of the windows admitted a dim, bleak light that glinted off the many copper pieces on display everywhere. The furniture was dark.

On the wall was a large portrait of a woman, signed *Jef*, full of awkward passages but imbued with a clear desire to present the model — presumably the artist's wife — in a flattering way.

When Maigret looked around the room he was not surprised to find more hanged men. The best ones, considered good enough to frame!

'You'll have a glass of genever?'

The inspector could feel Van Damme glaring coldly at him, obviously infuriated by the whole situation.

'You were saying a moment ago that you knew Jean Lecocq d'Arneville . . . '

Steps sounded on the floor above, probably from the lying-in room.

'But only casually,' the distracted father replied, listening intently to the faint whimpering of the newborn infant.

And raising his glass, he exclaimed, 'To the health of my little girl! And my wife!'

Turning abruptly away, he drained his glass in one go, then went to the sideboard and pretended to look for something while he recovered from his emotions, but Maigret still caught the soft hiccup of a stifled sob.

'I'm sorry, I have to go up there! On a day like today . . . '

Maigret and Van Damme had not exchanged one word. As they crossed the courtyard, passing by the fountain, the inspector glanced with a faint smile at the other man, wondering what he would do next.

Once out in the street, however, Van Damme simply touched the brim of his hat and strode off to the right.

There aren't many taxis in Liège. Unfamiliar with the tram lines, Maigret walked back to the Hôtel du Chemin de Fer, where he had lunch and made inquiries about the local newspapers.

At two o'clock, he entered the *La Meuse* newspaper building at the very moment when Joseph Van Damme was leaving it: the two men passed silently within arm's reach of each other.

'He's still one step ahead of me!' Maigret grumbled under his breath.

When he asked the usher with his silver chain of office about consulting the newspaper's archives, he was told to fill out an authorization form and wait for its approval.

Maigret thought over certain striking details in his case: Armand Lecocq d'Arneville had told him that his brother had left Liège at around the same time that Jef Lombard was drawing hanged men with such morbid fascination.

And clothing B, which the tramp of Neuschanz and Bremen had carried around in the yellow suitcase, was at least six years old, according to the German technician, *and perhaps even ten* . . .

And now Joseph Van Damme had turned up at *La Meuse*! Didn't that tell the inspector something?

The usher showed Maigret into a room with heavy formal furniture, where the parquet gleamed like a skating rink.

'Which year's collection do you wish to consult?'

Maigret had already noticed the enormous cardboard cases arrayed around the entire room, each containing the issues of a particular year.

'I'll find it myself, thank you.'

The room smelled of polish, musty paper and formal luxury. On the moleskin tabletop were reading stands to hold the cumbersome volumes. Everything was so neat, so clean, so austere that the inspector hardly dared take his pipe from his pocket.

In a few moments he was leafing page by page through the newspapers of the 'year of the hanged men'.

Thousands of headlines streamed past his gaze, some recalling events of worldwide importance, others dealing with local incidents: a big department store fire (a full page for three days running), an alderman's resignation, an increase in tram fares.

Suddenly: torn newsprint, all along the binding. The daily paper for 15 February had been ripped out.

Hurrying into the reception room, Maigret fetched the usher.

'Someone came here before I did, isn't that

88

right? And it was this same collection he asked for?'

'Yes. He was here only five minutes or so.'

'Are you from Liège? Do you remember what happened back then?'

'Ten years ago? Hmm . . . That's the year my sister-in-law died . . . I know! The big floods! We even had to wait a week for the burial because the only way you could get around in the streets down by the Meuse was by boat. Here, look at these articles: *The King and Queen visit the disaster victims* . . . There are photos, and — wait, we're missing an issue. How extraordinary! I'll have to inform the director about this . . . '

Maigret picked up a scrap of newsprint that had fallen to the floor while Joseph Van Damme — and there was no doubt about it — had been tearing out the pages for 15 February.

7

The Three Men

There are four daily papers in Liège. Maigret spent two hours checking their archives one after the other and, as he expected, they were all missing the 15 February issue.

With its luxury department stores, popular brasseries, cinemas and dance halls, the place to see and be seen in Liège is the busy quadrangle of streets known as the Carré. At least three times, the inspector caught sight of Joseph Van Damme strolling around there, walking stick in hand.

When Maigret returned to the Hôtel du Chemin de Fer, he found two messages waiting for him. The first was a telegram from Lucas, to whom he had given certain instructions just before leaving Paris.

Stove ashes found room Louis Jeunet Rue Roquette analysed by technician stop Identified remains Belgian and French banknotes stop Quantity suggests large sum

The other was a letter delivered to the hotel by messenger, typed on ordinary typing paper without any heading.

Detective Chief Inspector,

I beg to inform you that I am prepared to furnish the answers you seek in your inquiry.

I have my reasons for being cautious, and I would be obliged, if my proposal interests you, if you would meet me this evening at around eleven o'clock, at the Café de la Bourse, which is behind the Théâtre Royal.

Until then, I remain, sir, your most humble, loyal and obedient servant, etc., etc.

No signature. On the other hand, a rather surprising number of business turns of phrase for a note of this kind: *I beg to inform you . . . I would be obliged . . . if my proposal interests you . . . your most humble, loyal and obedient servant, etc., etc . . .*

Dining alone at his table, Maigret realized that, although he hadn't much noticed it before, the focus of his attention had shifted somewhat away from Jean Lecocq d'Arneville, who had killed himself in a hotel room in Bremen under the name of Louis Jeunet.

Now the inspector found himself haunted by the images Jef Lombard had hung up everywhere, those hanged men dangling from a church-steeple cross, from the trees in a wood, from a nail in an attic room, grotesque or sinister hanged men in the garb of many centuries, their faces livid or flushed crimson.

At half past ten he set out for the Théâtre Royal; it was five to eleven when he pushed open the door of the Café de la Bourse, a quiet little place frequented by locals and by card players in particular.

And there he found a surprise waiting for him. Three men were sitting at a table off in a corner, over by the counter: Maurice Belloir, Jef Lombard and Joseph Van Damme.

Things seemed to hang fire for a moment while the waiter helped Maigret out of his overcoat. Belloir automatically rose halfway in greeting. Van Damme didn't move a muscle. Lombard, grimacing with extraordinary nervous tension, could not keep still as he waited for his companions to make a move.

Was Maigret going to come over, shake hands, sit down with them? He knew them all: he had accepted Van Damme's invitation to lunch in Bremen, he'd had a glass of brandy at Belloir's house in Rheims, and only that morning he had visited Lombard's home.

'Good evening, gentlemen.'

He shook their hands with his customary firmness, which could at times seem vaguely threatening.

'Imagine, meeting you all again like this!'

There was space next to Van Damme on the banquette, so Maigret parked himself there.

'A glass of pale ale!' he called to the waiter.

Then silence fell. A strained, oppressive silence. Van Damme stared straight ahead, his teeth clenched. Lombard was still fidgeting, as if his clothes were too tight at his armpits. Belloir, cold and distant, was studying his fingertips and ran a wooden match end under the nail of one index finger to remove a speck.

'Madame Lombard is doing well?'

Jef Lombard darted a glance all around, as if

seeking something to cling to, then stared at the stove and stammered, 'Very well . . . Thank you.'

By the wall clock behind the counter, Maigret counted five whole minutes without anyone saying a word.

Van Damme, who had let his cigar go out, was the only man who allowed his face to burn with undisguised hatred.

Lombard was the most interesting one to observe. Everything that had happened that day had surely rubbed his nerves raw, and even the tiniest muscle in his face was twitching.

The four men were sitting in an absolute oasis of silence in a café where everyone else was loudly chattering away.

'And *belote* again!' crowed a card player on the right.

'High *tierce*,' said a fellow cautiously on the left. 'We're all agreed on that?'

'Three beers! Three!' shouted the waiter.

The whole café was a beehive of noise and activity except for that one table of four, around which an invisible wall seemed to be growing.

Lombard was the one who broke the spell. He'd been chewing on his lower lip when suddenly he leaped to his feet and gasped, 'The hell with it!'

After glancing briefly but piercingly at his companions, he grabbed his hat and coat and, flinging the door violently open, left the café.

'I bet he bursts into tears as soon as he gets off on his own,' said Maigret thoughtfully.

He'd sensed it, that sob of rage and despair

swelling inside the man's throat until his Adam's apple quivered.

Turning to Van Damme, who was staring at the marble tabletop, Maigret tossed down half his beer and wiped his lips with the back of his hand.

The atmosphere was the same — but ten times more concentrated — as in the house in Rheims, where the inspector had first imposed himself on these three people. And the man's imposing bulk itself helped make his stubborn presence all the more menacing.

Maigret was tall and wide, particularly broad-shouldered, solidly built, and his run-of-the-mill clothes emphasized his peasant stockiness. His features were coarse, and his eyes could seem as still and dull as a cow's. In this he resembled certain figures out of children's nightmares, those monstrously big blank-faced creatures that bear down upon sleepers as if to crush them. There was something implacable and inhuman about him that suggested a pachyderm plodding inexorably towards its goal.

He drank his beer, smoked his pipe, watched with satisfaction as the minute hand of the café clock snapped onwards with a metallic click. On a livid clock face!

He seemed to be ignoring everyone and yet he kept an eye on the slightest signs of life to either side.

This was one of the most extraordinary hours of his career. For this stand-off lasted almost one hour: exactly fifty-two minutes! A war of nerves.

Although Jef Lombard had been *hors de*

combat practically from the outset, the other two men were hanging on.

Maigret sat between them like a judge, but one who made no accusations and whose thoughts could not be divined. What did he know? Why had he come? What was he waiting for? A word, a gesture that would corroborate his suspicions? Had he already found out the whole truth — or was his confident manner simply a bluff?

And what could anyone say? More musings on coincidence and chance encounters?

Silence reigned. They waited even without any idea of what they were waiting for. They were waiting for something, and nothing was happening!

With each passing minute, the hand on the clock quivered as the mechanism within creaked faintly. At first no one had paid any attention. Now, the sound was incredibly loud — and the event had even separated into three stages: an initial click; the minute hand beginning to move; then another click, as if to slide the hand into its new slot. And as an obtuse angle slowly became an acute angle, the clock face changed: the two hands would eventually meet.

The waiter kept looking over at this gloomy table in astonishment. Every once in a while, Maurice Belloir would swallow — and Maigret would know this without even looking. He could hear him live, breathe, wince, carefully shift his feet a little now and again, as if he were in church.

Not too many customers were left. The red cloths and playing cards were vanishing from the pale marble table-tops. The waiter stepped outside to close the shutters, while the *patronne* sorted the chips into little piles, according to their value.

'You're staying?' Belloir finally asked, in an almost unrecognizable voice.

'And you?'

'I'm . . . not sure.'

Then Van Damme tapped the table sharply with a coin and called to the waiter, 'How much?'

'For the round? Nine francs seventy-five.'

The three of them were standing now, avoiding one another's eyes, and the waiter helped each of them in turn into his overcoat.

'Goodnight, gentlemen.'

It was so foggy outside that the streetlamps were almost lost in the mist. All the shutters were closed. Somewhere in the distance, footsteps echoed along the pavement.

There was a moment's hesitation, for none of the men wanted to take responsibility for deciding in which direction they would go. Behind them, someone was locking the doors of the café and setting the security bars in place.

Off to the left lay an alley of crookedly aligned old houses.

'Well, gentlemen,' announced Maigret at last, 'the time has come to wish you goodnight.'

He shook Belloir's hand first; it was cold, trembling. The hand Van Damme grudgingly extended was clammy and soft.

The inspector turned up the collar of his overcoat, cleared his throat and began walking alone down the deserted street. And all his senses were attuned to a single purpose: to perceive the faintest noise, the slightest ruffle in the air that might warn him of any danger.

His right hand gripped the butt of the revolver in his pocket. He had the impression that in the network of alleys laid out on his left, enclosed within the centre of Liège like a small island of lepers, people were trying to hurry along without making a sound.

He could just make out a low murmur of conversation but couldn't tell whether it was very near or far away, because the fog was muffling his senses.

Abruptly, he pitched to one side and flattened himself against a door just as a sharp report rang out — and someone, off in the night, took to his heels.

Advancing a few steps, Maigret peered down the alley from which the shot had come but saw only some dark blotches that probably led into blind side alleys and, at the far end 200 metres away, the frosted-glass globe announcing a shop selling *pommes frites*.

A few moments later, as he was walking past that shop, a girl emerged from it with a paper cone of golden *frites*. After propositioning him for form's sake, she headed off to a brighter street.

★ ★ ★

Grinding the pen-nib down on to the paper with his enormous index finger, Maigret was peacefully writing, pausing from time to time to tamp

97

down the hot ashes in his pipe.

He was ensconced in his room in the Hôtel du Chemin de Fer and according to the illuminated station clock, which he could see from his window, it was two in the morning.

Dear old Lucas,

As one never knows what may happen, I'm sending you the following information so that, if necessary, you will be able to carry on the inquiry I have begun.

1. Last week, in Brussels, a shabbily dressed man who looks like a tramp wraps up thirty thousand-franc notes and sends the package to his own address, Rue de la Roquette, in Paris. The evidence will show that he often sent himself similar sums but that *he did not make any use of the money himself.* The proof is that charred remains of large amounts of banknotes burned on purpose have been found in his room.

He goes by the name of Louis Jeunet and is more or less regularly employed by a workshop on his street.

He is married (contact Mme Jeunet, herbalist, Rue Picpus) and has a child. After some acute episodes of alcoholism, however, he leaves his wife and child under mysterious and troubling circumstances.

In Brussels, after posting the money, he buys a suitcase in which to transport some things he's been keeping in a hotel room. While he is on his way to Bremen, I replace his suitcase with another.

Then Jeunet, *who does not appear to have been contemplating suicide and who has already bought something for his supper*, kills himself upon realizing that the contents of his suitcase have been stolen.

The stolen property is an old suit that does not belong to him and which, years earlier, had been torn as if in a struggle and drenched with blood. This suit *was made in Liège*.

In Bremen, a man comes to view the corpse: Joseph Van Damme, an import-export commission agent, *born in Liège*.

In Paris, I learn that Louis Jeunet is in reality Jean Lecocq d'Arneville, *born in Liège*, where he studied to graduate level. He disappeared from Liège about ten years ago and no one there has had any news of him, but he has no black marks against his name.

2. In Rheims, before he leaves for Brussels, Jean Lecocq d'Arneville is observed one night entering the home of Maurice Belloir, deputy director of a local bank and *born in Liège*, who denies this allegation.

But the thirty thousand francs sent from Brussels were supplied by this same Belloir.

At Belloir's house I encounter: Van Damme, who has flown in from Bremen; Jef Lombard, a photoengraver *in Liège*; and Gaston Janin, who was also born *in that city*.

As I am travelling back to Paris with Van Damme, he tries to push me into the Marne.

And I find him again *in Liège*, in the home of Jef Lombard, who was an active painter around ten years ago and has covered the walls of his home with works from that period depicting hanged men.

When I consult the local newspaper archives, I find that all the papers of 15 February in the year of the hanged men have been stolen by Van Damme.

That evening, an unsigned letter promises to tell me everything and gives me an appointment in a local café. There I find not one man, but three: Belloir (in from Rheims), Van Damme and Jef Lombard.

They are not pleased to see me. I have the feeling that it's one of these men who has decided to talk; the others seem to be there simply to prevent this.

Lombard cracks under the strain and leaves abruptly. I stay with the other two men. Shortly past midnight, I take leave of them outside, in the fog, and a few moments later a shot is fired at me.

I conclude both that one of the three tried to talk to me and that one of the same three tried to eliminate me.

And clearly, given that this last action amounts to a confession, *the person in question has no recourse but to try again and not miss me.*

But who is it? Belloir, Van Damme, Lombard?

I'll find out when he tries again. Since accidents do happen, I'm sending you these notes on the off chance, so that you will be familiar with the inquiry from the very beginning.

To see the human side of this case, look in particular at Mme Jeunet and Armand Lecocq d'Arneville, the dead man's brother.

And now I'm going to bed. Give my best to everybody back there.

Maigret

The fog had faded away, leaving beads of pearly hoarfrost on the trees and every blade of grass in Square d'Avroy. A chilly sun gleamed in the pale-blue sky as Maigret crossed the square, and with each passing minute the melting frost fell in limpid drops to the gravel.

It was eight in the morning when the inspector strode through the still-deserted Carré, where the folded sandwich boards of film posters stood propped against closed shutters.

When Maigret stopped at a mailbox to post his letter to Sergeant Lucas, he took a moment to look around him and felt a pang at the thought that somewhere in the city, in those streets bathed in sunlight, a man was at that very moment thinking about him, a man whose salvation depended upon killing him. And the man had the home-ground advantage over the inspector, as he had proved the night before by vanishing into the maze of alleys.

He knew Maigret, too, and was perhaps even watching him where he stood, whereas the inspector did not know who he was.

Could he be Jef Lombard? Did the danger lie

in the ramshackle house in Rue Hors-Château, where a woman and her newborn lay sleeping upstairs, watched over by her loving old mother, while her husband's employees worked nonchalantly among the acid baths, hustled along by bicycle messengers from the newspapers?

Joseph Van Damme, a bold, moody and aggressive man, always scheming: was he not lying in wait for the inspector in a place *where he knew Maigret would eventually appear*?

Because that fellow had foreseen everything ever since Bremen! Three lines in a German newspaper — and he showed up at the morgue! He had lunch with Maigret and then beat him to Rheims!

And beat him again to Rue Hors-Château! Beat the investigator to the newspaper archives!

He was even at the Café de la Bourse!

True, there was nothing to prove that he was the one who had decided to talk to Maigret. But there was nothing to prove that he wasn't!

Perhaps it was Maurice Belloir, so cold and formal, the haughty provincial *grand bourgeois*, who had taken a shot at him in the fog. Maybe he was the one whose only hope was to polish off Maigret.

Or Gaston Janin, the little sculptor with the goatee: he hadn't been at the Café de la Bourse, but he could have been lying in ambush in the street . . .

And what connected all that to a hanged man swinging from a church-steeple cross? Or to clusters of hanged men? Or to forests of trees that bore no fruit but hanged men? Or to an old bloodstained suit with lapels clawed by desperate fingernails?

Typists were going off to work. A municipal street sweeper rolled slowly past, its double-nozzle sprayer and brush roller pushing rubbish into the gutter. At street corners, the local police in their white enamel helmets directed traffic with their shiny white gauntlets.

'Police headquarters?' Maigret inquired.

He followed the directions and arrived while the cleaning ladies were still busy, but a cheerful clerk welcomed his French colleague and, upon the inspector's request to examine some ten-year-old police records, but only for the month of February, the man exclaimed in surprise: 'You're the second person in twenty-four hours! You want to know if a certain Joséphine Bollant was in fact arrested for domestic larceny back then, right?'

'Someone came here?'

'Yesterday, towards five in the afternoon. A citizen of Liège who's made it big abroad even though he's still quite a young man! His father was a doctor, and him, he's got a fine business going, in Germany.'

'Joseph Van Damme?'

'The very man! But no matter how hard he looked, he couldn't find what he wanted.'

'Would you show me?'

It was a green index-book of daily reports bound in numerical order. Five entries were listed for 15 February: two for drunkenness and breach of the peace at night, one for shoplifting, one for assault and battery and the last one for breach of close and stealing rabbits.

Maigret didn't bother to look at them. He simply checked the numbers at the top of each form.

'Did Monsieur Van Damme consult the book himself?'

'Yes. He took it into the office next door.'

'Thank you!'

The five reports were numbered 237, 238, 239, 241 and 242.

In other words, number 240 was missing and had been torn out just as the archived newspapers had been ripped from their bindings.

A few minutes later, Maigret was standing in the square behind the town hall, where cars were pulling up to deliver a wedding party. In spite of himself, he was straining to catch the faintest sound, unable to shake a slight feeling of anxiety that he didn't like at all.

8

Little Klein

He had made it just in time: it was nine o'clock. The employees of the town hall were arriving for work, crossing the main courtyard there and pausing a moment to greet one another on the handsome stone steps, at the top of which a doorkeeper with a braided cap and nicely groomed beard was smoking his pipe.

It was a meerschaum. Maigret noticed this detail, without knowing why; perhaps because it was glinting in the morning sun, because it looked well seasoned and because for a moment the inspector envied this man who was smoking in voluptuous little puffs, standing there as a symbol of peace and joie de vivre.

For that morning the air was like a tonic that grew more bracing as the sun rose higher into the sky. A delightful cacophony reigned, of people shouting in a Walloon dialect, the shrill clanging of the red and yellow streetcars, and the splashing of the four jets in the monumental Perron Fountain doing its best to be heard over the hubbub of the surrounding Place du Marché.

And when Maigret happened to see Joseph Van Damme head up one side of the double staircase leading to the main lobby, he hurried after him. Inside the building, the two staircases continued up on opposite sides, reuniting on each floor. On one landing, the two men found themselves face to face, panting from their exertion, struggling to appear perfectly at ease before the usher with his silver chain of office.

What happened next was short and swift. A question of precision, of split-second timing.

While dashing up the stairs, Maigret had realized that Van Damme had come only to make something disappear, as he had at police headquarters and the newspaper archives.

One of the police reports for 15 February had already been torn out. But in most cities, didn't the police send a copy of all daily reports to the mayor the next morning?

'I would like to see the town clerk,' announced Maigret, with Van Damme only two steps behind him. 'It's urgent . . . '

Their eyes met. They hesitated. The moment for shaking hands passed. When the usher turned expectantly to the businessman from Bremen, he simply murmured, 'It's nothing, I'll come back later.'

He left. The sound of his footsteps died away as he crossed the lobby downstairs.

Shortly afterwards, Maigret was shown into an opulent office, where the town clerk — ramrod straight in his morning coat and a very high collar — quickly began the search for the ten-year-old daily police reports.

The room was warm, the carpets soft and springy. A sunbeam lit up a bishop's crozier in a historical painting that took up one whole section of wall.

After half an hour's hunting and a few polite exchanges, Maigret found the reports about the stolen rabbits, the public drunkenness, the shoplifting and then, between two minor incidents, the following lines:

Officer Lagasse, of Division No. 6, was proceeding this morning at six o'clock to the Pont des Arches to take up his post there when, on passing the main door of the Church of Saint-Pholien, he observed a body hanging from the door knocker.

A doctor was immediately summoned but could only confirm the death of the young man, one Émile Klein, born in Angleur, twenty years old, a house painter living in Rue du Pot-au-Noir.

Klein had hanged himself, apparently around the middle of the night, with the aid of a window-blind cord. His pockets held only a few items of no value and some small change.

The inquiry established that the deceased had not been regularly employed for three months, and he seems to have been driven to his action by destitution.

His mother, Madame Klein, a widow who lives in Angleur on a modest pension, has been notified.

There followed hours of feverish activity. Maigret vigorously pursued this new line of inquiry and yet, without being really aware of it, he was less interested in finding out about Klein than he was in finding Van Damme.

For only then, when he had the businessman again in his sights, would he be closing in on the truth. Hadn't it all started in Bremen? And from then on, whenever Maigret scored a point, hadn't he come up against Van Damme?

Van Damme, who had seen him at the town hall, now knew that he'd read the report, that he was tracking down Klein.

At Angleur, nothing! The inspector had taken a taxi deep into an industrial area where small working-class houses, all cast from the same mould in the same sooty grey, lined up on dismal streets at the feet of factory chimneys.

A woman was washing the doorstep of one such house, where Madame Klein had lived.

'It's at least five years since she passed away.'

Van Damme would not be skulking around that neighbourhood.

'Didn't her son live with her?'

'No! And he made a bad end of it: he did away with himself, at the door of a church.'

That was all. Maigret learned only that Klein's father had been a foreman in a coalfield and that after his death his wife lived off a small pension, occupying only a garret in the house, which she sublet.

'To Police Division No. 6,' he told the taxi driver.

As for Officer Lagasse, he was still alive, but he hardly remembered anything.

'It had rained the whole night, he was soaked, and his red hair was sticking to his face.'

'He was tall? Short?'

'Short, I'd say.'

Maigret went next to the gendarmerie, spending almost an hour in offices that smelled of leather and horse sweat.

'If he was twenty years old at the time, he must have been seen by an army medical board . . . Did you say Klein, with a K?'

They found Form 13, in the 'registrant not acceptable' file, and Maigret copied down the information: *height* 1.55 metres, *chest* .80 metres, and a note mentioning 'weak lungs'.

But Van Damme had still not shown up. Maigret had to look elsewhere. The only result of that morning's inquiries was the certainty that clothing B had never belonged to the hanged man of Saint-Pholien, who had been just a shrimp.

Klein had killed himself. There had been no struggle, not a drop of blood shed.

So what tied him to the Bremen tramp's suitcase and the suicide of Lecocq d'Arneville, alias Louis Jeunet?

★ ★ ★

'Drop me off here . . . And tell me how to find Rue Pot-au-Noir.'

'Behind the church, the street that runs down to Quai Sainte-Barbe.'

After paying off his taxi in front of Saint-Pholien, Maigret took a good look at the new church standing alone in a vast stretch of waste land.

To the right and left of it were boulevards lined by apartment houses built at about the same time as the present church, but behind it there still remained part of the old neighbourhood the city had cut into to make room for Saint-Pholien.

In a stationery shop window, Maigret found some postcards showing the old church, which had been lower, squatter and completely black. One wing had been shored up with timbers. On three sides, dumpy, mean little houses backed up against its walls and gave the whole place a medieval look.

Nothing was left of this Court of Miracles except a sprawl of old houses threaded with alleys and dead ends, all giving off a nauseating odour of poverty.

A stream of soapy water was running down the middle of Rue du Pot-au-Noir, which wasn't even two paces wide. Kids were playing on the doorsteps of houses teeming with life. And although the sun was shining brightly, its rays could not reach down into the alley. A cooper busy hooping barrels had a brazier burning right out in the street.

The house numbers had worn away, so the inspector had to ask for directions to number 7, which turned out to be all the way down a blind alley echoing with the whine of saws and planes, a workshop with a few carpenter's benches at which three men were labouring away. All the shop doors were open, and some glue was heating on a stove.

Looking up, one of the men put down his dead cigarette butt and waited for the visitor to speak.

'Is this the place where a man named Klein used to live?'

The man glanced knowingly at his companions, pointed to the open door of a dark staircase and grumbled, 'Upstairs! Someone's already there.'

'A new tenant?'

The man gave an odd little smile, which Maigret would understand only later.

'Go see for yourself . . . On the first floor, you can't miss it: there's only the one door . . . '

One of the other workmen shook with silent laughter as he worked his long, heavy plane. Maigret started up the stairs, but after a few steps there was no more banister, and the stairwell was completely shrouded in darkness. He struck a match and saw up ahead a door with no lock or doorknob, and only a string to secure it to a rusty nail.

With his hand in his revolver pocket, Maigret nudged the door open with his knee — and was promptly dazzled by light pouring in from a bay window missing a good third of its panes, a sight so surprising that, when he looked around, it took him a few moments to actually focus on anything.

Finally he noticed, off in a corner, a man leaning against the wall and glowering at him with savage fury: it was Joseph Van Damme.

'We were bound to wind up here, don't you think?' said the inspector, in a voice that resonated strangely in the raw, vacant air of the room.

Saying nothing, staring at him venomously, Van Damme never moved.

To understand the layout of the place, one would have had to know what kind of building — convent, barracks, private house — had once contained these walls, not one of which was smooth or square. And although half the room had wooden flooring, the rest was paved with uneven flagstones, as if it were an old chapel.

The walls were whitewashed, except for a rectangular patch of brown bricks apparently blocking up what had once been a window. The view from the bay window was of a gable, a gutter, and beyond them, some crooked roofs off in the direction of the Meuse.

But by far the most bizarre thing of all was that the place was furnished so incoherently that it might have been a lunatic asylum — or some elaborate practical joke.

Strewn in disorder on the floor were new but unfinished chairs, a door lying flat with one panel repaired, pots of glue, broken saws and crates from which straggled straw or shavings.

Yet off in one corner there was a kind of divan or, rather, a box spring, partly draped with a length of printed calico. And directly overhead hung a slightly battered lantern with coloured glass, the kind sometimes found in second-hand shops.

Separate sections of an incomplete skeleton like the ones medical students use had been tossed on to the divan, but the ribs and the pelvis were still hooked together and sat slumped forward like an old rag doll.

And then there were the walls! White walls, covered with drawings and even painted frescoes that presented perhaps the most arrestingly absurd aspect of the whole room: grinning, grimacing figures and inscriptions along the lines of *Long live Satan, grandfather of the world!*

On the floor lay a bible with a broken back. Elsewhere were crumpled-up sketches and papers yellow with age, all thick with dust.

Over the door, another inscription: *Welcome, damned souls!*

And amid this chaos of junk sat the unfinished chairs, the glue pots, the rough pine planks, smelling like a carpenter's shop. A stove lay on its side, red with rust.

Finally, there was Joseph Van Damme, meticulously groomed in his well-tailored overcoat and impeccable shoes, Van Damme who in spite of everything was still the man-about-town with a modern office at a prestigious address, at home in the great brasseries of Bremen, a lover of fine food and aged Armagnac . . .

. . . Van Damme who called and waved to the leading citizens of Liège from the wheel of his car, remarking that that man in the fur-lined coat was worth millions, that that one over there owned a fleet of thirty merchant ships, Van Damme who would later, serenaded by light music amid the clinking of glasses and saucers, shake the hands of all these magnates with whom he felt a growing fraternity . . .

. . . Van Damme who suddenly looked like a hunted animal, still frozen with his back against the wall, with white plaster marks on his

113

shoulder and one hand in his overcoat pocket, glaring steadily at Maigret.

'How much?'

Had he really spoken? Could the inspector, in that unreal atmosphere, have been imagining things?

Startled, Maigret knocked over a chair with a caved-in seat, which landed with a loud clatter.

Van Damme had flushed crimson, but not with the glow of health: his hypertensive face betrayed panic — or despair — as well as rage and the desire to live, to triumph at any cost, and he concentrated all his remaining will to resist in his defiant gaze.

'What do you mean?' asked Maigret, going over to the pile of crumpled sketches swept into a corner by the bay window, where he began spreading them out for a look. They were studies of a nude figure, a girl with coarse features, unruly hair, a strong, healthy body with heavy breasts and broad hips.

'There's still time,' Van Damme continued. 'Fifty thousand? . . . A hundred?'

When the inspector gave him a quizzical look, Van Damme, in a fever of ill-concealed anxiety, barked, 'Two hundred thousand!'

Fear shivered in the air within the crooked walls of that miserable room. A bitter, sick, morbid fear.

And perhaps there was something else, too: a repressed desire, the intoxicating temptation of murder . . .

Yet Maigret went on examining the old figure drawings, recognizing in various poses the same voluptuous girl, always staring sullenly into the distance. Once, the artist had tried draping her in the length of calico covering the divan. Another time, he had sketched her in black stockings. Behind her was a skull, which now sat at the foot of the box spring. And Maigret remembered having seen that macabre death's-head in Jef Lombard's self-portrait.

A connection was arising, still only vaguely, among all these people, these events, across time and space. With a faint tremor of excitement, the inspector smoothed out a charcoal sketch depicting a young man with long hair, his shirt collar wide open across his chest and the beginnings of a beard on his chin. He had chosen a Romantic pose: a three-quarter view of the head, and he seemed to be facing the future the way an eagle stares into the sun.

It was Jean Lecocq d'Arneville, the suicide of the sordid hotel in Bremen, the tramp who had never got to eat his last dinner.

'Two hundred thousand francs!'

And the voice added, even now betraying the businessman who thinks of every detail, of the fluctuations in the exchange rate, 'French francs! . . . Listen, inspector . . . '

Maigret sensed that pleading would give way to threats, that the fear quivering in his voice would soon become a growl of rage.

'There's still time, no official action has been taken, and we're in Belgium . . . '

There was a candle end in the lantern; beneath the pile of papers on the floor, the inspector found an old kerosene stove.

115

'You're not here in an official capacity . . . and even if . . . I'm asking you for a month.'

'*Which means it happened in December . . .* '

Van Damme seemed to draw back even closer to the wall and stammered, 'What do you mean?'

'It's November now. In February, it will have been ten years since Klein hanged himself, and you're asking me for only one month.'

'I don't understand . . . '

'Oh yes you do!'

And it was maddening, frightening, to see Maigret go on leafing through the old papers with his left hand — and the papers were crackling, rustling — while his right hand remained thrust into his overcoat pocket.

'You understand perfectly, Van Damme! If the problem were Klein's death, and if — for example — he'd been murdered, the statute of limitations would apply only in February, meaning ten years afterwards. Whereas you are asking me for only one month. So *whatever happened . . .* happened in December.'

'You'll never find out anything . . . '

His voice quavered like a wobbly phonograph record.

'Then why are you afraid?'

The inspector lifted up the box spring, underneath which he saw only dust and a greenish, mouldy crust of something barely recognizable as bread.

'Two hundred thousand francs! We could arrange it so that, later on . . . '

'*Do you want me to slap your face?*'

Maigret's threat had been so blunt and

unexpected that Van Damme panicked for a moment, raised his arm to protect himself and, in so doing, unintentionally pulled out the revolver he'd been clutching in his coat pocket. Realizing what he'd done, he was again overcome for a few seconds by that intoxicating temptation . . . but must have hesitated to shoot.

'Drop it!'

He let go. The revolver fell to the floor, near a pile of wood shavings.

And, turning his back to the enemy, Maigret kept on rummaging through the bewildering collection of incongruous things. He picked up a yellowish sock, also marbled with mildew.

'So tell me, Van Damme . . . '

Sensing a change in the silence, Maigret turned round and saw the man pass a hand over his face, where his fingers left wet streaks on his cheeks.

'You're crying?'

'Me?'

He'd said this aggressively, sardonically, despairingly.

'What branch of the army were you in?'

Van Damme was baffled by the inspector's question, but ready to snatch at any scrap of hope.

'I was in the École des Sous-Lieutenants de Réserve, at Beverloo.'

'Infantry?'

'Cavalry.'

'So you must have been between one metre sixty-five and one metre seventy. And you weren't over seventy kilos. It was later that you put on some weight.'

Maigret pushed away a chair he'd bumped into, then picked up another scrap of paper — it looked like part of a letter — with only a single line on it: *Dear old thing* . . .

But he kept an eye on Van Damme, who was still trying to figure out what Maigret had meant and who — in sudden understanding, his face haggard — cried out in horror, 'It wasn't me! I swear I've never worn that suit!'

Maigret's foot sent Van Damme's revolver spinning to the other side of the room.

Why, at that precise moment, did he count up the children again? A little boy in Belloir's house. Three kids in Rue Hors-Château, and the newest hadn't even opened her eyes yet! Plus the son of the false Louis Jeunet . . .

On the floor, the beautiful naked girl was arching her back, throwing out her chest on an unsigned sketch in red chalk.

There were hesitant footsteps, out on the stairs; a hand fumbled at the door, feeling for the string that served as a latch.

9

The Companions of the Apocalypse

In what happened next, everything mattered: the words, the silences, the looks they gave one another, even the involuntary twitch of a muscle. Everything had great meaning, and there was a sense that behind the actors in these scenes loomed an invisible pall of fear.

The door opened. Maurice Belloir appeared, and his first glance was for Van Damme, over in the corner with his back to the wall. The second glance took in the revolver lying on the floor.

It was enough; he understood. Especially when he saw Maigret, with his pipe, still calmly going through the pile of old sketches.

'Lombard's coming!' announced Belloir, without seeming to address anyone in particular. 'I grabbed a taxi.'

Hearing this was enough to tell Maigret that the bank deputy director had just given up. The evidence was slight: a gentle easing of tension in his face; a hint of shame in his tired voice.

The three of them looked at one another. Joseph Van Damme spoke first.

'What is he . . . ?'

'He's gone crazy. I tried to calm him down, but he got away from me. He went off talking to himself, waving his arms around . . . '

'He has a gun?' asked Maigret.

'He has a gun.'

Maurice Belloir tried to listen carefully, with the strained look of a stunned man struggling in vain to recover control of himself.

'Both of you were down in Rue Hors-Château? Waiting for the result of my conversation with . . .'

He pointed to Van Damme, and Belloir nodded.

'And all three of you agreed to offer me . . . ?'

He didn't need to say everything; they understood right away. They all understood even the silences and felt as if they could hear one another think.

Suddenly footsteps were racing up the stairs. Someone tripped, must have fallen, then moaned with rage. The next moment the door was kicked open and framed the figure of Jef Lombard, stock still for an instant as he gazed at the three men with terrifying intensity.

He was shaking, gripped by fever, perhaps by some kind of insanity.

What he saw must have been a mad vision of Belloir backing away from him, Van Damme's congested face, and then Maigret, broad-shouldered and absolutely immobile, holding his breath.

And there was all that bewildering junk to boot, with the lantern and the broken-down divan and the spread-out drawings covering all but the breasts and chin of the naked girl in that sketch . . .

The scene lasted for mere fractions of a second. Jef Lombard's long arm was holding out a revolver. Maigret watched him quietly. Still, he

120

did heave a sigh when Lombard threw the gun to the floor, grabbed his head with both hands and burst into great raw sobs.

'I can't, I can't!' he groaned. 'You hear me? God damn it, I can't!'

And he turned away to lean both arms against the wall, his shoulders heaving. They could hear him snuffling softly.

The inspector went over and closed the door, to shut off the noise of sawing and planing downstairs and the distant cries of children out in the street.

★   ★   ★

Jef Lombard wiped his face with his handkerchief, tossed back his hair and looked around with the empty eyes of someone whose nerves have just given way. He was not completely calm; his fingers were flexing like claws, he was breathing heavily, and when he tried to speak he had to bite his lip to suppress the sob welling in his throat.

'To end up like this!' he finally said, his voice dark and biting.

He tried to laugh, but sounded desperate.

'Nine years! Almost ten! I was left all alone, with no money, no job . . . '

He was talking to himself, probably unaware that he was staring hard at the figure drawing of the nude with that bare flesh . . .

'Ten years of slogging away, every day, with difficulties and disappointments of all kinds, but I got married anyway, I wanted kids . . . I drove

121

myself like an animal to give them a decent life. A house! And the workshop! Everything — you saw that! But what you didn't see is what it cost me to build it all, and the *heartbreaks* . . . The bills that kept me awake at night when I was just getting started . . . '

Passing his hand over his forehead, he swallowed hard, and his Adam's apple rose and fell.

'And now look: I've just had a baby girl and I can't remember if I've even seen her! My wife is lying in bed unable to understand what's going on, she sneaks frightened looks at me, she doesn't recognize me any more . . . My men ask me questions, and I don't know what to tell them.

'All gone! Suddenly, in a few days: wrecked, ruined, done for, smashed to pieces! *Everything!* Ten years of work! And all because . . . '

Clenching his fists, he looked down at the gun on the floor, then up at Maigret. He was at the end of his rope.

'Let's get it over with,' he sighed, wearily waving a hand. 'Who's going to do the talking? It's so stupid!'

And he might have been speaking to the skull, the heap of old sketches, the wild, outlandish drawings on the walls.

'Just so stupid . . . '

He seemed on the verge of tears again, but no, he was all done in. The fit had passed. He went over to sit on the edge of the divan, planted his elbows on his bony knees, his chin in his hands, and sat there, waiting.

He moved only to scrape a bit of mud off the bottom of a trouser leg with a fingernail.

★ ★ ★

'Am I disturbing you?' asked a cheery voice.

The carpenter entered, covered in sawdust, and, after looking around at the drawings decorating the walls, he laughed.

'So, you came back to look at all this?'

No one moved. Only Belloir tried to look as if nothing were wrong.

'Do you remember about those twenty francs you still owe me for that last month? Oh, not that I've come to ask you for them. It just makes me laugh, because when you left without taking all this old junk, I recall you saying, 'Maybe one day a single one of these sketches might well be worth as much as this whole dump.' I didn't believe you. Still, I did put off whitewashing the walls. One day I brought up a framer who sells pictures and he went off with two or three drawings. Gave me a hundred sous for them. Do you still paint?'

It finally dawned on him that something was wrong. Van Damme was staring stubbornly at the floor. Belloir was impatiently snapping his fingers.

'Aren't you the one who set himself up in Rue Hors-Château?' asked the carpenter, turning to Jef Lombard. 'I've a nephew worked with you. A tall blond fellow . . . '

'Maybe,' sighed Lombard, turning away.

'You I don't recognize . . . Were you with this lot?'

123

Now the landlord was speaking to Maigret.

'No.'

'What a weird bunch! My wife didn't want me to rent to them, and then she advised me to throw them out, especially since they didn't pay up very often. But they amused me. Always looking to be the one wearing the biggest hat, or smoking the longest clay pipe. And they used to sing together and drink all night long! And some pretty girls would show up sometimes . . . Speaking of which, Monsieur Lombard, that one there, on the floor, do you know what happened to her? . . .

'She married a shop walker at Le Grand Bazar and she lives about two hundred metres down the street from here. She has a son who goes to school with mine . . . '

Lombard stood up, went over to the bay window, and retraced his steps in such agitation that the carpenter decided to beat a retreat.

'Maybe I am disturbing you after all, so I'll leave you to it. And you know, if you're interested in anything here . . . Of course, I never held on to this stuff on account of the twenty francs! All I took was one landscape, for my dining room.'

Out on the landing, he seemed about to start chatting again, but was summoned from downstairs.

'Someone to see you, *patron*!'

'Later, then, gentlemen. Glad to have met — '

The closing door cut off his voice. Although inopportune, the carpenter's visit had eased some of the tension, and while he'd been talking,

Maigret had lit his pipe.

Now he pointed to the most puzzling drawing on the wall, an image encircled by an inscription that read: *The Companions of the Apocalypse.*

'Was this the name of your group?'

Sounding almost like himself again, it was Belloir who replied.

'Yes. I'll explain . . . It's too late for us, isn't it — and tough luck for our wives and children . . . '

But Lombard broke in: 'Let me tell him, I want to . . . '

And he began pacing up and down the room, now and then looking over at some object or other, as if to illustrate his story.

'Just over ten years ago, I was studying painting at the Académie, where I used to go around in a wide-brimmed hat and a *laval-lière* . . . Two others there with me were Gaston Janin, who was studying sculpture, and little Émile Klein. We would parade proudly around the Carré — because we were *artists*, you understand? Each of us thought he'd be at least another Rembrandt!

'It all started so foolishly . . . We read a lot, and favoured the Romantic period. We'd get carried away and idolize some writer for a week, then drop that one and adopt another . . .

'Little Klein, whose mother lived in Angleur, rented this studio we're in, and we started meeting here. We were really impressed by the medieval atmosphere of the neighbourhood, especially on winter evenings. We'd sing old songs and recite Villon's poetry . . .

'I don't remember any more who discovered the Book of Revelation — the Apocalypse of John — and insisted on reading us whole chapters from it.

'One evening we met a few university students: Belloir, Lecocq d'Arneville, Van Damme, and a Jewish fellow named Mortier, whose father has a shop selling tripe and sausage casings not far from here.

'We got to drinking and wound up bringing them back to the studio. The oldest of them wasn't even twenty-two. That was you, Van Damme, wasn't it?'

It was doing Lombard good to talk. His movements were less abrupt, his voice less hoarse, but his face was still blotched with red and his lips swollen from weeping.

'I think it was my idea to found a group, a society! I'd read about the secret societies in German universities during the eighteenth century. A club that would unite Science and Art!'

Looking around the studio walls, he couldn't help sneering.

'Because we were just full of that kind of talk! Hot air that puffed up our pride. On the one side were Klein, Janin and me, the paint-pushers: we were Art! On the other side, our new university friends. We drank to that. Because we drank a lot . . . We drank to feel even more gloriously superior! And we'd dim the lights to create an atmosphere of mystery.

'We'd lounge around right here, look: some of us on the divan, the others on the floor. We'd smoke pipe after pipe, until the air became a thick haze. Then we'd all start singing. There was almost always someone feeling sick who'd have to go and throw up in the courtyard. We'd still be going strong at two, three in the morning, working ourselves up into a frenzy. Helped along by the wine, some cheap rotgut that upset our stomachs, we used to soar off into the realm of metaphysics . . .

'I can still see little Klein . . . He was the most excitable one, the nervous type. He wasn't well. His mother was poor and he lived on nothing, went without food so he could drink. Because when we'd been drinking, we all felt like real geniuses!

'The university contingent was a little more level-headed, because they weren't as poor, except for Lecocq d'Arneville. Belloir would swipe a bottle of nice old Burgundy or liqueur from his parents, and Van Damme used to bring some charcuterie . . .

'We were convinced that people used to look at us out in the street with fear and admiration, and we chose an arcane, sonorous, lofty name: *The Companions of the Apocalypse*. Actually, I don't think any of us had read the Book of Revelation all the way through . . . Klein was the only one who could recite a few passages by heart, when he was drunk.

'We'd all decided to split the rent for the room, but Klein was allowed to live here.

'A few girls agreed to come pose for us for free . . . Pose and all the rest, naturally! And we tried to think of them as *grisettes* from *La Bohème*!

And all that half-baked folderol . . .

'There's one of the girls, on the floor. Dumb as they come. But we painted her as a Madonna anyway.

'Drinking — that was the main thing. We had to ginger up the atmosphere at all costs. Klein once tried to achieve the same effect by pouring sulphuric ether on the divan. And I remember all of us, working ourselves up, waiting for intoxication, expecting visions . . . Oh God Almighty!'

Lombard went over to cool his forehead against a misty windowpane, but when he came back there was a new quaver in his voice.

'Chasing after this frenzied exaltation, we wound up nervous wrecks — especially those of us who weren't eating enough, you understand? Little Klein, among others: a poor kid going without food to over-stimulate himself with drink . . .

'And it was as if we were rediscovering the world all on our own, naturally! We were full of opinions on every great problem, and full of scorn for society, established truths and everything bourgeois. When we'd had a few drinks and smoked up a storm, we'd spout the most cock-eyed nonsense, a hodgepodge of Nietzsche, Karl Marx, Moses, Confucius, Jesus Christ . . .

'Here's an example: I don't remember which one of us discovered that *pain doesn't exist*, the brain's simply imagining it. One night I became so enthralled with the idea that, surrounded by my excited audience, I stabbed myself in the upper arm with a pocket knife *and forced myself to smile about it*!

'And we had other wild inspirations like that . . . We were an elite, a coterie of geniuses who'd come together by chance and were way above the conventional world with its laws and preconceived opinions. A gathering of the gods, hey? Gods who were sometimes dying of hunger but who strode through the streets with their heads high, crushing passers-by with their contempt.

'And we had the future completely in hand: Lecocq d'Arneville would become a new Tolstoy, while Van Damme, who was taking boring courses at our university business school, would fundamentally redefine economics and upend all the accepted ideas about the social workings of humanity. And each one of us had a role to play, as poets, painters and future heads of state.

'All fuelled by booze! Or just fumes! Because by the end we were so used to flying high here that simply by walking through that door, into the alchemical light of the lantern, with a skeleton in the shadows and the skull we used as a communal drinking bowl, we'd catch the little fever we craved, all on our own.

'Even the most modest among us could already envision the marble plaque that would one day adorn this house: *Here met the famous Companions of the Apocalypse* . . . We all tried to come up with the newest great book or amazing idea. It's a miracle we didn't all wind up anarchists! Because we actually discussed that question, quite seriously. There'd been an incident in Seville; someone read the newspaper article about it aloud, and I don't remember any more who shouted, 'True genius is destructive!'

'Well, our kiddy club debated this subject for hours. We came up with ways to make bombs. We cast about for interesting things to blow up.

'Then little Klein, who was on his sixth or seventh glass, became ill, but not like the other times. This was some kind of nervous fit: he was writhing on the floor, and all we could think of any more was what would happen to us if something happened to him! And that girl was there! Henriette, her name was. She was crying . . .

'Oh, those were some nights, all right . . . It was a point of honour with us not to leave until the lamplighter had turned off the gas streetlamps, and then we'd head out shivering into the dreary dawn. Those of us who were better off would sneak home through a window, sleep, eat and more or less recover from our nightly excesses, but the others — Klein, Lecocq d'Arneville and I — would drag ourselves through the streets, nibbling on a roll and looking longingly into shop windows . . .

'That year I didn't have an overcoat because I wanted to buy a wide-brimmed hat that cost a hundred and twenty francs, and I pretended that, like everything else, cold was an illusion. And primed by all our discussions, I announced to my father, a good, honest man, a gunsmith's assistant — he's dead, now — that parental love is the worst form of selfishness and that a child's first duty is to reject his family.

'He was a widower. He used to go off to work in the morning at six o'clock, just when I was getting home. Well, he took to setting out earlier so he wouldn't run into me, because my big speeches frightened him. And he would leave me little notes on the table: *There's some cold meat in the cupboard. Father . . .* '

★ ★ ★

Lombard's voice broke for a moment. He looked over at Belloir, who was sitting on the edge of a staved-in chair, staring at the floor, and then at Van Damme, who was shredding a cigar to bits.

'There were seven of us,' said Lombard dully. 'Seven supermen! Seven geniuses! Seven kids!

'Janin's still sculpting, off in Paris — or rather, he makes shop-window mannequins for a big factory. Now and then he works off his frustration by doing something from a real model, his mistress of the moment . . . Belloir's in banking, Van Damme's in business, I'm a photoengraver . . . '

The fear in that silent room was now palpable. Lombard swallowed hard but went on, and his eyes seemed to sink even deeper into their dark sockets.

'Klein hanged himself at the church door . . . Lecocq d'Arneville shot himself in the mouth in Bremen . . . '

Another silence. This time, unable to sit still, Belloir stood up, hesitated, then went to stand by the bay window. A strange noise seemed to be rumbling in his chest.

'And the last one?' inquired Maigret. 'Mortier, I believe? The tripe dealer's son.'

Lombard now stared at him so frantically that the inspector thought he might have another fit. Van Damme somehow knocked over a chair.

'It was in December, wasn't it?'

As he was speaking, Maigret kept a close eye on the three men.

'In a month it will have been ten years. The statute of limitations will come into effect.'

He went first to pick up Van Damme's automatic, then collected the revolver Lombard had thrown away after he arrived.

Maigret had seen it coming: Lombard was breaking down, holding his head in his hands and wailing, 'My children! My three little ones!'

And with renewed hysteria, unashamed to show the tears streaming down his face, he yelled, 'It's because of you, you, only because of you, that I haven't even seen my newborn child, my little girl! I couldn't even say what she looks like . . . *Do you understand?*'

10

Christmas Eve in Rue du Pot-au-Noir

There must have been a passing shower, some swift low-lying clouds, because all the sunshine glinting off objects in the room vanished in an instant. As if a switch had been flicked, the light turned uniformly grey, while the clutter took on a glum look.

Maigret understood why those who'd gathered there had felt the need to doctor the light with a lantern of many colours, set their stage with mysterious shadows and muddle the atmosphere with drink and tobacco smoke.

And he could imagine how Klein would awaken in the morning after those sad orgies to find himself surrounded by empty bottles, broken glasses and rancid odours, all bathed in the murk from the bay window, which had no curtains.

Jef Lombard was too upset to go on, and it was Maurice Belloir who took up the story.

Everything shifted, as if they'd moved to a different register. Lombard had been shaken to his very core, his emotion expressed through wrenching sobs, shrill, wheezing catches in his voice, nervous pacing and periods of alternating agitation and calm that could have been plotted on a medical chart, while Belloir's entire person — his voice, his gaze, his every move — was under such taut control that it was painful to see, for it clearly demanded a gruelling effort of will and concentration.

This man could never have cried, or even tried to smile: he held himself completely still.

'May I take over, inspector? It will be dark soon and we'll have no light here.'

It was not Belloir's fault that he'd brought up a practical detail, and it wasn't from lack of feeling, for it was actually his own way of showing how he felt.

'I believe that we were all sincere in our arguments and endless discussions, and when we were dreaming out loud. But there were different degrees of sincerity involved.

'Jef has mentioned this. On the one hand, there were the wealthy ones, who went home afterwards to recover their balance in a stable environment: Van Damme, Willy Mortier and I. And even Janin, who had everything he needed.

'Willy Mortier was in a class by himself, however. A case in point: he was the only one who chose his mistresses from among professional nightclub singers and the dancers in second-rate theatres. He paid them.

'He was a practical, unsentimental person, like his father, who arrived in Liège with empty pockets, matter-of-factly chose the sausage-casing business — and made a fortune.

'Willy received a monthly allowance of 500 francs, which seemed a fabulous sum to the rest of us. He never set foot inside the university, paid poorer students to take notes for him in lectures and 'arranged' to pass his exams through favours and bribes.

'He came here simply out of curiosity, because he never shared our tastes or ideas. Look at his father: he'd buy paintings from artists even though he despised them, and he 'bought' city councilmen and even aldermen as well, to get what he wanted. He despised them, too.

'Well, Willy despised us in the same way. He was a rich boy who came here to see just how different he was from the rest of us.

'He didn't drink. And those who got drunk here disgusted him. During our epic discussions, he'd say only a few words, but they were like ice water, the kind of words that hurt because they're too blunt, because they ruined the fake poetic atmosphere we'd managed to create.

'He hated us! And we hated him! On top of everything else, he was stingy — and cynical about it. Klein didn't always get something to eat every day, so one or the other of us would help him out now and then. Mortier? He'd announce, 'I don't want any difficulties about money to come between us. I don't want to be welcomed simply because I'm well off.'

'And he'd cough up *exactly* his share when we were all turning our pockets inside out to buy something to drink.

'It was Lecocq d'Arneville who used to take lecture notes for him, and I once overheard Willy refuse to give him an advance on his payment.

'He was the alien, hostile element that crops up almost every time when men get together. We put up with him. Klein, though, when he was drunk, used to attack him savagely, really let

135

everything that bothered him come pouring out. Mortier would go a bit pale bur he'd just listen, with a faint sneer . . .

'I mentioned various kinds of sincerity. Klein and Lecocq d'Arneville were definitely the most forthright, unpretentious members of our group. They were close, like brothers. They'd both had difficult childhoods, with their mothers watching every sou . . . Both these fellows were desperate to better themselves and agonized over anything that stood in their way.

'Klein had to work during the day as a house painter to pay for his evening classes at the Académie, and he did tell us that it made him dizzy when he had to climb a ladder. Lecocq took lecture notes for others, gave French lessons to foreign students; he often came here to eat. The stove must still be around here somewhere . . . '

It was lying on the floor near the divan, where Lombard gave it a gloomy kick.

* * *

Not one hair was out of place on Maurice Belloir's sleek head, and his voice was flat, stripped down.

'Since those days, I've heard people in the middle-class drawing rooms of Rheims ask jokingly, 'In such-and-such a situation, would you be able to kill someone?' Sometimes it's the mandarin question, you know the one: *If all you had to do was push a button to kill a wealthy mandarin way off in China to inherit his riches, would you do it?*

'We took up the weirdest ideas here and talked for nights on end, so we inevitably came around to the enigma of life and death . . .

'It was almost Christmas; it had been snowing. A short item in a newspaper started us off. We always had to challenge the status quo, right? So we went all out on this idea: mankind is just a patch of mould on the earth's crust. So human life and death don't matter, pity is only a sickness, big animals eat the little ones, and we eat the big ones.

'Lombard told you about the pocket knife: stabbing himself to prove that pain didn't exist!

'Well, that night, shortly before Christmas, with three or four empty bottles lying around on the floor, we seriously debated the idea of killing someone. After all, weren't we off in the realm of pure theory, where anything goes? All bright-eyed, we kept quizzing one another with shivers of guilty excitement.

' "Would *you* be brave enough?"

' "Why not? If life is nothing, just some accident, a blemish on the face of the earth . . . "

' "A stranger, passing in the street?"

'And Klein — so pale, with those dark rings under his eyes — he'd drunk the most. And he yelled, 'Yes!'

'We were afraid to take another step: it felt like being at the edge of a cliff. We were dicing with danger, joking around with this murder we'd conjured up, and now that murder seemed to be stalking *us* . . .

'Someone who'd been an altar boy — I think

it was Van Damme — started singing the *Libera nos*, which the priest chants over a coffin, and we all took up the chorus, playing this ghoulish game with real relish.

'But we didn't kill anyone that night! At four a.m. I went over the garden wall to sneak home. By eight I was having coffee with my family. The whole thing was only a memory, you understand? Like remembering being scared watching a play in a theatre.

'But Klein stayed here, at Rue du Pot-au-Noir, where all those ideas kept seething in his sickly, swollen head. They were eating him alive. We could tell what was worrying him from the questions he kept popping at us over the next few days.

''Do you really think it's hard to kill someone?'

'We weren't drunk any more but we didn't want to back down, so we blustered, we said, 'Of course it isn't!'

'Maybe we were even getting a thrill out of his childish excitement, but get this straight: we had no intention of causing a tragedy! We were still seeing how far we could go . . .

'When there's a fire, onlookers can't help wanting it to last, to be a *spectacular* fire, and when the river is rising, newspaper readers hope for *major* flooding they can talk about for the next twenty years. *They want something interesting, and it doesn't matter what!*

'Christmas Eve arrived. Everybody brought some bottles. We drank, we sang, and Klein, already half-soused, kept pulling one after another of us aside.

' 'Do you think I'd be able to kill someone?'

'We weren't worried about it. By midnight no one was sober. We talked about going out for more bottles.

'That's when Willy Mortier showed up, in a dinner jacket, with a broad white shirt front that seemed to soak up all the light. His face was rosy, he was wearing scent, and he announced that he'd just come from a fancy society reception.

' 'Go and get some booze!' Klein yelled at him.

' 'You're drunk, chum! I just came along to pay my respects.'

' 'No, to look down your nose at us!'

'There still wasn't any reason to suspect that something might happen, although Klein's face was more frightening than it had ever been during his other drunken spells. He was so small, so thin next to the other man . . . His hair was a mess, his forehead was all sweaty, and he'd yanked his tie off.

' 'Klein,' said Willy, 'you're stinking drunk!'

' 'So what! This stinking drunk's telling you to go and get some booze!'

'I think that scared Willy. He'd begun to sense that this was no laughing matter, but he still tried to bluff his way out . . . His black hair had been curled and perfumed . . .

' 'You fellows don't seem to be having much fun here,' he told us. 'It was livelier back with the stuffed shirts I just left!'

' 'Go and get some booze . . . '

'Now Klein was circling him, staring at him,

all wound up. A few of us were off in a corner, talking about some Kantian theory or other. Someone else was weeping and swearing that he wasn't fit to live.

'Not one of us had all his wits about him, and no one saw the whole thing: Klein darting forward abruptly, a furious little bundle of nerves, and striking Mortier . . .

'It looked as if he'd butted him in the chest with his head, but we saw blood spurting out! Willy opened his mouth so wide . . . '

★ ★ ★

'No!' Lombard begged suddenly, now standing and staring at Belloir as if in a daze.

Van Damme had retreated back to the wall, his shoulders slumping. But nothing could have stopped Belloir, not even if he had wanted to himself. It was growing dark. Everyone's face looked grey.

'We were all frantic!' the voice went on. 'And Klein huddled there with a knife in his hand, stunned, gaping at Willy, who just stood swaying, tottering . . . These things don't happen the way people imagine — I can't explain . . .

'Mortier was still on his feet in spite of the blood streaming from the hole in his shirt front. He said — and I'm sure of this — 'Bastards!' And he kept standing in the same place, his legs slightly apart, as if to keep his balance. If he hadn't been bleeding, you'd have thought *he* was the drunk.

'He had big eyes, and now they seemed even

bigger . . . His left hand was clutching the button of his dinner jacket, while his right was fumbling around the back of his trousers.

'Someone — I think it was Jef — shouted in terror, and we saw Mortier's right hand pull a revolver slowly from a pocket, a small black thing, made of steel, that looked so *hard* . . .

'Klein was rolling on the floor in a fit. A bottle fell, smashing into pieces.

'And Willy was still alive! Just barely swaying, he looked at us, one after the other! Although he couldn't have been seeing clearly . . . He raised the revolver . . .

'Then someone stepped forwards to grab the gun from him, slipped in the blood, and the two of them fell to the floor.

'Mortier must have gone into convulsions — because he still wasn't dead, you hear me? His eyes, those big eyes, were wide open! He kept trying to shoot, and he said it again: 'Bastards!'

'The other man's hand was able to grip his throat . . . He hadn't much longer to live, anyway . . .

'*I got completely soaked . . . while the dinner jacket just lay there on the floor.*'

★   ★   ★

Van Damme and Lombard were now looking at their companion in horror. And Belloir finished what he had to say.

'That hand around his neck, it was mine! I was the man who slipped in that pool of blood . . . '

He was standing in the same place as he had

then. Now, though, he was dapper and soigné, his shoes polished, his suit impeccable. He wore a large gold signet ring on his white, well-cared-for hand with its manicured nails.

'We were in a state of shock. We made Klein go to bed, even though he wanted to go and give himself up. No one spoke. Again, I can't explain . . . And yet I was quite lucid! I'll say it again: people don't understand what such tragedies are really like. I dragged Van Damme out on to the landing, where we talked quietly, while Klein kept howling and struggling.

'The church bells rang the hour while three of us were going down the alley carrying the body, but I don't remember what time it was. The Meuse was in spate — Quai Sainte-Barbe was under half a metre of water — and the current was running fast. Both upstream and down, the barrage gates were open. We just caught a glimpse of a dark mass being swept past the nearest lamp post by the rushing water.

'My suit was stained and torn; I left it at the studio after Van Damme went home to get me some of his clothes. The next day, I concocted a story for my parents . . . '

'Did you all get together again?' Maigret asked slowly.

'No. Most of us bolted from Rue du Pot-au-Noir. Lecocq d'Arneville stayed on with Klein. And ever since then, we've all avoided one another, as if by mutual agreement. Whenever any of us met up by accident in town, we looked the other way.

'It turned out that Willy's body was never

found, thanks to the flood. Since he hadn't been proud of knowing us, he'd always been careful never to mention us at home. People thought he'd simply run off for a few days. Later, they did look for him in the seedy parts of town, where they thought he might have finished up that evening.

'I was the first to leave Liège, three weeks later. I suddenly broke off my studies and announced to my family that I wanted to pursue my career in France. I found work in a bank in Paris.

'I learned from the newspapers that Klein had hanged himself that February at the door of Saint-Pholien.

'One day I ran into Janin, in Paris. We didn't talk about the tragedy, but he told me that he, too, had moved to France.'

'I stayed on in Liège, alone,' muttered Lombard resentfully, his head hanging.

'You drew hanged men and church steeples,' Maigret said. 'Then you did sketches for the newspapers. Then . . .'

And he recalled the house in Rue Hors-Château, the windows with the small, green-tinged panes, the fountain in the courtyard, the portrait of the young woman, the photoengraving workshop, where posters and magazine illustrations were gradually invading the walls of hanged men . . .

And the kids! The newest one born only yesterday . . .

Hadn't ten years gone by? And little by little, more or less clumsily, hadn't life returned to normal everywhere?

Van Damme had roamed around Paris, like the other two. By chance, he'd wound up in Germany. His parents had left him an inheritance. He had become an important businessman in Bremen.

Maurice Belloir had made a fine marriage. Moving up the ladder, he was now a bank deputy director! Then there was the lovely new house in Rue de Vesle, where a little boy was studying the violin.

In the evening he played billiards with other town luminaries in the comfortable ambience of the Café de Paris.

Janin got by with a series of mistresses, earned his living by making shop-window mannequins and relaxed by working on portrait busts of his lady friends.

And hadn't even Lecocq d'Arneville got married? Didn't his wife and child live in the back of the herbalist's shop in Rue Picpus?

Willy Mortier's father was still buying, cleaning and selling whole truckloads of pig's entrails, bribing city councilmen and growing ever richer.

His daughter had married a cavalry officer, who hadn't wanted to join the family business, whereupon Mortier had refused to hand over the agreed-upon dowry.

The couple lived off somewhere in a small garrison town.

11

The Candle End

It was nearly dark. Their faces were receding into the shadows, but their features seemed all the more sharply etched.

Lombard was the one who burst out, as if alarmed by the gathering dusk, 'We need some light!'

There was still a candle end, left in the lantern that had hung from the same nail for ten years, kept along with the broken-down divan, the length of calico, the battered skeleton, the sketches of the girl with naked breasts and everything else saved as security by the landlord still waiting for his rent.

When Maigret lit the stump, shadows danced on the walls, which shone red, yellow and blue in light glowing through the tinted glass panes, as if from a magic lantern.

'When did Lecocq d'Arneville come to see you for the first time?' the inspector asked, turning towards Belloir.

'It must be about three years ago. I hadn't been expecting it . . . The house you saw had just been finished. My boy was barely walking yet.

'I was struck by how much he'd grown to resemble Klein: not so much physically as in his nature. That same feverish intensity, the same morbid uneasiness. He came as an enemy. He was furious and embittered, or desperate — I can't find exactly the right word. He sniggered at me, spoke aggressively, he was on edge; he pretended to admire my home, my position, my life and character, and yet . . . I had the feeling he might burst into tears, like Klein when he was drunk!

'He thought that I'd forgotten. Not true! I simply wanted to live, you understand me? And that's why I worked like a dog: to live . . .

'But he hadn't been able to get on with his life. He had lived with Klein for two months after that Christmas Eve, it's true . . . We left, they stayed behind: the two of them, here in this room, in . . .

'I can't explain what I felt in his presence. So many years had passed, but I had the feeling Lecocq d'Arneville had remained exactly the same. It was as if life had moved on for some, and stopped short for others.

'He told me that he'd changed his name because he didn't want to keep anything that reminded him of that awful night. He'd even changed his life! He'd never opened another book. He'd got it into his head to build a new life by becoming a manual labourer.

'I had to glean all this information on my own, weeding it out from all his reproaches, caustic remarks and truly monstrous accusations.

'He'd failed! Been a disaster at everything! And part of him was still rooted right here. It was the same for the rest of us, I think, but in our case it was less intense, not as painful, as unhealthy. I believe Klein's face haunted him

146

even more than Willy's did.

'Married, with a kid, he'd been through some tough times and had turned to drink. He was unable, not only to be happy, but even to be at any kind of peace. He screamed at me that he adored his wife and had left her because when he was near her, he felt like a thief! A thief stealing happiness! Happiness stolen from Klein . . . And the other man.

'You see, I've thought a lot about this since then. And I think I understand. We were fooling around with dangerous ideas, with mysticism and morbid thoughts. It was only a game, and we were just kids, playing, but at least two of us let themselves fall into the trap. The most excitable, fanatical ones.

'Klein and Lecocq d'Arneville. We'd all talked about killing someone? Klein went on to do it! And then he killed himself! And Lecocq, appalled, a broken man, was chained to this nightmare for the rest of his life.

'The others and I tried to escape, to find our way back to a normal life, whereas Lecocq d'Arneville threw himself recklessly into his remorse, in a rage of despair. He destroyed his own life! Along with those of his wife and son . . .

'So he turned on us. Because that's why he'd come looking for me. I hadn't understood that at first. He looked around at *my* house, *my* family, *my* bank. And I really did feel that he considered it his duty to destroy all that.

'To avenge Klein! To avenge himself.

'He threatened me. He had kept the suit, with

147

the rips, the bloodstains, and it was the only physical proof of what happened that Christmas Eve. He asked me for money. Lots of it! And asked for more later on.

'Because wasn't that where we were vulnerable? Van Damme, Lombard, myself, even Janin: everything we had achieved depended on money.

'It was the beginning of a new nightmare! Lecocq had known what he was doing, and he went from one to another of us, lugging along that sinister ruined suit. With diabolical cunning, he calculated precisely how much to ask us for, to make us feel the pinch.

'You saw my house, inspector. It's mortgaged! My wife thinks her dowry is sitting untouched at the bank, but there's not a centime of it left. And I've done other things like that.

'He went twice to Bremen, to see Van Damme. He came to Liège. Still consumed with fury, bent on destroying every last scrap of happiness.

'There were six of us around Willy's corpse. Klein was dead; Lecocq was trapped in a living nightmare. So we all had to be equally miserable. And he didn't even spend the money! He lived as wretchedly as before, when he was sharing a bit of cheap sausage with Klein. He burned all the money! And every banknote he burned meant unbelievable hardship for us all.

'For three years we've been struggling, each off in his own corner: Van Damme in Bremen, Jef in Liège, Janin in Paris, myself in Rheims. For three years we've hardly dared write to one another, while Lecocq d'Arneville was forcing us back into the madness of the Companions of the Apocalypse.

'I have a wife. So does Lombard. We've got kids. So we're trying to hang on, for them.

'The other day Van Damme sent us telegrams saying Lecocq had killed himself, and he told us to meet.

'We were all together when you turned up. After you left, we learned that you were the one who now had the bloodstained suit, and that you were determined to track down the truth.'

'Who stole one of my suitcases at Gare du Nord?' Maigret asked, and it was Van Damme who answered.

'Janin. I'd arrived before you and was hiding on one of the station platforms.'

Everyone was exhausted. The candle end would probably last about another ten minutes, if that. The inspector accidentally knocked over the skull, which fell to the floor and seemed to be trying to bite it.

'Who wrote to me at the Hôtel du Chemin de Fer?'

'I did,' Lombard replied without looking up. 'Because of my little girl. My little daughter I haven't seen yet . . . But Van Damme suspected as much. Belloir, too. Both of them were waiting at the Café de la Bourse.'

'And it was you who fired the shot?'

'Yes . . . I couldn't take it any more. I wanted to live! Live! With my wife, my kids . . . So I was waiting for you outside. I've debts of 50,000 francs at the moment. Fifty thousand francs that

Lecocq d'Arneville burned to ashes! But that's nothing — I'll pay the debts, I'll do whatever it takes, but to know that you were out there, hunting us . . . '

Maigret looked at Van Damme.

'And you were racing on ahead of me, trying to destroy the clues?'

No one spoke. The candle flame wavered . . . Lombard was the only one still illuminated, by a fading red gleam from the lantern.

It was then, for the first time, that Belloir's voice faltered.

'Ten years ago, right after the . . . the thing . . . I would have accepted my fate. I'd bought a revolver, in case anyone came to arrest me. But after ten years of living, striving, struggling! And with a wife and child now, well — I think I could have shoved you into the Marne myself. Or taken a shot at you that night outside the Café de la Bourse.

'Because in a month — not even that, in twenty-six days — the statute will be in force . . . '

Silence fell, and it was then that the candle suddenly flamed up and went out. They were left in utter darkness.

Maigret did not move. He knew that Lombard was standing at his left, Van Damme was leaning against the wall in front of him, with Belloir barely a step behind him.

He waited, without even bothering to slip his hand into the pocket holding his revolver. He definitely sensed that Belloir was trembling all over, even panting.

150

Maigret struck a match and said, 'Let's go, shall we?'

In the glimmer of the match, everyone's eyes seemed to shine especially brightly. The four of them brushed against one another in the doorway, and again on the stairs. Van Damme fell, because he'd forgotten that there was no handrail after the eighth step.

The carpenter's shop was closed. Through the curtains of one window, they could see an old woman knitting by the light of a small paraffin lamp.

'Was it along there?' asked Maigret, pointing to the roughly paved street leading to the embankment a hundred metres away, where a gas lamp was fixed to the corner of a wall.

'The Meuse had reached the third house,' Belloir replied. 'I had to wade into the water up to my knees to . . . so that he would go off with the current.'

Turning round, they walked back, passing the new church looming in the middle of vacant ground that was still bare and uneven dirt.

Suddenly they found themselves amid the bustle of passers-by, red and yellow trams, cars, shop windows.

To get to the centre of town they had to cross the Pont des Arches and heard the rushing river crashing noisily into the piers.

Back in Rue Hors-Château, people would be waiting for Jef Lombard: his men downstairs, amid their acid baths, their photoengraved plates waiting to be picked up by bicycle messengers; the new mother upstairs, with the sweet old

151

mother-in-law and, nestled in the white bed sheets, the tiny girl who hadn't yet opened her eyes; the two older boys, trying not to make too much noise in the dining room decorated with hanged men.

And wasn't there another mother, in Rheims, giving her son a violin lesson, while the maid was polishing all the brass stair-rods and dusting the china pot holding the big green plant?

In Bremen, the commercial building was closing up for the day. The typist and two clerks were leaving their modern office, and when they turned off the electricity, the porcelain letters spelling *Joseph Van Damme, Import-Export Commission Agent* would vanish into the night.

Perhaps, in the brasseries alive with Viennese music, some businessman with a shaved head would remark, 'Huh! That Frenchman isn't here . . . '

In Rue Picpus, Madame Jeunet was selling a toothbrush, or a hundred grams of dried chamomile, its pale flowers crackling in their packet.

The little boy was doing his homework in the back of the shop.

The four men were walking along in step. A breeze had come up and was driving so many clouds through the sky that the bright moon shone through for only a few seconds at a time.

Did they have any idea where they were going?

When they passed in front of a busy café, a drunk staggered out.

'I'm due back in Paris!' Maigret announced, stopping abruptly.

And while the other three stood staring at him, not daring to speak and uncertain whether to rejoice or despair, he shoved his hands into his coat pockets.

'There are five kids at stake here . . . '

The men weren't even sure they'd heard him correctly, because Maigret had been muttering to himself through clenched teeth.

And the last they saw of him was his broad back in his black overcoat with the velvet collar, walking away.

'One in Rue Picpus, three in Rue Hors-Château, one in Rheims . . . '

★ ★ ★

In Rue Lepic, where he went after leaving the train station, the concierge told him, 'There's no point in going upstairs, Monsieur Janin isn't there. They thought he had bronchitis, but now that it's turned into pneumonia, they've taken him off to the hospital.'

So the inspector had himself driven to Quai des Orfèvres, where he found Sergeant Lucas phoning the owner of a bar that had racked up some violations.

'Did you get my letter, *vieux*?'

'It's all over? You figured it out?'

'Fat chance!'

It was one of Maigret's favourite expressions.

'They ran off? You know, that letter really had me worried . . . I almost dashed up to Liège. Well, what was it? Anarchists? Counterfeiters? An international gang?'

'Kids,' he sighed.

And he tossed into his cupboard the suitcase containing what a German technician had called, in a long and detailed report, clothing B.

'Come along and have a beer, Lucas.'

'You don't look too happy . . . '

'Says who? There's nothing funnier than life, *vieux*! Well, are you coming?'

A few moments later, they were pushing through the revolving door of Brasserie Dauphine.

Lucas had seldom felt so anxious and bewildered. Skipping the beer, his companion put away six ersatz absinthes just about non-stop, which didn't prevent him from announcing in a fairly steady voice, and with only a slightly blurry and most unfamiliar look in his eye, 'You know, *vieux*, ten more cases like that one and I'll hand in my resignation. Because it would prove that there's a good old Good Lord up there who's decided to take up police work.'

When he called over the waiter, though, he did add, 'But don't you worry! There won't be ten like that one . . . So, what's new around the shop?'

The Carter of
La Providence

Translated by
DAVID COWARD

1

Lock 14

The facts of the case, though meticulously reconstructed, proved precisely nothing — except that the discovery made by the two carters from Dizy made, frankly, no sense at all.

On the Sunday — it was 4 April — it had begun to rain heavily at three in the afternoon.

At that moment, moored in the reach above Lock 14, which marks the junction of the river Marne and the canal, were two motor barges, both heading downstream, a canal boat which was being unloaded and another having its bilges washed out.

Shortly before seven, just as the light was beginning to fade, a tanker-barge, the *Éco-III*, had hooted to signal its arrival and had eased itself into the chamber of the lock.

The lock-keeper had not been best pleased, because he had relatives visiting at the time. He had then waved 'no' to a boat towed by two plodding draught horses which arrived in its wake only minutes later.

He had gone back into his house but had not been there long when the man driving the horse-drawn boat, who he knew, walked in.

'Can I go through? The skipper wants to be at Juvigny for tomorrow night.'

157

'If you like. But you'll have to manage the gates by yourself.'

The rain was coming down harder and harder. Through his window, the lock-keeper made out the man's stocky figure as he trudged wearily from one gate to the other, driving both horses on before making the mooring ropes fast to the bollards.

The boat rose slowly until it showed above the lock side. It wasn't the barge master standing at the helm but his wife, a large woman from Brussels, with brash blonde hair and a piercing voice.

By 7.20 p.m., the *Providence* was tied up by the Café de la Marine, behind the *Éco-III*. The tow-horses were taken on board. The carter and the skipper headed for the café where other boat men and two pilots from Dizy had already assembled.

At eight o'clock, when it was completely dark, a tug arrived under the lock with four boats in tow.

Its arrival swelled the crowd in the Café de la Marine. Six tables were now occupied. The men from one table called out to the others. The newcomers left puddles of water behind them as they stamped the mud off their boots.

In the room next door, a store lit by an oil-lamp, the women were buying whatever they needed.

The air was heavy. Talk turned to an accident that had happened at Lock 8 and how much of a hold-up this would mean for boats travelling upstream.

158

At nine o'clock, the wife of the skipper of the *Providence* came looking for her husband and their carter. All three of them then left after saying goodnight to all.

By ten o'clock, the lights had been turned out on most of the boats. The lock-keeper accompanied his relations as far as the main road to Épernay, which crosses the canal two kilometres further on from the lock.

He did not notice anything out of the ordinary. On his way back, he walked past the front of the café. He looked in and was greeted by a pilot.

'Come and have a drink! Man, you're soaked to the skin . . . '

He ordered rum, but did not sit down. Two carters got up, heavy with red wine, eyes shining, and made their way out to the stable adjoining the café, where they slept on straw, next to their horses.

They weren't exactly drunk. But they had had enough to ensure that they would sleep like logs.

There were five horses in the stable, which was lit by a single storm lantern, turned down low.

At four in the morning, one of the carters woke his mate, and both began seeing to their animals. They heard the horses on the *Providence* being led out and harnessed.

At the same time, the landlord of the café got up and lit the lamp in his bedroom on the first floor. He also heard the *Providence* as it got under way.

At 4.30, the diesel engine of the tanker-barge

159

spluttered into life, but the boat did not leave for another quarter of an hour, after its skipper had swallowed a bracing hot toddy in the café which had just opened for business.

He had scarcely left and his boat had not yet got as far as the bridge when the two carters made their discovery.

One of them was leading his horses out to the towpath. The other was ferreting through the straw looking for his whip when one hand encountered something cold.

Startled, because what he had touched felt like a human face, he fetched his lantern and cast its light on the corpse which was about to bring chaos to Dizy and disrupt life on the canal.

★　★　★

Detective Chief Inspector Maigret of the Flying Squad was running through these facts again, putting them in context.

It was Monday evening. That morning, magistrates from the Épernay prosecutor's office had come out to make the routine inspection of the scene of the crime. The body, after being checked by the people from Criminal Records and examined by police surgeons, had been moved to the mortuary.

It was still raining, a fine, dense, cold rain which had gone on falling without stopping all night and all day.

Shadowy figures came and went around the lock gates, where a barge was rising imperceptibly.

The inspector had been there for an hour and had got no further than familiarizing himself with a world which he was suddenly discovering and about which, when he arrived, he had had only mistaken, confused ideas.

The lock-keeper had told him:

'There was hardly anything in the canal basin: just two motor barges going downstream, one motorized barge heading up, which had gone through the lock in the afternoon, one boat cleaning out its bilges and two panamas. Then the tin tub turned up with four vessels in tow . . . '

In this way did Maigret learn that a 'tin tub' is a tug and a 'panama' a boat without either an engine or its own horses on board, which employs a carter with his own animals for a specified distance, known in the trade as 'hitching a lift'.

When he arrived at Dizy all he'd seen was a narrow canal, three miles from Épernay, and a small village near a stone bridge.

He had had to slog through the mud of the towpath to reach the lock, which was two kilometres from Dizy.

There he had found the lock-keeper's house. It was made of grey stone, with a board that read: 'Office'.

He had walked into the Café de la Marine, which was the only other building in the area.

On his left was a run-down café-bar with brown oil-cloth-covered tables and walls painted half brown and half a dirty yellow.

But it was full of the characteristic odour

which marked it out as different from the usual run of country cafés. It smelled of stables, harness, tar, groceries, oil and diesel.

There was a small bell just by the door on the right. Transparent advertisements had been stuck over the glass panels.

Inside was full of stock: oilskins, clogs, canvas clothes, sacks of potatoes, kegs of cooking oil and packing cases containing sugar, dried peas and beans cheek-by-jowl with fresh vegetables and crockery.

There were no customers in sight. The stable was empty except for the horse which the landlord only saddled up when he went to market, a big grey as friendly as a pet dog. It was not tethered and at intervals would walk around the yard among the chickens.

Everywhere was sodden with rainwater. It was the most striking thing about the place. And the people who passed by were black, gleaming figures who leaned into the rain.

A hundred metres away, a narrow-gauge train shunted backwards and forwards in a siding. The carter had rigged up an umbrella on the back of the miniature engine and he crouched under it, shivering, with shoulders hunched.

A barge hauled by boat hooks slid along the canal bank heading for the lock chamber, from which another was just emerging.

How had the woman got here? And why? That was what had baffled the police at Épernay, the prosecutor's people, the medics and the specialists from Records. Maigret was now turning it over and over in his heavy head.

She had been strangled, that was the first sure fact. Death had occurred on the Sunday evening, probably around 10.30.

And the body had been found in the stable a little after four in the morning.

There was no road anywhere near the lock. There was nothing there to attract anyone not interested in barges and canals. The towpath was too narrow for a car. On the night in question anyone on foot would have had to wade knee deep through the puddles and mud.

It was obvious that the woman belonged to a class where people were more likely to ride in expensive motor-cars and travel by sleeper than walk.

She had been wearing only a beige silk dress and white buckskin shoes designed more for the beach than for city streets.

The dress was creased, but there was no trace of mud on it. Only the toe of the left shoe was wet when she was found.

'Between thirty-eight and forty,' the doctor had said after he'd examined the body.

Her earrings were real pearls worth about 15,000 francs. Her bracelet, a mixture of gold and platinum worked in the very latest style, was more artistic than costly even though it was inscribed with the name of a jeweller in the Place Vendôme.

Her hair was brown, waved and cut very short at the nape of the neck and temples.

The face, contorted by the effects of strangulation, must have been unusually pretty.

No doubt a bit of a tease.

Her manicured, varnished fingernails were dirty.

Her handbag had not been found near her. Police officers from Épernay, Rheims and Paris, armed with a photograph of the body, had been trying all day to establish her identity but without success.

Meanwhile the rain continued to fall with no let-up over the dreary landscape. To left and right, the horizon was bounded by chalk hills streaked with white and black, where at this time of year the vines looked like wooden crosses in a Great War cemetery.

The lock-keeper, recognizable only because he wore a silver braided cap, trudged wearily around the chamber of the lock, in which the water boiled every time he opened the sluices.

And every time a vessel was raised or lowered he told the tale to each new bargee.

Sometimes, after the official papers had been signed, the two of them would hurry off to the Café de la Marine and down a couple or three glasses of rum or a half litre of white wine.

And every time, the lock-keeper would point his chin in the direction of Maigret, who was prowling around with no particular purpose and thus probably made people think he did not know what he was doing.

Which was true. There was nothing normal about the case. There was not even a single witness who could be questioned.

For once the people from the prosecutor's office had interviewed the lock-keeper and spoken to the Waterways Board's civil engineer, they had decided that all the boats were free to go on their way.

The two carters had been the last to leave, around noon, each in charge of a 'panama'.

Since there is a lock every three or four kilometres, and given that they are all connected by telephone, the location of any boat at any given time could be established and any vessel stopped.

Besides which, a police inspector from Épernay had questioned everyone, and Maigret had been given transcripts of their written statements, which told him nothing except that the facts did not add up.

Everyone who had been in the Café de la Marine the previous day was known either to the owner of the bar or the lock-keeper and in most cases to both.

The carters spent at least one night each week in the same stable and invariably in the same, semi-drunken state.

'You know how it is! You take a drop at every lock . . . Nearly all the lock-keepers sell drink.'

The tanker-barge, which had arrived on Sunday afternoon and moved on again on Monday morning, was carrying petrol and was registered to a big company in Le Havre.

The *Providence*, which was owned by the skipper, passed this way twenty times a year with the same pair of horses and its old carter. And this was very much the case with all the others.

Maigret was in a tetchy mood. He entered the stable and from there went to the café or the shop any number of times.

He was seen walking as far as the stone bridge looking as though he was counting his steps or looking for something in the mud. Grimly, dripping with water, he watched as ten vessels were raised or lowered.

People wondered what he had in mind. The answer was: nothing. He didn't even try to find what might be called clues, but rather to absorb the atmosphere, to capture the essence of canal life, which was so different from the world he knew.

He had made sure that someone would lend him a bicycle if he should need to catch up with any of the boats.

The lock-keeper had let him have a copy of the *Official Handbook of Inland Waterways*, in which out-of-the-way places like Dizy take on an unsuspected importance for topographical reasons or for some particular feature: a junction, an intersection, or because there is a port or a crane or even an office.

He tried to follow in his mind's eye the progress of the barges and carters:

Ay — Port — Lock 13.

Mareuil-sur-Ay — Shipyard — Port — Turning dock — Lock 12 — Gradient 74, 36 . . .

Then Bisseuil, Tours-sur-Marne, Condé, Aigny . . .

Right at the far end of the canal, beyond the Langres plateau, which the boats reached by going up through a series of locks and then were lowered down the other side, lay the Sâone, Chalon, Mâcon, Lyons . . .

'What was the woman doing here?'

In a stable, wearing pearl earrings, her stylish bracelet and white buckskin shoes!

She must have been alive when she got there because the crime had been committed after ten in the evening.

But how? And why? And no one had heard a thing! She had not screamed. The two carters had not woken up.

If the whip had not been mislaid, it was likely the body might not have been discovered for a couple of weeks or a month, by chance when someone turned over the straw.

And other carters passing through would have snored the night away next to a woman's corpse!

Despite the cold rain, there was still a sense of something heavy, something forbidding in the atmosphere. And the rhythm of life here was slow.

Feet shod with boots or clogs shuffled over the stones of the lock or along the towpath. Tow-horses streaming with water waited while barges were held at the lock before setting off again, taking the strain, thrusting hard with their hind legs.

Soon evening would swoop down as it had the previous day. Already, barges travelling upstream had come to a stop and were tying up for the night, while their stiff-limbed crews made for the café in groups.

Maigret followed them in to take a look at the room which had been prepared for him. It was next door to the landlord's. He remained there for about ten minutes, changed his shoes and cleaned his pipe.

At the same time as he was going back downstairs, a yacht steered by a man in oilskins close to the bank slowed, went into reverse and slipped neatly into a slot between two bollards.

The man carried out all these manoeuvres himself. A little later, two men emerged from the cabin, looked wearily all round them and eventually made their way to the Café de la Marine.

They too had donned oilskins. But when they took them off, they were seen to be wearing open-necked flannel shirts and white trousers.

The watermen stared, but the newcomers gave no sign that they felt out of place. The very opposite. Their surroundings seemed to be all too familiar to them.

One was tall, fleshy, turning grey, with a brick-red face and prominent, greenish-blue eyes, which he ran over people and things as if he weren't seeing them at all.

He leaned back in his straw-bottomed chair, pulled another to him for his feet and summoned the landlord with a snap of his fingers.

His companion, who was probably twenty-five or so, spoke to him in English in a tone of snobbish indifference.

It was the younger man who asked, with no trace of an accent:

'You have still champagne? I mean without bubbles?'

'I have.'

'Bring us a bottle.'

They were both smoking imported cork-tipped Turkish cigarettes.

The watermen's talk, momentarily suspended, slowly started up again.

Not long after the landlord had brought the wine, the man who had handled the yacht arrived, also in white trousers and wearing a blue-striped sailor's jersey.

'Over here, Vladimir.'

The bigger man yawned, exuding pure, distilled boredom. He emptied his glass with a scowl, indicating that his thirst was only half satisfied.

'Another bottle!' he breathed at the young man.

The young man repeated the words more loudly, as if he was accustomed to passing on orders in this way.

'Another bottle! Of the same!'

Maigret emerged from his corner table, where he had been nursing a bottle of beer.

'Excuse me, gentlemen, would you mind if I asked you a question?'

The older man indicated his companion with a gesture which meant:

'Talk to him.'

He showed neither surprise nor interest. The sailor poured himself a drink and cut the end off a cigar.

'Did you get here along the Marne?'

'Yes, of course, along the Marne.'

'Did you tie up last night far from here?'

The big man turned his head and said in English:

'Tell him it's none of his business.'

Maigret pretended he had not understood and, without saying any more, produced a photograph of the corpse from his wallet and laid it on the brown oilcloth on the table.

The bargees, sitting at their tables or standing at the bar, followed the scene with their eyes.

The yacht's owner, hardly moving his head, looked at the photo. Then he stared at Maigret and murmured:

'Police?'

He spoke with a strong English accent in a voice that sounded hoarse.

'Police Judiciaire. There was a murder here last night. The victim has not yet been identified.'

'Where is she now?' the other man asked, getting up and pointing to the photo.

'In the morgue at Épernay. Do you know her?'

The Englishman's expression was impenetrable. But Maigret registered that his huge, apoplectic neck had turned reddish blue.

The man picked up his white yachting cap, jammed it on his balding head, then muttered something in English as he turned to his companion.

'More complications!'

Then, ignoring the gawping watermen, he took a strong pull on his cigarette and said:

'It's my wife!'

The words were less audible that the patter of the rain against the window panes or even the creaking of the windlass that opened the lock gates. The ensuing silence, which lasted a few seconds, was absolute, as if all life had been suspended.

'Pay the man, Willy.'

The Englishman threw his oilskin over his shoulders, without putting his arms in the sleeves, and growled in Maigret's direction.

'Come to the boat.'

The sailor he had called Vladimir polished off the bottle of champagne and then left, accompanied by Willy.

The first thing the inspector saw when he arrived on board was a woman in a dressing gown dozing on a dark-red velvet bunk. Her feet were bare and her hair uncombed.

The Englishman touched her on the shoulder and with the same poker face he had worn earlier he said in a voice entirely lacking in courtesy:

'Out!'

Then he waited, his eye straying to a folding table, where there was a bottle of whisky and half a dozen dirty glasses plus an ashtray overflowing with cigarette ends.

In the end, he poured himself a drink mechanically and pushed the bottle in Maigret's direction with a gesture which meant:

'If you want one . . . '

A barge passed on a level with the portholes, and fifty metres further on the carter brought his horses to a halt. There was the sound of bells on their harness jangling.

2

The Passengers on Board the *Southern Cross*

Maigret was almost as tall and broad as the Englishman. At police headquarters on Quai des Orfèvres, his imperturbability was legendary. But now he was exasperated by the calm of the man he wanted to question.

Calm seemed to be the order of the day on the boat. From Vladimir, who sailed it, to the woman they had roused from her sleep, everyone on board seemed either detached or dazed. They were like people dragged out of bed after a night of serious drinking.

One detail among many: as she got up and looked round for a packet of cigarettes, the woman noticed the photo which the Englishman had put down on the table. During the short walk from the Café de la Marine to the yacht, it had got wet.

'Mary?' She put the question scarcely batting an eye.

'Yes. Mary.'

And that was it! She went out through a door which opened into the cabin and presumably was the door to the bathroom.

Willy appeared on deck and poked his head in through the hatchway. The cabin was cramped. Its varnished mahogany walls were thin and anyone forward could hear every word, for its owner looked first in that direction, frowning, then at the young man saying impatiently:

'Come in . . . and sharp about it!'

Then, turning to Maigret, he added curtly:

'Sir Walter Lampson, Colonel, Indian Army, retired.'

He accompanied this introduction of himself with a stiff little bow and a motion of the hand towards the bench seat along the cabin wall.

'And you are . . . ?' said the inspector, turning towards Willy.

'A friend . . . Willy Marco.'

'Spanish?'

The colonel gave a shrug. Maigret scanned the young man's visibly Jewish features.

'My father is Greek and my mother Hungarian.'

'Sir Walter, I'm afraid I have to ask you some questions.'

Willy had sat down casually on the back of a chair and was rocking backwards and forwards, smoking a cigarette.

'I'm listening.'

But just as Maigret was about to open his mouth, the yacht's owner barked:

'Who did it? Do you know?'

He meant the perpetrator of the crime.

'We haven't come up with anything so far. That's why you can be useful to our inquiries by filling me in on a number of points.'

'Was it a rope?' he continued, holding one hand against his throat.

'No. The murderer used his hands. When was the last time you saw Mrs Lampson?'

'Willy . . . ?'

Willy was obviously his general factotum, expected to order the drinks and answer questions put to the colonel.

'Meaux. Thursday evening,' he said.

'And you did not report her disappearance to the police?'

Sir Walter helped himself to another whisky.

'Why should I? She was free to do whatever she pleased.'

'Did she often go off like that?'

'Sometimes.'

The sound of rain pattered on the deck overhead. Dusk was turning into night. Willy Marco turned the electric light on.

'Batteries been charged up?' the colonel asked him in English. 'It's not going to be like the other day?'

Maigret was trying to maintain a coherent line of questioning. But he was constantly being distracted by new impressions.

Despite his best efforts, he kept looking at everything, thinking about everything simultaneously. As a result his head was filled with a jumble of half-formed ideas.

He was not so much annoyed as made to feel uneasy by this man who, in the Café de la Marine, had cast a quick glance at the photo and said without flinching:

'It's my wife.'

And he recalled the woman in the dressing gown saying:

'Mary?'

Willy went on rocking to and fro, a cigarette

glued to his lips, while the colonel was worrying about the boat's batteries!

In the neutral setting of his office, the inspector would have doubtless conducted a properly structured interview. But here, he began by taking off his overcoat without being invited to and picked up the photo, which was disturbing in the way all photographs of corpses are disturbing.

'Do you live here, in France?'

'In France, England . . . Sometimes Italy . . . Always on my boat, the *Southern Cross*.'

'And you've just come from . . . ?'

'Paris!' replied Willy who had got the nod from the colonel to do the talking. 'We stayed there two weeks after spending a month in London.'

'Did you live on board?'

'No. The boat was moored at Auteuil. We stayed at the Hotel Raspail, in Montparnasse.'

'You mean the colonel, his wife, the lady I saw just now, plus yourself?'

'Yes. The lady is the widow of a member of the Chilean parliament, Madame Negretti.'

Sir Walter gave an impatient snort and lapsed into English again:

'Get on with it or else he'll still be here tomorrow morning.'

Maigret did not flinch. But from then on, he put his questions with more than a touch of bloody-mindedness.

'So Madame Negretti is no relation?' he asked Willy.

'Absolutely not.'

'So she is not connected in any way with you

and the colonel . . . Would you tell me about accommodation arrangements on board?'

Sir Walter swallowed a mouthful of whisky, coughed and lit a cigarette.

'Forward are the crew's quarters. That's where Vladimir sleeps. He's a former cadet in the Russian navy . . . He served in Wrangel's White Russian fleet.'

'Any other crew? No servants?'

'Vladimir does everything.'

'Go on.'

'Between the crew's quarters and this cabin are, on the right, the galley, and on the left the bathroom.'

'And aft?'

'The engine.'

'So there were four of you in this cabin?'

'There are four bunks . . . First, the two that you see. They convert to day couches . . . Then . . . '

Willy crossed to a wall panel, pulled out a kind of deep drawer which was in fact a bed.

'There's one of these on each side . . . Do you see?'

Actually, Maigret was indeed beginning to see a little more clearly. He was beginning to feel that it wouldn't be long before he got to the bottom of these unusual living arrangements.

The colonel's eyes were a dull grey and watered like a drunk's. He seemed to have lost interest in the conversation.

'What happened at Meaux? But first, when exactly did you get there?'

'Wednesday evening . . . Meaux is a one-day

stage from Paris. We'd brought along a couple of girls, just friends, with us from Montparnasse.'

'And?'

'The weather was marvellous. We played some records and danced outside, on deck. Around four in the morning I took the girls to their hotel, and they must have caught the train back the next morning.'

'Where was the *Southern Cross* moored?'

'Near the lock.'

'Anything happen on Thursday?'

'We got up very late, we were woken several times in the night by a crane loading stone into a barge nearby. The colonel and I went for a drink before lunch in town. Then, in the afternoon, let me see . . . the colonel had a nap . . . and I played chess with Gloria . . . Gloria is Madame Negretti.'

'On deck?'

'Yes. I think Mary went for a walk.'

'And she never came back?'

'Yes she did: she had dinner on board. The colonel suggested we all spend the evening at the palais de danse. Mary didn't want to come with us . . . When we got back, which was around three in the morning, she wasn't here.'

'Didn't you look for her?'

Sir Walter was drumming his fingers on the polished top of the table.

'As the colonel told you, his wife was free to come and go as she pleased. We waited for her until Saturday and then we moved on . . . She knew our route and could have caught up with us later.'

'Are you going down to the Mediterranean?'

'Yes, to the island of Porquerolles, off Hyères. It's where we spend most of the year. The colonel bought an old fort there. It's called the Petit Langoustier.'

'Did everybody stay on board all day Friday?'

Willy hesitated for a moment then almost blurted out his answer:

'I went to Paris.'

'Why?'

He laughed unpleasantly, which gave his mouth an odd twist.

'I mentioned our friends, the two girls . . . I wanted to see them again. Or at least one of them.'

'Can you give me their names?'

'First names . . . Suzy and Lia . . . You'll find them any night at La Coupole. They live at the hotel on the corner of Rue de la Grande-Chaumière.'

'Working girls?'

'They're both decent sorts . . . '

The door opened. It was Madame Negretti. She had put on a green silk dress.

'May I come in?'

The colonel answered with a shrug. He must now have been on to his third whisky and was drinking them more or less neat.

'Willy . . . Ask him . . . The formalities . . . '

Maigret had no need to have it translated to understand. But this roundabout, offhand way of being asked questions was beginning to irritate him.

'Obviously as a first step you will be expected

178

to identify the body. After the post-mortem, you will no doubt be given a death certificate authorizing burial. You will choose the cemetery and . . . '

'Can we go now, straightaway? Is there a garage around here where I can hire a car?'

'There's one in Épernay.'

'Willy, phone for a car . . . right now.'

'There's a phone at the Café de la Marine,' said Maigret while the young man badtemperedly put on his oilskin jacket.

'Where's Vladimir?'

'I heard him come back a little while ago.'

'Tell him we'll have dinner at Épernay.'

Madame Negretti, who was running to fat and had glossy black hair and very light skin, had found a chair in a corner, under the barometer, and had observed what was happening with her chin cupped in one hand. She looked as if her mind was elsewhere or perhaps she was deep in thought.

'Are you coming with us?' asked Sir Walter.

'I'm not sure . . . Is it still raining?'

Maigret was already bristling, and the colonel's last question did nothing to calm him down.

'How many days do think you'll need us for? To wind everything up?'

To this came the blunt answer:

'Do you mean including the funeral?'

'Yes . . . Three days?'

'If the police doctors produce a burial certificate and if the examining magistrate has no objection, you could be all done in practical terms inside twenty-four hours.'

Did the colonel feel the bitter sarcasm of the words?

Maigret needed to take another look at the photo: a body that was broken, dirty, crumpled, a face which had once been pretty, carefully made up, with scented rouge applied to lips and cheeks, and a macabre grimace which you couldn't look at without feeling an icy chill run up and down your spine.

'Like a drink?'

'No thanks.'

'In that case . . . '

Sir Walter stood up to indicate that he considered that the interview was over. Then he called:

'Vladimir! . . . A suit!'

'I'll probably have to question you again,' the inspector said. 'I may even need to have your boat thoroughly searched.'

'Tomorrow . . . Épernay first, right? . . . How long will the car be?'

'Will I have to stay here by myself?' said Madame Negretti in alarm.

'With Vladimir . . . But you can come . . . '

'I'm not dressed.'

Willy suddenly burst in and shrugged off his streaming oilskins.

'The car will be here in ten minutes.'

'Perhaps, inspector, if you wouldn't mind . . . ?'

The colonel motioned to the door.

'We must dress.'

As he left, Maigret felt so frustrated that he would gladly have punched someone on the nose. He heard the hatch close behind him.

From the outside, all that could be seen was the glow of eight portholes and the light of the white lantern fixed to the mast. Not ten metres away was the outline of the squat stern of a barge and, on the left, a large heap of coal.

Perhaps it was an illusion but Maigret had the impression that the rain was coming down twice as hard and that the sky was the darkest and most threatening he'd ever seen.

He made his way to the Café de la Marine, where everyone stopped talking the moment he walked in. All the watermen were there, huddled round the cast-iron stove. The lock-keeper was leaning against the bar, near the landlord's daughter, a tall girl with red hair who wore clogs.

The tables were covered with waxy cloths and were littered with wine bottles, tumblers and standing pools of drink.

'So, was it his missus?' the landlord finally asked, taking his courage in both hands.

'Yes. Give me a beer. On second thoughts, no. Make it something hot. A grog.'

The watermen's talk started up again, very gradually. The girl brought Maigret the steaming glass and in doing so brushed against his shoulder with her apron.

The inspector imagined those three characters getting dressed in that cramped space. Vladimir too.

He imagined a number of other things, idly and without great relish.

He was familiar with the lock at Meaux, which is bigger than most locks because, like the one at

Dizy, it is situated at the junction of the Marne and the canal, where there is a crescent-shaped port which is always full of barges packed closely together.

There, among the watermen, the *Southern Cross* would have been moored, all lit up, and on board the two women from Montparnasse, the curvaceous Gloria Negretti, Madame Lampson, Willy and the colonel dancing on the deck to the strains of the gramophone and drinking . . .

In a corner of the Café de la Marine, two men in blue overalls were eating sausage and bread, cutting slices off each with their knives and drinking red wine.

And someone was talking about an accident which had happened that morning in the 'culvert', that is a stretch of the canal which, as it crosses the high part of the Langres plateau, passes through a tunnel for eight kilometres.

A barge hand had got one foot caught in the horses' tow-line. He'd called out but hadn't been able to make the carter hear. So when the animals set off again after a rest stop, he'd been yanked into the water.

The tunnel was not lit. The barge carried only one lamp which reflected faintly in the water. The barge hand's brother — the boat was called *Les Deux Frères* — had jumped into the canal.

Only one of them had been fished out, and he was dead. They were still looking for the other.

'They only had two more instalments on the boat to pay. But it looks like, going by the contract, that the wives won't have to fork out another penny.'

A taxi-driver wearing a leather cap came in and looked round.

'Who was it ordered a car?'

'Me!' said Maigret.

'I had to leave it at the bridge. I didn't fancy finishing up in the canal.'

'Will you be eating here?' the landlord asked the inspector.

'I don't know yet.'

He went out with the taxi-driver. Through the rain, the white-painted *Southern Cross* was a milky stain. Two boys from a nearby barge, out despite the downpour, were staring at it admiringly.

'Joseph!' came a woman's voice. 'Bring your brother here! . . . You're going to get a walloping! . . .'

'*Southern Cross*,' the taxi-driver read on the bow. 'English, are they?'

Maigret walked across the gangplank and knocked. Willy opened the door. He was already dressed, looking elegant in a dark suit. Inside, Maigret saw the colonel, red-faced and jacket-less, having his tie knotted by Gloria Negretti. The cabin smelled of eau de Cologne and brilliantine.

'Has the car come?' asked Willy. 'Is it here?'

'It's at the bridge, a short distance from here.'

Maigret stayed outside. He half heard the colonel and the young man arguing in English. Eventually Willy came out.

'He won't traipse through mud,' he said. 'Vladimir's going to launch the dinghy. We'll meet you there.'

183

'Thought so,' muttered the taxi-driver, who had heard.

Ten minutes later, Maigret and he were walking to and fro on the stone bridge just by the parked taxi, which had its sidelights on. Nearly half an hour went by before they heard the putt-putt of a small two-stroke engine.

Eventually Willy's voice shouted:

'Is this the place? . . . Inspector!'

'Yes, over here!'

The dinghy, powered by a removable motor, turned a half circle and pulled in to the bank. Vladimir helped the colonel out and made arrangements to pick them up when they got back.

In the car, Sir Walter did not speak. Despite his bulk, he was remarkably elegant. Ruddy-faced, well turned-out and impassive, he was every inch the English gentleman as portrayed in nineteenth-century prints.

Willy was chain-smoking.

'Some jalopy!' he muttered as they lurched over a drain.

Maigret noticed he was wearing a platinum ring set with a large yellow diamond.

When they got to the town, where the cobbled streets gleamed in the rain, the taxi-driver lifted the glass separating him and his fare and asked:

'Where do you want me to . . . ?'

'The mortuary!' replied the inspector.

It didn't take long. The colonel barely said a word. There was only one attendant in the building, where three bodies were laid out on stone slabs.

All the doors were locked. The locks creaked as they were opened. The light had to be switched on.

It was Maigret who lifted the sheet.

'Yes!'

Willy was the most upset, the most anxious to turn away from the sight.

'Do you recognize her too?'

'It's her all right . . . She looks so . . . '

He did not finish. The colour was visibly draining from his face. His lips were dry. If the inspector had not dragged him away, he would probably have passed out.

'You don't know who . . . ?' the colonel said distinctly.

Was a barely noticeable hint of distress just detectable in his tone of voice? Or wasn't it just the effect of all those glasses of whisky?

Even so, Maigret made a mental note of this small shift.

Then they were outside, on a pavement poorly lit by a single lamp-post near the car. The driver had not budged from his seat.

'You'll have dinner with us, won't you?' Sir Walter asked, again without turning to face Maigret.

'Thank you, no. Since I'm here, I'll make the most of it to sort out a few matters.'

The colonel bowed and did not insist.

'Come, Willy.'

Maigret remained for a moment in the doorway of the mortuary while the young man, after conferring with the Englishman, turned to the taxi-driver.

He was obviously asking which was the best restaurant in town. People walked past while brightly lit, rattling trams trundled by.

A few kilometres from there, the canal stretched away, and all along it, near the locks, there were barges now asleep which would set off at four in the morning, wrapped in the smell of hot coffee and stables.

3

Mary Lampson's Necklace

When Maigret got into bed, in his room, with its distinctive, slightly nauseating smell, he lay for some time aligning two distinct mental pictures.

First, Épernay: seen through the large, brightly lit windows of La Bécasse, the best restaurant in town, the colonel and Willy elegantly seated at a table surrounded by high-class waiters . . .

It was less than half an hour after their visit to the mortuary. Sir Walter Lampson was sitting ramrod straight, and the aloof expression on that ruddy face under its sparse thatch of silver hair was phenomenal.

Beside his elegance, or more accurately his pedigree, Willy's smartness, though he wore it casually enough, looked like a cheap imitation.

Maigret had eaten elsewhere. He had phoned the Préfecture and then the police at Meaux.

Then, alone and on foot, he had headed off into the rainy night along the long ribbon of road. He had seen the illuminated portholes of the *Southern Cross* opposite the Café de la Marine.

He had been curious and called in, using a forgotten pipe as an excuse.

It was there that he had acquired the second mental picture: in the mahogany cabin, Vladimir, still wearing his striped sailor's jersey, a cigarette hanging from his lips, was sitting opposite Madame Negretti, whose glossy hair again hung down over her cheeks.

They were playing cards — 'sixty-six', a game popular in central Europe.

There had been a brief moment of utter stupefaction. But no shocked reaction! Both had just stopped breathing for a second.

Then Vladimir had stood up and begun hunting for the pipe. Gloria Negretti had asked, in a faint lisp:

'Aren't they back yet? Was it Mary?'

The inspector had thought for a moment of getting on his bicycle, riding along the canal and catching up with the barges which had passed through Dizy on Sunday night. The sight of the sodden towpath and the black sky had made him change his mind.

When there was a knock on the door of his room, he was aware, even before he opened his eyes, that the bluey-grey light of dawn was percolating through the window of his room.

He had spent a restless night full of the sound of horses' hooves, confused voices, footsteps on the stairs, clinking glass in the bar underneath him and finally the smell of coffee and hot rum which had wafted up to him.

'What is it?'

'Lucas! Can I come in?'

Inspector Lucas, who almost always worked with Maigret, pushed the door open and shook the clammy hand which his chief held out through a gap in the bedclothes.

'Got something already? Not too worn out, I hope?'

'I'll survive, sir. After I got your phone call, I went straight to the hotel you talked about, on the corner of Rue de la Grande-Chaumière. The girls weren't there, but at least I got their names. Suzanne Verdier, goes under the name of Suzy, born at Honfleur in 1906. Lia Lauwenstein, born in the Grand Duchy of Luxembourg in 1903. The first arrived in Paris four years ago, started as a housemaid, then worked for a while as a model. The Lauwenstein girl has been living mainly on the Côte d'Azur . . . Neither, I checked, appears in the Vice Squad's register of prostitutes. But they might as well be on it.'

'Lucas, would you pass me my pipe and order me coffee?'

The sound of rushing water came from the chamber of the lock and over it the chug of a diesel engine idling. Maigret got out of bed and stood at a poor excuse for a washstand where he poured cold water into the bowl.

'Don't stop.'

'I went to La Coupole, like you said. They weren't there, but the waiters all knew them. They sent me to the Dingo, then La Cigogne. I ended up at a small American bar, I forget what it's called, in Rue Vavin, and found them there, all alone, looking very sorry for themselves. Lia is quite a looker. She's got style. Suzy is blonde, girl-next-door type, not a nasty bone in her body. If she'd stayed back in the sticks where she came from, she'd have got married and made a good wife and mother. She had got

189

freckles all over her face and . . . '

'See a towel anywhere?' interrupted Maigret. His face was dripping with water, and his eyes were shut. 'By the way, is it still raining?'

'It wasn't raining when I got here, but it looks like it could start up again at any moment. At six this morning there was a fog which almost froze your lungs . . . Anyway, I offered to buy the girls a drink. They immediately asked for sandwiches, which didn't surprise me at first. But after a while I noticed the pearl necklace the Lauwenstein girl was wearing. As a joke I managed to get a bite on it. They were absolutely real! Not the necklace of an American millionairess, but even so it must have been worth all of 100,000 francs. Now when girls of that sort prefer sandwiches and hot chocolate to cocktails . . . '

Maigret, who was smoking his first pipe of the day, answered the knock of the girl who had brought his coffee. Then he glanced out of the window and registered that there was as yet no sign of life outside. A barge was passing close to the *Southern Cross*. The man leaning his back against the tiller was staring at the yacht with reluctant admiration.

'Right. Go on.'

'I drove them to another place, a quiet café.

'There, without warning, I flashed my badge, pointed to the necklace and asked straight out: 'Those are Mary Lampson's pearls, aren't they?'

'I don't suppose they knew she was dead. But if they did, they played their parts to perfection.

'It took them a few moments to admit everything. In the end it was Suzy who said to her friend: 'Best tell him the truth, seeing as he knows so much about it already.'

'And a pretty tale it was too . . . Need a hand, chief?'

Maigret was flailing his arms wildly in his efforts to catch his braces, which were dangling down his thighs.

'The main point first. They both swore that it was Mary Lampson herself who gave them the pearls last Friday, in Paris, where she'd come to meet them. You'll probably understand this better than I do, because all I know about the case is what you told me over the phone.

'I asked if Madame Lampson had come there with Willy Marco. They said no. They said they hadn't seen Willy since last Thursday, when they left him at Meaux.'

'Just a moment,' Maigret broke in as he knotted his tie in a milky mirror which distorted his reflection. 'The *Southern Cross* arrives at Meaux on Wednesday evening. Our two girls are on board. They spend a lively night with the colonel, Willy, Mary Lampson and Gloria.

'It's very late when Suzy and Lia are taken off to a hotel, and they leave by train on Thursday morning . . . Did anyone give them money?'

'They said 500 francs.'

'Had they got to know the colonel in Paris?'

'A few days earlier.'

'And what happened on the yacht?'

Lucas gave a knowing smile.

'Assorted antics, none very savoury. Apparently the Englishman lives only for whisky and women. Madame Negretti is his mistress.'

'Did his wife know?'

'Oh, she knew all right! She herself was Willy's mistress. None of which stopped them bringing Suzy and Lia to join the party, if you follow me. And then there was Vladimir, who danced with all the women. In the early hours there was a row because Lia Lauwenstein said that 500 francs was charity. The colonel did not answer, leaving that to Willy. They were all drunk. The Negretti woman fell asleep on the roof, and Vladimir had to carry her into the cabin.'

Standing at the window, Maigret let his eye wander along the black line of the canal. To his left, he could see the small-gauge railway, which was still used to transport earth and gravel.

The sky was grey and streaked low down with shreds of blackish cloud. But it had stopped raining.

'What happened then?'

'That's more or less it. On Friday, Mary Lampson supposedly travelled to Paris and met up with both girls at La Coupole, when she must have given them the necklace.'

'My, my! A teeny-weeny little present . . . '

'Not a present. She handed it over for them to sell on. They were to give her half of whatever cash they got for it. She told them her husband didn't let her have much in the way of ready money.'

The paper on the walls of the room was patterned with small yellow flowers. On it the basin was a splash of dirty white.

Maigret saw the lock-keeper hurrying his way along with a bargee and his carter, clearly intending to drink a tot of rum at the bar.

'That's all I could get out of them,' said Lucas in conclusion. 'I left them at two this morning. I sent Inspector Dufour to keep a discreet eye on their movements. Then I went back to the Préfecture to check the records as per your instructions. I found the file on Willy Marco, who was kicked out of Monaco four years ago after some murky business to do with gambling. The following year he was questioned after an American woman claimed he had relieved her of some items of jewellery. But the charge was dropped, I don't know why, and Marco stayed out of jail. Do you think that he's . . . '

'I don't think anything. And that's the honest truth, I swear. Don't forget the murder was committed on Sunday after ten at night, when the *Southern Cross* was moored at La Ferté-sous-Jouarre.'

'What do you make of the colonel?'

Maigret shrugged his shoulders and pointed to Vladimir, who had just popped out through the forward hatch and was making for the Café de la Marine. He was wearing white trousers, rope sandals and a sweater. An American sailor's cap was pulled down over one ear.

'Phone call for Monsieur Maigret,' the red-haired serving girl called through the door.

'Come down with me, Lucas.'

The phone was in the corridor, next to a coat stand.

'Hello? . . . Meaux? . . . What was that? . . . Yes, the *Providence* . . . At Meaux all day Thursday loading? . . . Left at three o'clock

Friday morning . . . Did any others? . . . The *Éco-III* . . . That's a tanker-barge, right? . . . Friday night at Meaux . . . Left Saturday morning . . . Thanks, inspector! . . . Yes, carry on with the questioning, you never know . . . Yes, I'll still be at this address . . . '

Lucas had listened to this conversation without understanding a word of it. Before Maigret could open his mouth to tell him, a uniformed officer on a bicycle appeared at the door.

'Message from Records . . . It's urgent!'

The man was spattered with mud to the waist.

'Go and dry off for a moment and while you're at it drink my health with a hot grog.'

Maigret led Lucas out on to the towpath, opened the envelope and read out in a half-whisper:

Summary of preliminary analyses relating to inquiries into the murder at Dizy:
— victim's hair shows numerous traces of resin and also the presence of horsehairs, dark brown in colour;
— the stains on the dress are fuel oil;
— stomach contents at time of death: red wine and tinned meat similar in type to what is commercially available as corned beef.

'Eight out of ten horses have dark brown coats!' sighed Maigret.

★ ★ ★

In the café, Vladimir was asking what was the nearest place where he could buy the supplies he needed. There were three people who were telling him, including the cycling policeman from Épernay, who eventually set off with the Russian in the direction of the stone bridge.

Maigret, with Lucas in tow, headed for the stable, where, in addition to the landlord's grey, a broken-kneed mare possibly intended for slaughter had been kept since the night before.

'It wasn't here that she would have picked up traces of resin,' said the inspector.

He walked twice along the path that led round the buildings from the canal to the stable.

'Do you sell resin?' he asked when he saw the landlord pushing a wheelbarrow full of potatoes.

'It's not exactly proper resin . . . We call it Norwegian pitch. It's used for coating the sides of wooden barges above the waterline. Below it they use coal-tar, which is twenty times cheaper.'

'Have you got any?'

'There are still about twenty cans in the shop . . . But in this sort of weather there's no call for it. The bargees wait for the sun to come out before they start doing up their boats.'

'Is the *Eco-III* made of wood?'

'Iron, like most boats with motors.'

'How about the *Providence?*'

'Wood. Have you found out something?'

Maigret did not reply.

'You know what they're saying?' said the man, who had set down his wheelbarrow.

'Who are 'they'?'

'Everybody on the canal, the bargees, pilots, lock-keepers. Goes without saying that a car would have a hard time driving along the towpath, but what about a motorbike? A motorbike could come from a long way off and leave no more trace than a pushbike.'

The door of the *Southern Cross*'s cabin opened. But no one came out.

For one brief moment, a patch of sky turned yellowish, as if the sun was at last about to break through. Maigret and Lucas walked up and down the canal bank without speaking.

No more than five minutes had gone by before the wind was bending the reeds flat, and one minute later rain was coming down in earnest.

Maigret held out one hand, an automatic reaction. With an equally mechanical gesture Lucas produced a packet of grey pipe tobacco from his pocket and handed it to his companion.

They paused a moment by the lock. The chamber was empty but it was being made ready, for an invisible tug still some distance off had hooted three times, which meant that it was towing three boats.

'Where do you reckon the *Providence* is now?' Maigret asked the lock-keeper.

'Half a mo' . . . Mareuil, Condé . . . and just before Aigny there's a string of about ten boats. That'll hold her up . . . Only two sluices of the lock at Vraux are working . . . So I'd say she's at Saint-Martin.'

'Is that far?'

'Exactly thirty-two kilometres.'

'And the *Éco-III*?'

'Should be at La Chaussée. But a barge coming downstream told us last night that she'd broken her propeller at Lock 12. Which means you'll find her at Tours-sur-Marne, which is fifteen kilometres upstream. It's their own fault . . . It's clear. Regulations state no loads should exceed 280 tons, but they all go on doing it.'

★ ★ ★

It was ten in the morning. As Maigret clambered on to the bicycle he had hired, he saw the colonel sitting in a rocking chair on the deck of the yacht. He was opening the Paris papers, which the postman had just delivered.

'No special orders,' he told Lucas. 'Stay around here. Don't let them out of your sight.'

The showers became less frequent. The towpath was dead straight. When he reached the third lock, the sun came out, still rather watery, but making the droplets of water on the reeds sparkle.

From time to time, Maigret had to get off his bike to get past horses towing a barge. Harnessed side by side, they took up the full width of the towpath and plodded forward, one step at a time, with an effort which made their muscles swell visibly.

Two of these animals were being driven by a little girl of eight or ten. She wore a red dress and carried a doll which dangled at the end of one arm.

The villages were, for the most part, some distance from the canal so that the long ribbon of flat water seemed to unfurl in an absolutely empty landscape.

Here and there was an occasional field with men bent over the dark earth. But most of it was woods. Reeds a metre and a half or two metres high further added to the mood of calm.

A barge taking on a cargo of chalk near a quarry sent up clouds of dust which whitened its hull and the toiling men.

There was a boat in the Saint-Martin lock, but it wasn't the *Providence*.

'They'll have stopped for their dinners in the reach above Châlons!' the lock-keeper's wife said as she went, with two young children clinging to her skirts, from one dock-gate to the other.

Maigret was not a man who gave up easily. Around eleven o'clock he was surprised to find himself in springlike surroundings, where the air pulsed with sun and warmth.

Ahead of him, the canal cut a straight line across a distance of six kilometres. It was bordered with woods of fir on both sides.

At the far end the eye could just make out the light-coloured stonework of a lock. Through its gates spurted thin jets of water.

Halfway along, a barge had halted, at a slight angle. Its two horses had been unharnessed and, their noses in a feedbag, were munching oats and snorting.

The first impression was cheerful or at least restful. Not a house in sight. The reflections in the calm water were wide and slow.

A few more turns of the pedals and the inspector saw a table set up under the awning over the tiller in the stern of the barge. On it was a blue and white checked waxed tablecloth. A woman with fair hair was setting a steaming dish in the middle of it.

He got off his bike after reading, on the rounded bows in gleaming polished letters: *Providence*.

One of the horses, taking its time, stared at him, then twitched its ears and let out a peculiar growl before starting to eat again.

$$\star \quad \star \quad \star$$

Between the barge and the side of the canal was a thin, narrow plank, which sagged under Maigret's weight. Two men were eating, following him with their eyes, while the woman advanced towards him.

'Yes, what do you want?' she asked as she buttoned her blouse, which was part open over her ample bosom.

She spoke with a singsong intonation almost as strong as a southern accent. But she wasn't at all bothered. She waited. She seemed to be protecting the two men with the fullness of her brazen flesh.

'Information,' said the inspector. 'I expect you know there was a murder at Dizy?'

'The crew of the *Castor et Pollux* told us about it. They overtook us this morning. Is it true? It doesn't hardly seem possible, does it? How could anybody have done such a thing? And on the canal too, where it's always so peaceful.'

Her cheeks were blotchy. The two men went on eating, never taking their eyes off Maigret, who glanced involuntarily down at the dish which contained dark meat and gave off an aroma which startled his nostrils.

'A kid goat. I bought it this morning at the lock at Aigny . . . You were looking for information? About us, I suppose? We'd gone long before any dead body was discovered. Speaking of which, anybody know who the poor woman was?'

One of the men was short, dark-haired, with a drooping moustache and a soft, submissive air about him.

He was the husband. He'd merely nodded vaguely at the intruder, leaving his wife to do the talking.

The other man was around sixty years of age. His hair, thick and badly cut, was white. A beard three or four centimetres long covered his chin and most of his cheeks, and he had very thick eyebrows. He looked as hairy as an animal.

In contrast, his eyes were bright but without expression.

'It's your carter I'd like to talk to.'

The woman laughed.

'Talk to Jean? I warn you, he don't talk much to anyone. He's our tame bear! Look at the way he's eating! But he's also the best carter you could hope to find.'

The old man's fork stopped moving. He looked at Maigret with eyes that were disturbingly clear.

Village idiots sometimes have eyes like that.

And also animals who are used to being treated with kindness and then without warning are beaten without pity.

There was something vacant about them. But something else too, something beyond words, almost withdrawn.

'What time did you get up to see to your horses?'

'Same time as always . . . '

Jean's shoulders were unusually broad and looked even broader because his legs were short.

'Jean gets up every day at half past two!' the woman broke in. 'Take a look at the horses. They are groomed every day like they're thoroughbreds. And of an evening, you won't get him to go near a drop of white wine until he's rubbed them down.'

'Do you sleep in the stable?'

Jean did not seem to understand. So it was again the woman who pointed to a structure, taller than the rest, in the middle of the boat.

'That's the stable,' she said. 'He always sleeps there. Our cabin is in the stern. Would you like to see it?'

The deck was spotlessly clean, the brasses more highly polished than those on the *Southern Cross*. And when the woman opened a double door made of pine with a sky-light of coloured glass over it, Maigret saw a touching sight.

Inside was a small parlour. It contained exactly the same oak Henri III-style furniture as is found in the most traditional of lower-middle-class front rooms. The table was covered with a cloth embroidered with silks of various colours, and on it were vases, framed photographs and a stand overflowing with green-leaved plants.

There was more embroidery on a dresser. Over the armchairs were draped thin dust covers.

'If Jean had wanted, we could have rigged up a bed for him near us . . . But he always says he can only sleep in the stable, though we're afraid that he'll get kicked one of these days. No good saying the horses know him, is it? When they're sleeping . . . '

She had started eating, like the housewife who makes other people's dinners and gives herself the worst portion without a second thought . . .

Jean had stood up and kept staring at his horses and then at the inspector while the skipper rolled a cigarette.

'And you didn't see anything, or hear anything?' asked Maigret, looking the carter directly in the eye.

The man turned to the skipper's wife, who replied with her mouth full:

'If he'd seen something, he'd have said, 'course he would.'

'Here's the *Marie*!' said her husband anxiously.

The chugging of an engine had become audible in the last few moments. Now the form of a barge could be made out astern of the *Providence*.

Jean looked at the woman, who was looking uncertainly at Maigret.

'Listen,' she said finally, 'if you've got to talk to Jean, would you mind doing it as we go? The

Marie has got an engine, but she's slower than us. If she gets in front of us before we get to the lock, she'll hold us up for two days.'

Jean had not waited to hear her last words. He had already taken the feedbags containing the horses' oats from over their heads and was now driving them a hundred metres ahead of the barge.

The bargee picked up a tin trumpet and blew a few quavering notes.

'Are you staying on board? Listen, we'll tell you what we know. Everybody on the canals knows who we are, from Liège to Lyons.'

'I'll meet up with you at the lock,' said Maigret, whose bicycle was still on the bank.

The gangplank was stowed on board. A distant figure had just appeared on the lock gates, and the sluices started to open. The horses set off with a jangle of tinkling bells, and the red pompons tied to the top of their heads bobbed and jounced.

Jean walked by the side of them, unconcerned.

Two hundred metres astern, the motor barge slowed as it realized it had come too late.

Maigret followed, holding the handlebars of his bicycle with one hand. He could see the skipper's wife rushing to finish eating and her husband, short, thin and frail, leaning, almost lying, on the long tiller, which was too heavy for him.

4

The Lover

'I've had lunch,' said Maigret as he strode into the Café de la Marine, where Lucas was sitting at a table in the window.

'At Aigny?' asked the landlord. 'My brother-in-law's the inn-keeper at Aigny . . . '

'Bring us two beers.'

It had been a narrow escape. The inspector, pedalling hard, was barely in sight of Dizy when the weather had turned overcast again. And now thick rain was being drawn like curtains over the last rays of the sun.

The *Southern Cross* was still in its berth. There was no one to be seen on deck. And no sound came from the lock so that, for the first time, Maigret was aware of being truly in the country. He could hear chickens clucking in the yard outside.

'Got anything for me?' he asked Lucas.

'The Russian came back with supplies. The woman put in a brief appearance in a blue dressing gown. The colonel and Willy came for a drink before lunch. They gave me some odd looks, I think.'

Maigret took the tobacco pouch which his companion was holding out for him, filled his pipe and waited until the landlord, who had served them, had vanished into his shop.

'I didn't get anything either,' he muttered. 'Of the two boats which could have brought Mary Lampson here, one has broken down about fifteen kilometres from here, and the other is ploughing along the canal at three kilometres an hour.'

'The first one is iron-built, so no chance of the body coming into contact with pitch there.

'The other one is made of wood . . . The master and his wife are called Canelle. A fat motherly sort, who tried her level best to get me to drink a glass of disgusting rum, with a pint-sized husband who runs round after her like a spaniel.

'Which leaves just their carter.

'Either he's pretending to be stupid, in which case he does a brilliant turn, or else he's a complete half-wit. He's been with them for eight years. If the husband is a spaniel, he's a bulldog.

'He gets up at half past two every morning, sees to his horses, downs a bowl of coffee and then starts walking alongside his animals.

'He does his daily thirty or forty kilometres like that, every day, at the same pace, with a swig of white wine at every lock.

'Every evening he rubs the horses down, eats without speaking a word and then collapses on to a straw truss, most times still in his clothes.

'I've checked his papers. An old army pay book with pages so stuck together with filth they can hardly be opened. The name in it is Jean Liberge, born in Lille in 1869.

'And that's it . . . no, just a moment. The *Providence* would have had to get Mary

Lampson on board on Thursday evening at Meaux. So she was alive then. She was still alive when she got here on Sunday evening.

'It would be physically impossible to hide a grown woman for two days against her will in the stable on the boat.

'In which case all three of them would be guilty.'

The scowl on Maigret's face showed that he did not believe that was the case.

'But let's suppose the victim did get on the boat of her own free will. Do you know what you are going to do, Lucas? You're going to ask Sir Walter what his wife's maiden name was. Then get on the phone and find out what you can about her.'

There were two or three patches of sky where the sunlight still lingered, but the rain was coming down more and more heavily. Lucas had hardly left the Café de la Marine and was heading towards the yacht, when Willy Marco stepped off it, wearing a suit and tie, loose-limbed and casual, looking at nothing in particular.

It was definitely a trait shared by all the passengers on the *Southern Cross* that they always looked as though they hadn't had enough sleep or as if large amounts of alcohol did not agree with them.

The two men passed each other on the towpath. Willy appeared to hesitate when he saw Lucas go aboard. Then, lighting a fresh cigarette with the one he had just finished, he made straight for the café.

He was looking for Maigret and did not pretend otherwise.

He did not take off his soft felt hat but touched it absently with one finger as he murmured:

'Hello, inspector. Sleep well? I wanted a quick word . . . '

'I'm listening.'

'Not here, if it's all the same to you. Could we possibly go up to your room, do you think?'

He had lost nothing of his relaxed, confident manner. His small eyes sparkled with something not far from gleeful elation, or perhaps it was malevolence.

'Cigarette?'

'No thanks.'

'Of course! You're a pipe man.'

Maigret decided to take him up to his room, though it hadn't yet been cleaned. After a glance out at the yacht, Willy sat down at once on the edge of the bed and began:

'Naturally you've already made inquiries about me.'

He looked round for an ashtray, failed to locate one and flicked his ash on to the floor.

'Not much to write home about, eh? But I've never claimed to be a saint. Anyway the colonel tells me what a rotter I am three times a day.'

What was remarkable about this was the completely frank expression on his face. Maigret was forced to admit that he was beginning to warm to Willy, who he hadn't been able to stomach at first.

A strange mixture. Sly and foxy. Yet at the

same time a spark of decency which redeemed the rest, plus an engaging touch of humour.

'But you will have noted that I went to Eton, like the Prince of Wales. If we'd been the same age, we would have been the best of pals. But the truth is my father is a fig wholesaler in Smyrna. I can't bear the thought! I've been in some scrapes. The mother of one of my Eton friends, if you must know, got me out of one of them.

'You do understand if I don't give you her name, don't you? A delectable lady . . . But her husband became a government minister, and she was afraid of compromising his position.

'After that . . . They must have told you about Monaco, then that unpleasantness in Nice. Actually the truth isn't as bad as all that . . . Here's a tip: never believe anything you're told by a middle-aged American woman who lives it up on the Riviera and has a husband who arrives unexpectedly from Chicago. Stolen jewels have not always been stolen. But let's move on.

'Now, about the necklace. Either you know already or maybe you've not yet heard. I would have preferred to talk to you about it last night, but in the circumstances it might not have been the decent thing to do.

'The colonel is nothing if not a gentleman. He may be a touch over-fond of whisky, I grant. But he has some justification.

'He should have ended up a general. He was one of the men most in the public eye in Lima. But there was a scandal involving a woman, the wife of a highly placed local bigwig, and he was pensioned off.

'You've seen him. A magnificent specimen, with vigorous appetites. Out there, he had thirty native boys, orderlies, secretaries and God knows how many cars and horses for his own use.

'Then all of a sudden, all gone! Something like a hundred thousand francs a year, wiped out.

'Did I say that he'd already been married twice before he met Mary? His first wife died in India. Second time round, he got a divorce by taking all the fault on himself after finding his lady in bed with one of the boys.

'A real gentleman!'

Willy, now leaning well back, was swinging one leg lethargically, while Maigret, his pipe between his teeth, stood with his back against the wall without moving.

'That's how it goes. Nowadays, he passes the time as well as he can. Down at Porquerolles, he lives in his old fort, which the locals call the Petit Langoustier. When he's saved up enough money, he goes to Paris or London.

'And just think that in India he used to give dinners for thirty or forty guests every week!'

'Was it about the colonel you wanted to talk to me?' murmured Maigret.

Willy did not bat an eyelid.

'Actually, I was trying to put you in the picture. I mean, you've never lived in India or London or had thirty native servants and God knows how many pretty girls at your beck and call . . . I'm not trying to get under your skin . . .

'Be that as it may, I met him two years ago.

'You didn't know Mary when she was alive . . . An adorable creature but a brain like a bird's

209

. . . And a touch loud. If you weren't waiting hand and foot on her all the time, she'd have a fit or cause a scene.

'By the way, do you know how old the colonel is? Sixty-eight.

'She wore him out, if you follow me. She happily indulged his fantasies — he's not past it yet! — but she could be a bit of a nuisance.

'Then she got a thing about me. I quite liked her.'

'I take it that Madame Negretti is Sir Walter's mistress?'

'Yes,' the young man agreed with a scowl. 'It's hard to explain . . . He can't live or drink on his own. He has to have people round him. We met her when we put in once at Bandol. The next morning, she didn't leave. As far as he's concerned, that was it. She'll stay as long as she likes.

'But me, I'm different. I'm one of those rare men who can hold his whisky as well as the colonel.

'Except perhaps for Vladimir, who you've seen. Nine times out of ten, he's the one who puts us both to bed in our bunks.

'I don't know if you have grasped my position. It's true that I have no material worries. Still, there are times when we get stuck in a port for a fortnight waiting for a cheque from London so that we can buy petrol!

'Yes, and that necklace, which I shall come back to in a moment, has seen the inside of a pawnshop a score of times.

'Never mind! The whisky rarely runs out.

'It's not exactly a lavish lifestyle. But we sleep for as long as we want. We come and we go.

'Speaking personally, I much prefer it to being knee-deep in my father's figs.

'At the beginning, the colonel bought several items of jewellery for his wife. From time to time she would ask him for money.

'To buy clothes and so that she had a little pocket-money, if you follow me.

'But whatever you might think, I swear I got a colossal shock yesterday when I realized it was her in that awful photo! So did the colonel, actually . . . But he'd go through fire and water rather than show his feelings. That's his style. And so very English!

'When we left Paris last week — it's Tuesday today, isn't it — the cash was running low. The colonel sent a cable to London asking for an advance on his pension. We waited for it at Épernay. The draft arrived at around this time of day, I think.

'Thing is, I'd left a few debts unpaid in Paris. I'd asked Mary once or twice why she didn't sell her necklace. She could easily have told her husband she'd lost it or said it had been stolen.

'Thursday evening was the party, as you know. But you really shouldn't get any wrong ideas about what went on. The moment Lampson catches sight of pretty women, he has to invite them on board.

'Then a couple of hours later, when he's had too much to drink, he tells me to get rid of them as cheaply as possible.

'On Thursday, Mary got up much earlier than

211

usual, and by the time we'd all staggered out of our bunks, she'd already gone outside.

'After lunch, there was a brief moment when the two of us were alone. She was very affectionate. Affectionate in a special way, a sad way.

'At one point, she put her necklace in my hand and said: 'Just sell it.'

'I'm sorry if you don't believe me . . . I felt awkward, had a qualm or two. If you'd known her, you'd understand.

'Although she could be a real bitch at times, at others she could be quite touching.

'Don't forget that she was over forty. She was looking out for herself. But she must have had an inkling that her time had gone.

'Then someone came in. I slipped the necklace into my pocket. In the evening, the colonel dragged us all off to the palais de danse, and Mary stayed on board by herself.

'When we got back, she wasn't there. Lampson wasn't worried. It wasn't the first time she'd run off like that.

'And not for the reasons you might think. On one occasion, for instance, during the festival of Porquerolles, there was a rather jolly orgy at the Petit Langoustier which lasted the best part of a week. For the first couple of days, Mary was the life and soul of the party. But on day three, she disappeared.

'And do you know where we found her? Staying at an inn at Giens, where she was happily passing the time playing mummies with a couple of unwashed brats.

'I was not comfortable with the business of the necklace. On Friday, I went up to Paris. I nearly sold it. But then I told myself that if there were problems I could land myself in serious trouble.

'Then I remembered the two girls from the night before. With girls like that, you can get away with anything. Besides, I'd already met Lia in Nice and knew I could count on her.

'I gave the necklace to her. Just in case, I told her that if anyone asked, she was to say that Mary herself had given it to her to sell.

'It's as simple as that, and very stupid! I would have been far better off keeping quiet. All the same, if I come up against policemen who aren't very bright, it's the sort of thing that could well land me in court.

'I realized this yesterday the minute I heard that Mary had been strangled.

'I won't ask you what you think. To be honest, I'm expecting to be arrested.

'That would be a mistake, a big mistake! Look, if you want me to help, I'm ready to lend you a hand.

'There are things that may strike you as odd but are quite straightforward really.'

He was now almost flat on the bed, still smoking, with his eyes fixed on the ceiling.

Maigret took up a position by the window to cover his perplexity.

'Does the colonel know that you're here telling me all this?' he asked, turning round suddenly.

'No more than he knows about the business with the necklace. Actually, though I'm obviously in no position to ask, I would prefer if he went on not knowing.'

'And Madame Negretti?'

'A dead weight. A beautiful woman who is incapable of existing except on a couch, smoking cigarettes and drinking sweet liqueurs. She started the day she first came on board and has been doing it ever since . . . Oh sorry: she also plays cards. I think it's the only thing that really interests her.'

The screech of rusted iron indicated that the lock gates were being opened. Two mules trudged past the front of the house then stopped a little further on, while an empty barge continued moving, swinging as it lost way, looking as though it were trying to climb up the bank.

Vladimir, bent double, was baling out the rainwater which threatened to swamp the dinghy.

A car crossed the stone bridge, attempted to drive on to the towpath, stopped, then made several clumsy attempts to turn before coming to a complete stop.

A man dressed all in black got out. Willy, who had got off the bed, glanced out of the window and said:

'It's the undertaker.'

'When is the colonel thinking of leaving?'

'Immediately after the funeral.'

'Which will take place here?'

'Anywhere'll do! He already has one wife buried near Lima and another now married to a New Yorker who will finish up under six feet of American soil.'

Maigret glanced across at him instinctively, as if he was trying to work out if he was joking. But Willy Marco was perfectly serious, though that little ambiguous spark still flickered in his eye.

'If, that is, the money draft has come through! Otherwise, the funeral will have to wait.'

The man in black halted uncertainly by the yacht, put a question to Vladimir, who answered without stopping what he was doing, then finally climbed aboard and vanished into the cabin.

Maigret had not seen Lucas come out.

'You'd better go,' he said to Willy.

Willy hesitated. For a moment, a look of anxiety flitted across his face.

'Are you going to ask him about the necklace?'

'I don't know.'

The moment had passed. Willy, his usual cool self once more, knocked out the dent in his felt hat, waved a goodbye with one hand and went downstairs.

When, shortly after, Maigret followed him down, there were two bargees leaning on the bar nursing bottles of beer.

'Your mate's on the phone,' said the landlord. 'Asked for a Moulins number.'

A tug sounded its hooter several times in the distance. Maigret counted mechanically and muttered:

'Five.'

On the canal it was business as usual. Five barges approaching. The lock-keeper, wearing clogs, emerged from his house and made for the sluices.

Lucas came out of the phone booth. His face was red.

'Whew! That was hard work . . . '

'What is it?'

'The colonel told me his wife's maiden name was Marie Dupin. For the wedding, she produced a birth certificate with that name on it issued at Moulins. Now I've just phoned them there, pulling rank . . . '

'And?'

'There's only one Marie Dupin on their register. She is forty-two years old, has three children and is married to a man called Piedbœf, who is a baker in the high street. The clerk in the town hall I talked to said she had seen her serving in the shop only yesterday. Apparently she weighs all of 180 pounds.'

Maigret said nothing. Looking like a well-to-do bystander with time on his hands, he wandered over to the lock without another thought for his companion and followed every stage of the operation closely. All the while, one thumb angrily tamped down the tobacco in his pipe.

A little later, Vladimir approached the lock-keeper. He touched his white forage cap with one hand and asked where he could fill up with fresh water.

5

The YCF Badge

Maigret had gone to bed early, while Inspector Lucas, who had his orders, went off to Meaux, Paris and Moulins.

When he left the bar, there had been three customers, two bargees and the wife of one of them who had joined her husband and was sitting in a corner, knitting.

The atmosphere was cheerless and heavy. Outside, a barge had tied up less than two metres from the *Southern Cross*, whose portholes were all lit up.

Now, suddenly, the inspector was dragged from a dream so confused that even as he opened his eyes he could remember nothing of it. Someone was knocking urgently on his door, and a voice was calling in a panic:

'Inspector! Inspector! Come quickly! My father . . . '

He ran to the door in his pyjamas and opened it. Outside he was surprised to see the landlord's daughter looking distraught. She leaped on him and literally buried herself in his arms.

'Ah! . . . You must go, hurry! . . . No, stay here! . . . Don't leave me by myself! . . . I couldn't bear it! . . . I'm scared! . . . '

He had never paid much attention to her. He'd thought she was a sturdy girl, well upholstered, but without a nerve in her body.

And here she was, face convulsed, heaving for breath, hanging on to him with an insistence that was embarrassing. Still trying to extricate himself, he moved towards the window and opened it.

It was probably about six in the morning. It was barely first light and cold as a winter dawn.

A hundred metres beyond the *Southern Cross*, in the direction of the stone bridge and the Épernay road, four or five men were using a heavy boat hook to fish out something floating in the water, while one of the barge men untied his dinghy and began rowing across.

Maigret's pyjamas had seen better days. He threw his overcoat over his shoulders, located his ankle boots and inserted his bare feet into them.

'You realize . . . It's *him*! . . . They've . . . '

With a sudden movement, he broke free of the clutches of this strange girl, hurried down the stairs and was going outside just as a woman carrying a baby in her arms was bearing down on the group.

He hadn't been there when Mary Lampson's body had been found. But this new discovery was if anything more grim because, as an effect of this recurrence of crime, a feeling of almost mystical anguish now hung over this stretch of the canal.

The men called to each other. The landlord of the Café de la Marine, who had been first to spot a body floating in the water, was directing operations.

Twice the boat hook had snagged the corpse

and each time the metal end had slipped. Each time, the body had dipped a few centimetres before returning to the surface.

Maigret had already recognized Willy's dark suit. He could not see the face because the head, being heavier, remained submerged.

The man in the dinghy suddenly nudged it, grabbed the body by the chest and raised it with one hand. But he had to haul it over the side of the boat.

The man was not squeamish. He lifted the legs one after the other, threw his mooring rope on to the bank then wiped his streaming forehead with the back of his hand.

For one moment, Maigret had a glimpse of Vladimir's sleep-dulled head appearing through a hatch on the yacht. The Russian rubbed his eyes. Then he vanished.

'Don't touch anything!'

Behind him, one of the men protested, saying that back in Alsace his brother-in-law had been revived after being in the water for nearly three hours.

The landlord of the café pointed to the corpse's throat. There was no doubt: two finger marks, black, just like the ones on the neck of Mary Lampson.

This death was the more shocking of the two. Willy's eyes were wide open, looking much, much larger than usual. His right hand was still clutching a handful of reeds.

Maigret suddenly sensed an unexpected presence behind him. He turned and saw the colonel, also in pyjamas with a silk dressing gown thrown over them and blue kid slippers on his feet.

His silver hair was dishevelled and his face slightly puffy. He was a strange sight dressed like that, surrounded by canal men wearing clogs and thick coarse clothes, in the mud and damp of the early morning.

He was the tallest and broadest there. He gave off a faint whiff of eau de Cologne.

'It's Willy!' he said in a hoarse whisper.

Then he said a few words in English, too fast for Maigret to understand, bent down and touched the face of the young man.

The girl who had woken the inspector was leaning on the café door for support, sobbing. The lock-keeper came running.

'Phone the police at Épernay . . . And a doctor . . . '

Even Madame Negretti came out, barely decent, with nothing on her feet. But she did not dare leave the bridge of the yacht and called to the colonel:

'Walter! Walter!'

In the background were people who had arrived unseen: the driver of the little train, a group of navvies and a man with a cow which went ambling along the towpath by itself.

'Take him inside the café . . . And don't touch him more than you have to.'

He was obviously dead. The elegant suit, now no more than a limp rag, trailed along the ground when the body was lifted.

The colonel followed slowly. His dressing gown, blue slippers and ruddy scalp, across which the wind stirred a few long wisps of hair, made him an absurd but also priestly figure.

The girl's sobs came faster when the body passed in front of her. Then she ran off and shut herself away in the kitchen. The landlord was yelling down the phone:

'No, operator! . . . Police! . . . Hurry up! . . . There's been a murder! . . . Don't hang up! . . . Hello? Hello?'

Maigret kept most of the onlookers out. But the barge men who had discovered the body and helped to fish it out had all crowded into the café where the tables were still littered with glasses and bottles from the night before. The stove roared. A broom was lying in the middle of the floor.

The inspector caught a glimpse of Vladimir peering in through one of the windows. He'd had time to put his American sailor's forage cap on his head. The barge men were talking to him, but he was not responding.

The colonel was still staring at the body, which had been laid out on the red stone flags of the café floor. Whether he was upset or bored or scared it was impossible to say. Maigret went up to him:

'When was the last time you saw him?' he asked.

Sir Walter sighed and seemed to look around him for the man he usually relied on to answer for him.

'It's all so very terrible . . . ' he said eventually.

'Didn't he sleep on board last night?'

With a gesture of the hand, the Englishman

pointed to the barge men who were listening to them. It was like a reminder of the conventions. It meant: 'Do you think it right and proper for these people . . . '

Maigret ordered them out.

'It was ten o'clock last night. We had no whisky left on board. Vladimir hadn't been able to get any at Dizy. I decided to go to Épernay.'

'Did Willy go with you?'

'Not very far. He went off on his own just after the bridge.'

'Why?'

'We had words . . . '

And as the colonel said this, his eyes still drawn to the pinched, pallid, twisted features of the dead man, his own face crumpled.

Was it because he had not slept enough and that his flesh was puffy that he looked more upset? Perhaps. But Maigret would have sworn that there were tears lurking under those heavy eyelids.

'Did you have a bust-up?'

The colonel gave a shrug, as if resigning himself to hearing such a vulgar, ugly expression.

'Were you angry with him about something?'

'No! I wanted to know . . . I kept saying: 'Willy, you're a rotter . . . But you've got to tell me . . . ''

He stopped, overcome. He looked around him so that he would not be mesmerized by the dead man.

'Did you accuse him of murdering your wife?'

He shrugged and sighed:

'He went off by himself. It's happened before,

now and again. Next morning we'd drink the first whisky of the day together and put it out of our minds . . . '

'Did you walk all the way to Épernay?'

'Yes.'

'Did you drink a lot?'

The lingering look which the colonel turned on the inspector was abject.

'I also tried my luck at the tables, at the club . . . They'd told me at La Bécasse that there was a gambling club . . . I came back in a cab.'

'At what time?'

With a motion of the hand he intimated that he had no idea.

'Willy wasn't in his bunk?'

'No. Vladimir told me as he was helping me undress for bed.'

A motorcycle and sidecar pulled up outside the door. A police sergeant dismounted, and the passenger, a doctor, climbed out. The café door opened and then closed.

'Police Judiciaire,' said Maigret, introducing himself to his colleague from Épernay. 'Could you get these people to keep back and then phone the prosecutor's office . . . ?'

The doctor needed only a brief look at the body before saying:

'He was dead before he hit the water. Take a look at these marks.'

Maigret had already seen them. He knew. He glanced mechanically at the colonel's right hand. It was muscular, with the nails cut square and prominent veins.

★ ★ ★

It would take at least an hour to get the public prosecutor and his people together and ferry them to the crime scene. Policemen on cycles arrived and formed a cordon around the Café de la Marine and the *Southern Cross*.

'May I get dressed?' the colonel asked.

Despite his dressing gown, slippers and bare ankles, he made a surprisingly dignified figure as he passed through the crowd of bystanders. He had no sooner gone into the cabin than he poked his head out again and shouted:

'Vladimir!'

Then all the hatches on the yacht were shut.

Maigret was interviewing the lock-keeper, who had been called out to man his gates by a motorboat.

'I imagine that there is no current in a canal? So a body will stay in the place where it was thrown in?'

'In long stretches of the canal, ten or fifteen kilometres, that would be true. But this particular stretch doesn't go even five. If a boat passes through Lock 13, which is the one above mine, I smell water that's released arrive here a few minutes later. And if I put a boat going downstream through my lock, I take a lot of water out of the canal, and that creates a short-lived current.'

'What time do you start work?'

'Officially at dawn but actually a lot earlier. The horse-drawn boats, which move pretty slowly, set off at about three in the morning.

More often than not, they put themselves through the lock without me hearing a thing . . . Nobody says anything because we know them all . . . '

'So this morning . . . ?'

'The *Frédéric*, which spent the night here, must have left around half past three and went through the lock at Ay at five.'

Maigret turned and retraced his steps. Outside the Café de la Marine and along the towpath, a few groups of men had gathered. As the inspector passed them on his way to the stone bridge, an old pilot with a grog-blossom nose came up to him:

'Want me to show you the spot where that young feller was thrown into the water?'

And looking very proud of himself, he glanced round at his comrades, who hesitated a moment before falling into step behind him.

The man was right. Fifty metres from the stone bridge, the reeds had been trampled over an area of several metres. They hadn't simply been walked on. A heavy object had been dragged across the ground. The tracks were wide where the reeds had been flattened.

'See that? I live half a kilometre from here, in one of the first houses you come to in Dizy. When I was coming in this morning, to check if there were any boats going down the Marne that needed me, it struck me as unusual. And then I found this on the towpath just by it.'

The man was tiresome, for he kept pulling funny faces and looking back at his companions, who were following at a distance.

But the object he produced from his pocket was of the greatest interest. It was a finely worked enamel badge. On it was a kedge anchor and the initials 'YCF'.

'Yachting Club de France,' said the pilot. 'They all wear them in their lapels.'

Maigret turned to look at the yacht, which was clearly visible some two kilometres away. Under the words *Southern Cross* he could just make out the same initials: YCF.

Paying no further attention to the man who had given him the badge, he walked slowly to the bridge. On his right, the Épernay road stretched away in a straight line, still glistening with last night's rain. Traffic drove along it at high speeds.

To the left, the road formed a bend as it entered the village of Dizy. On the canal beyond, several barges were lying up, undergoing repairs, just by the yards owned by the Compagnie Générale de Navigation.

Maigret walked back the way he'd come, feeling the tension mounting. The public prosecutor's officials would be arriving soon, and for an hour or two there would be the usual chaos, questions, comings and goings and a spate of wild theories.

When he was level with the yacht, everything was still all closed up. A uniformed officer was pacing up and down a little distance away, telling bystanders to move along, but failing to prevent two journalists from Épernay taking pictures.

The weather was neither fine nor foul. A luminous grey morning sky, unbroken, like a frosted glass ceiling.

Maigret walked across the gangplank and knocked on the door.

'Who is it?' came the colonel's voice.

He went in. He was in no mood to argue. He saw the Negretti woman, wearing no more clothes than before, hair hanging down over her face and neck, wiping away her tears and snivelling.

Sir Walter was sitting on the bench seat, holding out his feet to Vladimir, who was helping him on with a pair of chestnut-brown shoes.

Water had to be boiling somewhere on a stove because there was the hiss of escaping steam.

The two bunks slept in by the colonel and Gloria were still unmade. Playing cards were scattered on the table beside a map of France's navigable waterways.

And still there was that elusive, spicy smell which evoked bar, boudoir and secret amours. A white canvas yachting cap hung from the hat stand next to a riding crop with an ivory handle.

'Was Willy a member of the Yacht Club de France?' asked Maigret in as neutral a tone as he could manage.

The way the colonel shrugged his shoulders told him his question was absurd. And so it was. The YCF is one of the most exclusive clubs.

'But I am,' Sir Walter said casually. 'And of the Royal Yacht Club in England.'

'Would you mind showing me the jacket you were wearing last night?'

'Vladimir . . . '

He now had his shoes on. He stood up, bent down and opened a small cupboard, which had been turned into a liquor cabinet. There was no whisky in sight. But there were other bottles of spirits, over which he hesitated.

Finally he brought out a bottle of liqueur brandy and murmured off handedly:

'What will you have?'

'Not for me, thanks.'

He filled a silver goblet which he took from a rack above the table, looked for the siphon, and frowned darkly like a man all of whose habits have been turned upside down and who feels hard done by.

Vladimir emerged from the bathroom with a black tweed suit. A nod from his master instructed him to hand it to Maigret.

'The YCF badge was usually pinned to the lapel of this jacket?'

'Yes. How long are they going to be over there? Is Willy still on the floor of that café?'

He had emptied his glass while still standing, a sip at a time, and hesitated about whether he'd pour himself another.

He glanced out of the porthole, saw legs and grunted indistinctly.

'Will you listen to me for a moment, colonel?'

The colonel indicated that he was listening. Maigret took the enamel badge from his pocket.

'This was found this morning at the spot where Willy's body was dragged through a bank of reeds and dumped in the canal.'

Madame Negretti uttered a cry, threw herself on the plum-coloured plush of the bench seat and there, holding her head in her hands, she began to sob convulsively.

Vladimir, however, did not move. He waited for the jacket to be returned to him so that he could hang it back up in its place.

The colonel gave an odd sort of laugh and repeated four or five times:

'Yes! Yes!'

As he did so, he poured himself another drink.

'Where I come from, the police ask questions differently. They have to say that everything you say may be used as evidence against you. I'll say it once . . . Shouldn't you be writing this down? I won't say it again . . .

'I was with Willy. We had words. I asked . . . It doesn't matter what I asked.

'He wasn't a rotter like the rest of them. Some rotters are decent fellows.

'I spoke too harshly. He grabbed my jacket just here . . . '

He indicated the lapels and looked out irritably at the feet encased in clogs or heavy shoes which were still visible through the portholes.

'That's all. I don't know, maybe the badge fell off then . . . It happened on the other side of the bridge.'

'Yet the badge was found on this side.'

Vladimir hardly seemed to be listening. He gathered up things that were lying about, went forward and returned unhurriedly.

In a very strong Russian accent, he asked Gloria, who wasn't crying any more but was lying flat on her back without moving, clutching her head with both hands:

'You want anything?'

Steps were heard on the gangplank. There was a knock on the door, and the sergeant said:

'Are you in there, inspector? It's the prosecutor's office . . . '

'I'm coming!'

The sergeant did not move, an unseen presence behind the mahogany door with brass handles.

'One more thing, colonel. When is the funeral?'

'Three o'clock.'

'Today?'

'Yes! I have no reason to stay on here.'

When he had drunk his third glass of three-star cognac, his eyes looked more clouded. Maigret had seen those eyes before.

Then, just as the inspector was about to leave, he asked, cool, casual, every inch the master of all he surveyed:

'Am I under arrest?'

At once, Madame Negretti looked up. She was deathly pale.

6

The American Sailor's Cap

The conclusion of the interview between the magistrate and the colonel was almost a solemn moment. Maigret, who stood slightly apart, was not the only one to notice it.

He caught the eye of the deputy public prosecutor and saw that he too had picked up on it.

The public prosecutor's team had gathered in the bar room of the Café de la Marine. One door led to the kitchen, from which came the clatter of saucepans. The other door, glass-panelled, was covered with stuck-on transparent adverts for pasta and rock soap through which the sacks and boxes in the shop could be seen.

The peaked cap of a policeman in uniform marched to and fro outside the window. Onlookers, silent but determined, had grouped a little further away.

A half-litre glass, with a small amount of liquid in it, was still standing beside a pool of wine on one of the tables.

The clerk of the court, seated on a backless bench, was writing. There was a peevish look on his face.

Once the statements had all been taken, the body had been placed as far from the stove as possible and temporarily covered with one of the brown oilcloths taken from a tabletop, leaving its disjointed boards exposed.

The smell had not gone away: spices, stables, tar and wine lees.

The magistrate, who was reckoned to be one of the most unpleasant in Épernay — he was a Clairfontaine de Lagny and proud of the aristocratic 'de' in the name — stood with his back to the fire and wiped his pince-nez.

At the start of the proceedings, he had said in English:

'I imagine you'd prefer us to use your language?'

He himself spoke it quite well with, perhaps, a hint of affectation, a slight screw of the lips standard among those who try — and fail — to reproduce the correct accent.

Sir Walter had accepted the offer. He had responded to every question slowly, his face turned to the clerk, who was writing, pausing from time to time to allow him to catch up.

He had repeated, without adding anything new, what he had told Maigret during their two interviews.

For the occasion, he had chosen a dark-blue double-breasted suit of almost military cut. To one lapel was pinned a single medal: the Order of Merit.

In one hand he held a peaked cap. On it was a broad gilt crest bearing the insignia of the Yachting Club de France.

It was very simple. One man asked questions and the other man invariably gave a slight, deferential nod before answering.

Even so, Maigret looked on admiringly but could not help feeling mortified as he remembered his own intrusive probings on board the *Southern Cross*.

His English was not good enough for him to grasp all the finer points. But he at least understood the broad meaning of the concluding exchanges.

'Sir Walter,' said the magistrate, 'I must ask you to remain available until we have got to the bottom of both these appalling crimes. I am afraid, moreover, that I have no choice but to withhold permission for the burial of Lady Lampson.'

Another slight bow of the head.

'Do I have your authorization to leave Dizy in my boat?'

With one hand the colonel gestured towards the onlookers who had gathered outside, the scenery, even the sky.

'My home is on Porquerolles . . . it will take me a week just to reach the Saône.'

This time it was the turn of the magistrate to offer a respectful nod.

They did not shake hands, though they almost did. The colonel looked around him, appeared not to see either the doctor, who seemed bored, or Maigret, who avoided his eye, but he did acknowledge the deputy prosecutor.

The next moment he was walking the short distance between the Café de la Marine and the *Southern Cross*.

He made no attempt to go inside the cabin. Vladimir was on the bridge. He gave him his orders and took the wheel.

Then, to the amazement of the canal men and the bargees, they saw the Russian in the striped jersey disappear into the engine room, start the motor and then, from the deck, with a neat flick of the wrist, yank the mooring ropes free of the bollards.

Within moments, a small, gesticulating group began moving off towards the main road, where their cars were waiting. It was the public prosecutor's team.

Maigret was left standing on the canal bank. He had finally managed to fill his pipe and now thrust both hands into his pockets with a gesture that was distinctly proletarian, even more proletarian than usual, and muttered:

'Well, that's that!'

It was back to square one!

The investigation of the prosecutor's office had come up with only a few points. It was too early to tell if they were significant.

First: the body of Willy Marco, in addition to the marks of strangulation, also had bruises to the wrists and torso. The police surgeon ruled out an ambush but thought that a struggle with an exceptionally strong attacker was more likely.

Second: Sir Walter had stated that he had met his wife in Nice, where, although she had divorced her Italian husband, she was still using her married name of Ceccaldi.

The colonel's account had not been clear. His wilfully ambiguous statement let it be supposed that Marie Dupin, or Ceccaldi, was at that time virtually destitute and living on the generosity of a few friends, though without ever actually selling her body.

He had married her during a trip to London, and it was then that she had obtained from France a copy of her birth certificate in the name of Marie Dupin.

'She was a most enchanting woman.'

In his mind's eye Maigret saw the colonel's fleshy, dignified, ruddy face as he said these words, without affectation and with a sober simplicity which had seemed to impress the magistrate favourably.

He stepped back to allow the stretcher carrying Willy's body to pass.

Suddenly he shrugged his shoulders and went into the café, sat down heavily on a bench and called:

'Bring me a beer!'

★   ★   ★

It was the girl who served him. Her eyes were still red, and her nose shone. He looked up at her with interest and, before he could question her, she looked this way and that to make sure no one was listening, then murmured:

'Did he suffer much?'

She had a lumpish, unintelligent face, thick ankles and red beefy arms. Yet she was the only one who had given a second thought to the suave Willy, who perhaps had squeezed her waist as a joke the evening before — if, indeed, he had.

Maigret was reminded of the conversation he had had with the young man when he had been half stretched out on the unmade bed in his room, chain-smoking.

The girl was wanted elsewhere. One of the watermen called to her:

'Seems like you're all upset, Emma!'

She tried to smile and gave Maigret a conspiratorial look.

The canal traffic had been held up all morning. There were now seven vessels, three with engines, tied up outside the Café de la Marine. The bargees' wives came to the shop, and each one made the door bell jangle.

'When you're ready for lunch . . . ' the landlord said to Maigret.

'In a while.'

And from the doorway, he looked at the spot where the *Southern Cross* had been moored only that morning.

The previous evening, two men, two healthy men, had stepped off it. They had walked off towards the stone bridge. If the colonel was to be believed, they'd separated after an argument, and Sir Walter had gone on his way along the three kilometres of empty, dead-straight road which led to the first houses of Épernay.

No one had ever seen Willy alive again. When the colonel had returned in a cab, he had not noticed anything unusual.

No witnesses! No one had heard anything! The butcher at Dizy, who lived 600 metres from the bridge, said his dog had barked, but he hadn't investigated and could not say what time it had been.

The towpath, awash with puddles and pools,

had been used by too many men and horses for there to be any hope of finding any useful tracks.

The previous Thursday, Mary Lampson, also fit and well to all appearances, had left the *Southern Cross*, where she had been alone.

Earlier — according to Willy — she had given him a pearl necklace, the only valuable item of jewellery she owned.

After this there was no trace of her. She had not been seen alive again. Two days had gone by when no one had reported seeing her.

On Sunday evening, she lay strangled under a pile of straw in a stable at Dizy, a hundred kilometres from her point of departure, with two carters snoring just feet from her corpse.

That was all! The Épernay magistrate had ordered both bodies to be transferred to cold storage in the Forensic Institute.

The *Southern Cross* had just left, heading south, for Porquerolles, for the Petit Langoustier, which was no stranger to orgies.

Maigret, head down, walked all round the building of the Café de la Marine. He beat off a bad-tempered goose which bore down on him, its beak open and shrieking with rage.

There was no lock on the stable door, only a simple wooden latch. The hunting dog with an overfed paunch, which prowled round the yard, turned joyful circles and greeted him deliriously, as it did all visitors.

When he opened the door, the inspector was confronted by the landlord's grey horse, which was no more tethered now than on the other days, and made the most of the opportunity to go for a walk outside.

The broken-winded mare was still lying in its box, looking miserable.

Maigret moved the straw with his foot, as though hoping to find something he had missed on his first examination of the place.

Two or three times he repeated to himself crossly:

'Back to square one!'

He had more or less made up his mind to return to Meaux, even Paris, and retrace step by step the route followed by the *Southern Cross*.

There were all kinds of odds and ends lying around: old halters, bits of harness, the end of a candle, a broken pipe . . .

From a distance he noticed something white poking out of a pile of hay. He went over not expecting anything much. The next moment he was holding an American sailor's forage cap just like the one worn by Vladimir.

The material was spattered with mud and horse droppings and misshapen as though it had been stretched in all directions.

Maigret searched all around but failed to come up with anything else.

Fresh straw had been put down over the spot where the body had been found to make it seem less sinister.

'*Am I under arrest?*'

As he walked towards the stable door, he could not have said why the colonel's question should suddenly surface in his memory. He also saw Sir Walter, as boorish as he was aristocratic, his eyes permanently watering, the drunkenness always just beneath the surface and his amazing composure.

He thought back to the brief talk he had had with the supercilious magistrate in the bar of the café, with its tables covered in brown oilcloth, which, through a sprinkling of polite voices and refined manners, had been magically transformed for a short time into a sophisticated drawing room.

He kept turning the cap round and round in his hands, suspicious, with a calculating look in his eye.

'Tread carefully,' Monsieur de Clairfontaine de Lagny had told him as he took Maigret's hand lightly.

The goose, still furious, followed the horse, screeching abuse at it.

The horse, letting its large head hang down, snuffled among the rubbish littering the yard.

On each side of the door was an old milestone. The inspector sat down on one of them, still holding the cap and his pipe, which had gone out.

Directly ahead of him was a large dung heap, then a hedge with occasional gaps in it, and beyond were fields in which nothing was yet growing and hills streaked with black and white on which a cloud with a dark centre seemed to have rested its full weight.

From behind one edge of it sprang an oblique shaft of sunlight which created sparkles of light on the dung heap.

'*An enchanting woman,*' the colonel had said of Mary Lampson.

'*Nothing if not a gentleman!*' Willy had said of the colonel.

Only Vladimir had said nothing. He had just kept busy, buying supplies, petrol, filling up the tanks of drinking water, baling out the dinghy and helping his employer to dress.

A group of Flemings passed along the road, talking in loud voices. Suddenly, Maigret bent down. The yard was paved with irregular flagstones. Two metres in front of him, in the crack between two of them, something had just been caught by the sun and glinted.

It was a cufflink, gold with a platinum hatching. Maigret had seen a pair just like it the day before, on Willy's wrists, when he was lying on his bed blowing cigarette smoke at the ceiling and talking so unconcernedly.

He took no more interest in the horse or the goose or any of his surroundings. Moments later, he was turning the handle that cranked the phone.

'Épernay . . . Yes, the mortuary! . . . This is the police!'

One of the Flemings was just coming out of the café. He stopped and stared at the inspector, who was extraordinarily agitated.

'Hello? . . . Inspector Maigret here, Police Judiciaire . . . You've just had a body brought in . . . No, not the car accident, this is about the man drowned at Dizy . . . That's right . . . Find the custody officer . . . Go through his effects, you'll find a cufflink . . . I want you to describe it to me . . . Yes, I'll hang on.'

Three minutes later, he replaced the receiver.

He had the information. He was still holding the forage cap and the cufflink.

'Your lunch is ready.'

He didn't bother to answer the girl with red hair, though she had spoken as politely as she could. He went out feeling that perhaps he was now holding one end of the thread but also fearing he would drop it.

'The cap in the stables . . . The cufflink in the yard . . . And the YCF badge near the stone bridge . . . '

It was that way he now started walking, very fast. Ideas formed and faded in turns in his mind.

He had not gone a kilometre when he was astonished by what he saw dead ahead.

The *Southern Cross*, which had set off in a great haste a good hour before, was now moored on the right-hand side of the bridge, among the reeds. He couldn't see anyone on board.

But when the inspector was less than a hundred metres short of it, a car coming from the direction of Épernay pulled up on the opposite bank. It stopped near the yacht. Vladimir, still wearing sailor's clothes, was sitting next to the driver. He got out and ran to the boat. Before he reached it, the hatch opened, and the colonel came out on deck, holding his hand out to someone inside.

Maigret made no attempt to hide. He couldn't tell whether the colonel had seen him or not.

Then things happened fast. The inspector could not hear what was said, but the way the people were behaving gave him a clear enough

241

idea of what was happening.

It was Madame Negretti who was being handed out of the cabin by Sir Walter. Maigret noted that this was the first time he had seen her wearing town clothes. Even from a distance it was obvious that she was very angry.

Vladimir picked up the two suitcases which stood ready and carried them to the car.

The colonel held out one hand to help her negotiate the gangplank, but she refused it and stepped forward so suddenly that she almost fell head first into the reeds.

She walked on without waiting for him. He followed several paces behind, showing no reaction. She jumped into the car still in the same furious temper, thrust her head angrily out of the window and shouted something which must have been either an insult or a threat.

However, just as the car was setting off, Sir Walter bowed courteously, watched her drive off and then went back to his boat with Vladimir.

Maigret had not moved. He had a very strong feeling that a change had come over the Englishman.

He did not smile. He remained his usual imperturbable self. But, for example, just as he reached the wheelhouse in the middle of saying something, he put one friendly, even affectionate, hand on Vladimir's shoulder.

Their cast-off was brilliantly executed. There were just the two men on board now. The Russian pulled in the gangplank and with one smooth action yanked the mooring ring free.

The prow of the *Southern Cross* was fast in

the reeds. A barge coming up astern hooted.

Lampson turned round. There was no way now he could not have seen Maigret but he gave no sign of it. With one hand, he let in the clutch. With the other, he gave the brass wheel two full turns, and the yacht reversed just far enough to free herself, avoided the bow of the barge, stopped just in time and then moved forward, leaving a wake of churning foam.

It had not gone a hundred metres when it sounded its hooter three times to let the lock at Ay know that its arrival was imminent.

* * *

'Don't waste time . . . Just drive . . . Catch up with that car if you can.'

Maigret had flagged down a baker's van, which was heading in the direction of Épernay. About a kilometre ahead they could see the car carrying Madame Negretti. It was moving slowly: the road was wet and greasy.

When the inspector had stated his rank, the van driver had looked at him with amused curiosity.

'Hop in. It won't take me five minutes to catch them up.'

'No, not too fast.'

Then it was Maigret's turn to smile when he saw that his driver was crouching over the steering wheel just like American cops do in car chases in Hollywood crime films.

There was no need to risk life and limb, nor any kind of complication. The car stopped briefly

243

in the first street it came to, probably to allow the passenger to confer with the driver. Then it drove off again and halted three minutes later outside what clearly was a rather expensive hotel.

Maigret got out of the van a hundred metres behind it, thanked the baker, who refused a tip and, having decided he wanted to see more, parked a little nearer the hotel.

A porter carried both bags in. Gloria Negretti walked briskly across the pavement.

Ten minutes later, Maigret was talking to the manager.

'The lady who has just checked in?'

'Room 9. I thought there was something not quite right about her. I never saw anybody more on edge. She talked fast and used lots of foreign words. As far as I could tell, she didn't want to be disturbed and asked for cigarettes and a bottle of kümmel to be taken up to her room. I hope at least there's not going to be any scandal . . . ?'

'None at all!' said Maigret. 'Just some questions I need to ask her.'

He could not help smiling as he neared the door with the number 9 on it, for there was lots of noise coming from inside. The young woman's high heels clacked on the wooden floor in a haphazard way.

She was walking to and fro, up and down, in all directions. She could be heard closing a window, tipping out a suitcase, running a tap, throwing herself on to the bed, getting up and kicking off a shoe to the other end of the room.

Maigret knocked.

'Come in!'

Her voice was shaking with anger and impatience. Madame Negretti had not been there ten minutes and yet she had found time to change her clothes, to muss up her hair and, in a word, to revert to the way she had looked on board the *Southern Cross*, but to an even messier degree.

When she saw who it was, a flash of rage appeared in her brown eyes.

'What do you want with me? What are you doing here? This is my room! I'm paying for it and . . . '

She continued in a foreign language, probably Spanish, unscrewed the top off a bottle of eau de Cologne and poured most of the contents over her hands before dabbing her fevered brow with it.

'May I ask you a question?'

'I told them I didn't want to see anybody. Get out! Do you hear?'

She was walking around in her silk stockings. She was most likely not wearing garters, for they began to slide down her legs. One had already uncovered a podgy, very white knee.

'Why don't you go and put your questions to people who can give you the answers? But you don't dare, do you? Because he's a colonel. Because he's *Sir* Walter! Don't you just love the *Sir*! Ha ha! If I told you only half of what I know . . .

'Look at this!'

She rummaged feverishly in her handbag and produced five crumpled 1,000-franc notes.

'This is what he just gave me! For what? For two years, for the two years that I've been living with him! That . . . '

She threw the notes on the carpet then, changing her mind, picked them up again and put them back in her bag.

'Of course, he promised he'd send me a cheque. But everybody knows what his promises are worth. A cheque! He won't even have enough money to get him to Porquerolles . . . though that won't stop him getting drunk on whisky every day!'

She wasn't crying, but there were tears in her voice. There was something unnerving about the distress exhibited by this woman who, when Maigret had seen her previously, had always seemed steeped in blissful sloth, supine in a hothouse atmosphere.

'And his precious Vladimir's just the same! He tried to kiss my hand and had the cheek to say: 'It's adieu, madame, not au revoir.'

'By God, they've got a nerve . . . But when the colonel wasn't around, Vladimir . . .

'But it's none of your business! Why are you still here? What are you waiting for? Are you hoping I'm going to tell you something?'

'Not at all!'

'But you can't deny that I'd be perfectly within my rights if I did . . . '

She was still walking up and down agitatedly, taking things out of her case, putting them down somewhere then a moment later picking them up again and putting them somewhere else.

'Leaving me at Épernay! In that disgusting

hole, where it never stops raining! I begged him at least to take me to Nice, where I have friends. It was on his account that I left them.

'Still, I should be glad they didn't kill me.

'I won't talk! Got that? Why don't you clear off! Policemen make me sick! As sick as the English! If you're man enough, why don't you go and arrest him?

'But you wouldn't dare! I know all about how these things work . . .

'Poor Mary! She'll be called all sorts now. Of course, she had her bad side and she'd have done anything for Willy. Me, I couldn't stand him.

'But to finish up dead like that . . .

'Have they gone? . . . So who are you going to arrest, then? Maybe me?

'Well, you just listen. I'll tell you something. Just one thing and you can make of it whatever you like. This morning, when he was getting dressed to appear before that magistrate — because he's forever trying to impress people and flashing his badges and medals — when he was dressing, Walter told Vladimir, in Russian, because he thinks I don't understand Russian . . .'

She was now speaking so quickly that she ran out of breath, stumbled over her words and reverted to throwing in snatches of Spanish.

'He told him to try and find out where the *Providence* was. Are you with me? It's the barge that was tied up near us at Meaux.

'They want to catch up with it and they're afraid of me.

'I pretended I hadn't understood.

'But I know you'd never ever dare to . . . '

She stared at her disembowelled suitcases and then around the room, which in only a few minutes she had succeeded in turning into a mess and filling with her acrid perfume.

'I don't suppose you've got any cigarettes? What sort of hotel is this? I told them to bring some, and a bottle of kümmel.'

'When you were in Meaux, did you ever see the colonel talking to anybody from the *Providence*?'

'I never saw a thing. I never paid attention to any of that . . . All I heard was what he said this morning. Why otherwise would they be worrying about a barge? Does anybody know how Walter's first wife died in India? The second one divorced him, so she must have had her reasons.'

A waiter knocked at the door with the cigarettes and a bottle. Madame Negretti reached for the packet and then hurled it into the corridor yelling:

'I asked for Abdullahs!'

'But madame . . . '

She clasped her hands together in a gesture which seemed like the prelude to an imminent fit of hysterics and shrieked:

'Ah! . . . Of all the stupid . . . Ah!'

She turned to face Maigret, who was looking at her with interest, and screamed at him:

'What are you still doing here? I'm not saying any more! I don't know anything! I haven't said anything! Got that? I don't want to be bothered any more with this business! . . . It's bad enough knowing that I've wasted two years of my life in . . . '

As the waiter left, he gave the inspector a knowing wink. And while the young woman, now a bundle of frayed nerves, was throwing herself on to the bed, he too took his leave.

The baker was still parked in the street outside.

'Well? Didn't you arrest her?' he asked in a disappointed voice. 'I thought . . . '

Maigret had to walk all the way to the station before he could find a taxi to take him back to the stone bridge.

7

The Bent Pedal

When the inspector overtook the *Southern Cross*, whose wash left the reeds swaying long after it had passed, the colonel was still at the wheel, and Vladimir, in the bow, was coiling a rope.

Maigret waited for the yacht at Aigny lock. The boat entered it smoothly, and, when it was made fast, the Russian got off to take his papers to the lock-keeper and give him his tip.

The inspector approached him and said: 'This cap belongs to you, doesn't it?'

Vladimir examined the cap, which was now dirty and ragged, then looked up at him.

'Thank you,' he said after a moment and took the cap.

'Just a moment! Can you tell me where you lost it?'

The colonel had been watching them carefully, without showing the least trace of emotion.

'I dropped it in the water last night,' Vladimir explained. 'I was leaning over the stern with a boat hook, clearing weeds which had fouled the propeller. There was a barge behind us. The woman was kneeling in their dinghy, doing her washing. She fished out my cap, and I left it on the deck to dry.'

'So it was left out all night on the deck.'

'Yes. This morning I didn't notice it was gone.'

'Was it already as dirty as this yesterday?'

'No! When the woman on the barge fished it out she put it in her wash with the rest.'

The yacht was rising by degrees. The lock-keeper already had both hands on the handle of the upper sluice gate.

'If I remember correctly, the boat behind you was the *Providence*, wasn't it?'

'I think so. I haven't seen it today.'

Maigret turned away with a vague wave of his hand then walked to his bicycle, while the colonel, as inscrutable as ever, engaged the motor and nodded to him as he passed through the lock.

The inspector remained where he was for a while, watching the yacht leave, thinking, puzzled by the astonishing ease and speed with which things happened on board the *Southern Cross*.

The yacht went on its way without paying any attention to him. The most that happened was that the colonel, from the wheel, asked the Russian the occasional question. The Russian returned short answers.

'Has the *Providence* got very far?' asked Maigret.

'She's maybe in the reach above Juvigny, five kilometres from here. She don't go as fast as that beauty there.'

Maigret reached there a few minutes before the *Southern Cross*, and from a distance Vladimir must have seen him talking to the bargee's wife.

The details she gave were clear. The day before, while doing her washing, which she then hung out on a line stretched across the barge, where it could be seen ballooning in the wind, she had indeed rescued the Russian's cap. Later, the man had given her little boy two francs.

It was now four in the afternoon. The inspector got back on his bike, his head filled with a jumble of speculations. The gravel of the towpath crunched under the tyres. His wheels parted the grit into furrows.

When he got to Lock 9, Maigret had a good lead over the Englishman.

'Can you tell me where the *Providence* is at this moment?'

'Not far off Vitry-le-François . . . They're making good time. They've got a good pair of horses and especially a carter who is no slouch.'

'Did they look as if they were in a hurry?'

'No more or less than usual. Oh, everybody's always in a hurry on the canal. You never know what might happen next. You can be held up for hours at a lock or go through in ten minutes. And the faster you travel the more money you earn.'

'Did you hear anything unusual last night?'

'No, nothing. Why? What happened?'

Maigret left without answering and from now on stopped at every lock, every boat.

He'd had no trouble making his mind up about Gloria Negretti. Though she'd done her level best to avoid saying anything damaging about the colonel, she had told everything she knew.

252

She was incapable of holding back! And equally incapable of lying! Otherwise, she would have made up a much more complicated tale.

So she really had heard Sir Walter ask Vladimir to find out about the *Providence*.

The inspector had also started to take an interest in the barge which had come from Meaux on Sunday evening, just before Mary Lampson was murdered. It was wood-built and treated with pitch and tar. Why did the colonel want to catch up with it? What was the connection between the *Southern Cross* and the heavy barge which could not go faster than the slow pace set by two horses?

As Maigret rode along the canal through monotonous countryside, pushing down harder and harder on the pedals, he came up with a number of hypotheses. But they led to conclusions which were fragmentary or implausible.

But hadn't the matter of the three clues been cleared up by Madame Negretti's furious accusations?

Maigret tried a dozen times to piece together the movements of all concerned during the previous night, about which nothing was known, except for the fact that Willy was dead.

Each time he tried, he was left with a poor fit, a gap. He had the impression that there was a person missing who was not the colonel, nor the dead man, nor Vladimir.

And now the *Southern Cross* was on the trail of someone on board the *Providence*.

Someone obviously who was mixed up in

recent events! Could it be assumed that this someone had had a hand in the second crime, that is, in the murder of Willy, as well as in the first?

A lot of ground can be covered quickly at night on a canal towpath, by a bike for example.

'Did you hear anything last night? Did you notice anything unusual on the *Providence* when it passed through?'

It was laborious, discouraging work, especially in the drizzling rain that fell out of the low clouds.

'No, nothing.'

The gap between Maigret and the *Southern Cross*, which lost a minimum of twenty minutes at each lock, grew wider. The inspector kept getting back on his bicycle with growing weariness and, as he pedalled through a deserted reach of the canal, stubbornly picked up the threads of his reasoning.

He had already covered forty kilometres when the lock-keeper at Sarry said, in answer to his question:

'My dog barked. I think something must have happened on the road. A rabbit running past, maybe? I just went back to sleep.'

'Any idea where the *Providence* stopped last night?'

The man did a calculation in his head.

'Hang on a minute. I wouldn't be surprised if she hadn't got as far as Pogny. The skipper wanted to be at Vitry-le-François tonight.'

Another two locks. Result: nothing! Maigret now had to follow the lock-keepers on to their gates, for the further he went the busier the traffic became. At Vésigneul, three boats were waiting their turn. At Pogny, there were five.

'Noises, no,' grumbled the man in charge of the lock there. 'But I'd like to know what swine had the nerve to use my bike!'

The inspector had time to wipe the sweat from his face now that he had a glimpse of what looked like light at the end of the tunnel. He was breathing hard and was hot. He had just ridden fifty kilometres without once stopping for a beer.

'Where is your bike now?'

'Open the sluices, will you, François?' the lock-keeper shouted to a carter.

He led Maigret to his house. The outside door opened straight into the kitchen, where men from the boats were drinking white wine which was being poured by a woman who did not put her baby down.

'You're not going to report us, are you? Selling alcohol isn't allowed. But everybody does it. It's just to do people a good turn. Here we are.'

He pointed to a lean-to made of wooden boards clinging to one side of the house. It had no door.

'Here's the bike. It's the wife's. Can you imagine, the nearest grocer's is four kilometres from here? I'm always telling her to bring the bike in for the night. But she says it makes a mess in the house. But I'll say that whoever used it must be a rum sort. I would never have noticed it myself . . .

'But as a matter of fact, the day before

yesterday, my nephew, who's a mechanic at Rheims, was here for the day. The chain was broken. He mended it and at the same time cleaned the bike and oiled it.

'Yesterday no one used it. Oh, and he'd put a new tyre on the back wheel.

'Well, this morning, it was clean, though it had rained all night. And you've seen all that mud on the towpath.

'But the left pedal is bent, and the tyre looks as if it's done at least a hundred kilometres.

'What do you make of it? The bike's been a fair old way, no question. And whoever brought it back took the trouble to clean it.'

'Which boats were moored hereabouts?'

'Let me see . . . The *Madeleine* must have gone to La Chaussée, where the skipper's brother-in-law runs a bistro. The *Miséricorde* was tied up here, under the lock . . . '

'On its way from Dizy?'

'No, she's going downstream. Came from the Saône. I think there was just the *Providence*. She passed through last night around seven. Went on to Omey, two kilometres further along. There's good mooring there.'

'Do you have another bike?'

'No. But this one is still rideable.'

'No it isn't. You're going to have to lock it up somewhere. Hire another one if you need to. Can I count on you?'

The barge men were coming out of the kitchen. One of them called to the lock-keeper.

'Deserting your mates, Désiré?'

'Half a tick, I'm with this gentleman.'

'Where do you think I can catch up with the *Providence*?'

'Lemme see. She'll still be making pretty good time. I'd be surprised if you'd be up with her before Vitry.'

Maigret was about to leave. But he turned, came back, took a spanner from his tool bag and removed both pedals from the lock-keeper's wife's bicycle.

As he set off, the pedals he had pushed into his pockets made two unsightly bulges in his jacket.

The lock-keeper at Dizy had said to him jokingly:

'When it's dry everywhere else, there are at least two places where you can be sure of seeing rain: here and Vitry-le-François.'

Maigret was now getting near Vitry, and it was starting to rain again, a fine, lazy, never-ending drizzle.

The look of the canal was now changing. Factories appeared on both banks, and the inspector rode for some time through a swarm of mill girls emerging from one of them.

There were boats almost everywhere, some being unloaded, while others, which were lying up having their bilges emptied, were waiting.

And here again were the small houses which marked the outskirts of a town, with rabbit hutches made from old packing-cases and pitiful gardens.

Every kilometre there was a cement works or a quarry or a lime kiln. The rain mixed the white powder drifting in the air into the mud of the towpath. The cement dust left a film on everything, on the tiled roofs, the apple trees and the grass.

Maigret had started to weave right to left and left to right the way tired cyclists do. He was thinking thoughts, but not joined-up thoughts. He was putting ideas together in such ways that they could not be linked to make a solid picture.

When he at last saw the lock at Vitry-le-François, the growing dusk was flecked with the white navigation lights of a string of maybe sixty boats lined up in Indian file.

Some were overtaking others, some were hove to broadside on. When barges came from the opposite direction, the crew members exchanged shouts, curses and snippets of news as they passed.

'Ahoy, there, *Simoun*! Your sister-in-law, who was at Chalon-sur-Saône, says she'll catch up with you on the Burgundy canal . . . They'll hold back the christening . . . Pierre says all the best!'

By the lock gates a dozen figures were moving about busily.

And above it all hung a bluish, rain-filled mist, and through it could be seen the shapes of horses which had halted and men going from one boat to another.

Maigret read the names on the sterns of the boats. One voice called to him:

'Hello, inspector!'

It was a moment or two before he recognized the master of the *Éco-III*.

'Got your problem sorted?'

'It was something and nothing! My mate's a

dimwit. The mechanic, who came all the way from Rheims, fixed it in five minutes.'

'You haven't seen the *Providence*, have you?'

'She's up ahead. But we'll be through before her. On account of the logjam, they'll be putting boats through the lock all tonight and maybe tomorrow night as well. Fact is there are at least sixty boats here, and more keep coming. As a rule, boats with engines have right of way and go before horse-boats. But this time, the powers that be have decided to let horse barges and motorized boats take turns.'

A friendly kind of man, with an open face, he pointed with one arm.

'There you go! Just opposite that crane. I recognize its white tiller.'

As he rode past the line of barges, he could make out people through open hatches eating by the yellow light of oil-lamps.

Maigret found the master of the *Providence* on the lock-side, arguing with other watermen.

'No way should there be special rules for boats with engines! Take the *Marie*, for example. We can gain a kilometre on her in a five-kilometre stretch. But what happens? With this priority system of theirs, she'll go through before us . . . Well, look who's here . . . it's the inspector!'

And the small man held out his hand, as if greeting a friend.

'Back with us again? The wife's on board. She'll be glad to see you. She said that, for a policeman, you're all right.'

In the dark, the ends of cigarettes glowed red, and the lights on the boats seemed so densely packed together that it was a mystery how they could move at all.

Maigret found the skipper's fat wife straining her soup. She wiped her hand on her apron before she held it out to him.

'Have you found the murderer?'

'Unfortunately no. But I came to ask a few more questions.'

'Sit down. Fancy a drop of something?'

'No thanks.'

'Go on, say yes! Look, in weather like this it can't do any harm. Don't tell me you've come from Dizy on a bike?'

'All the way from Dizy.'

'But it's sixty-eight kilometres!'

'Is your carter here?'

'He's most likely out on the lock, arguing. They want to take our turn. We can't let them push us around, not now. We've lost enough time already.'

'Does he own a bike?'

'Who, Jean? No!'

She laughed and, resuming her work, she explained: 'I can't see him getting on a bike, not with those little legs! My husband's got one. But he hasn't ridden a bike for over a year. Anyway I think the tyres have got punctures.'

'You spent last night at Omey?'

'That's right! We always try to stay in a place where I can buy my groceries. Because if, worse luck, you have to make a stop during the day, there are always boats that will pass you and get ahead.'

'What time did you get there?'

'Around this time of day. We go more by the sun than by clock time, if you follow me. Another little drop? It's gin. We bring some back from Belgium every trip.'

'Did you go to the shop?'

'Yes, while the men went for a drink. It must have been about eight when we went to bed.'

'Was Jean in the stable?'

'Where else would he have been? He's only happy when he's with his horses.'

'Did you hear any noises during the night?'

'Not a thing. At three, as usual, Jean came and made the coffee. It's our routine. Then we set off.'

'Did you notice anything unusual?'

'What sort of thing do you mean? Don't tell me you suspect poor old Jean? I know he can seem a bit, well, funny, when you don't know him. But he's been with us now for eight years, and I tell you, if he went, the *Providence* wouldn't be the same!'

'Does your husband sleep with you?'

She laughed again. And since Maigret was within range, she gave him a sharp dig in the ribs.

'Get away! Do we look as old as that?'

'Could I have a look inside the stable?'

'If you want. Take the lantern. It's on deck. The horses are still out because we're still hoping to go through tonight. Once we get to Vitry, we'll be fine. Most boats go down the Marne canal to the Rhine. It's a lot quieter on the run to the Saône — except for the culvert, which is eight kilometres long and always scares me stiff.'

261

Maigret made his way by himself towards the middle of the barge, where the stable loomed. Taking the storm lantern, which did service as a navigation light, he slipped quietly into Jean's private domain, which was full of a strong smell of horse manure and leather.

But his search was fruitless, though he squelched around in it for a quarter of an hour, during which time he could hear every word of what the skipper of the *Providence* was discussing on the wharf-side with the other men from the barges.

When a little while later he walked to the lock, where, to make up lost time, all hands were working together amid the screech of rusty crank-handles turning and the roar of roiling water, he spotted the carter at one of the gates, his horse whip coiled round his neck like a necklace, operating a sluice.

He was dressed as he had been at Dizy, in an old suit of ribbed corduroy and a faded slouch hat which had lost its band an age ago. A barge was emerging from the lock chamber, propelled by means of boat hooks because there was no other way of moving forward through the tangle of boats. The voices that called from one barge to another were rough and irritable, and the faces, lit at intervals by a navigation light, were deeply marked by fatigue.

All these people had been on the go since three or four in the morning and now had only one thought: a meal followed by a bed on to which they would at last be able to drop.

But they all wanted to be first through the

congested lock so that they would be in the right place to start the next day's haul. The lock-keeper was everywhere, snatching up documents here and there as he passed through the crowd, dashing back to his office to sign and stamp them, and stuffing his tips into his pocket.

'Excuse me!'

Maigret had tapped the carter on the arm. The man turned slowly, stared with eyes that were hardly visible under his thicket of eyebrows.

'Have you got any other boots than the ones you've got on?'

Jean didn't seem to understand the words. His face wrinkled up even more. He stared at his feet in bewilderment.

Eventually he shook his head, removed his pipe from his mouth and muttered:

'Other boots?'

'Have you just got those, the ones you're wearing now?'

A yes, nodded very slowly.

'Can you ride a bike?'

A crowd started to gather, intrigued by their conversation.

'Come with me!' said Maigret. 'I want a word.'

The carter followed him back to the *Providence*, which was moored 200 metres away. As he walked past his horses, which stood, heads hanging, rumps glistening, he patted the nearest one on the neck.

'Come on board.'

The skipper, small and puny, bent double over a boat hook driven into the bottom of the canal, was pushing the vessel closer to the bank to allow a barge going downstream to pass.

He saw the two men step into the stable but had no time to wonder what was happening.

'Did you sleep here last night?'

A grunt that meant yes.

'All night? You didn't borrow a bike from the lock-keeper at Pogny, did you?'

The carter had the unhappy, cowering look of a simpleton who is being tormented or a dog which has always been well treated and then brutally thrashed for no good reason.

He raised one hand and pushed his hat back, scratching his head through his white mop, which grew as coarse as horse hair.

'Take off your boots.'

The man did not budge but looked out at the bank, where the legs of his horses were visible. One of them whinnied, as if it knew the carter was in some sort of trouble.

'Boots! And quick about it!'

And joining the action to the word, Maigret made Jean sit down on the plank which ran along the whole length of one wall of the stable.

Only then did the old man become amenable. Giving his tormentor a look of reproach, he set about removing one of his boots.

He was not wearing socks. Instead, strips of canvas steeped in tallow grease were wound round his feet and ankles, seeming to merge with his flesh.

The lantern shed only a dim light. The skipper, who had completed his manoeuvre, came forward and squatted on the deck so that he could see what was going on inside the stable.

While Jean, grumbling, scowling and bad-tempered, lifted his other leg, Maigret was using a handful of straw to clean the sole of the boot he held in his hand.

He took the left pedal from his pocket and held it against the boot.

A bemused old man staring at his bare feet made a strange sight. His trousers, which either had been made for a man even shorter than he was or had been altered, stopped not quite halfway down his calf.

And the strips of canvas greasy with tallow were blackish and pock-marked with wisps of straw and dirty sweepings.

Maigret stood close to the lantern and held the pedal, from which some of the metal teeth were missing, against faint marks on the leather.

'Last night, at Pogny, you took the lock-keeper's bike,' he said, making the accusation slowly, without taking his eyes off the two objects in his hands. 'How far did you ride?'

'Ahoy! *Providence!* . . . Move up! . . . The *Étourneau* is giving up its turn and will be spending the night here, in the lower reach.'

Jean turned and looked at the men who were now rushing about outside and then at the inspector.

'You can go and help get the boat through the lock,' said Maigret. 'Here! Put your boots on.'

The skipper was already pushing on his boat hook. His wife appeared:

'Jean! The horses! If we miss out turn . . . '

The carter had thrust his feet into his boots,

was now on deck and was crooning in a strange voice:

'Hey! . . . Hey! . . . Hey up!'

The horses snorted and began moving forward. He jumped on to the bank, fell into step with them, treading heavily, his whip still wound round his shoulders.

'Hey! . . . Hey up!'

While her husband was heaving on the boat hook, the bargee's wife leaned on the tiller with all her weight to avoid colliding with a barge which was bearing down on them from the opposite direction, all that was visible of it being its rounded bows and the halo around its stern light.

The voice of the lock-keeper was heard shouting impatiently:

'Come on! . . . Where's the *Providence?* . . . What are you waiting for?'

The barge slid silently over the black water. But it bumped the lock wall three times before squeezing into the chamber and completely filling its width.

8

Ward 10

Normally, the four sluices of any lock are opened one after the other, gradually, to avoid creating a surge strong enough to break the boat's mooring ropes.

But sixty barges were waiting. Masters and mates whose turn was coming up helped with the operation, leaving the lock-keeper free to take care of the paper-work.

Maigret was on the side of the lock, holding his bicycle in one hand, watching the shadowy figures as they worked feverishly in the darkness. The two horses had continued on then stopped fifty metres further along from the upper gates, all by themselves. Jean was turning one of the crank handles.

The water rushed in, roaring like a torrent. It was visible, a foaming white presence, in the narrow gaps left vacant by the *Madeleine*.

But just as the cascading water was running most strongly, there was a muffled cry followed by a thud on the bow of the barge, which was followed by an unexplained commotion.

The inspector sensed rather than understood what was happening. The carter was no longer at his post, by the gate. Men were running along the walls. They were all shouting at the same time.

To light the scene there were only two lamps, one in the middle of the lift-bridge at the front of the lock and one on the barge, which was now rising rapidly in the chamber.

'Close the sluices!'

'Open the gates!'

Someone passed across an enormous boat hook, which caught Maigret a solid blow on the cheek.

Men from even distant boats came running. The lock-keeper came out of his house, shaking at the thought of his responsibilities.

'What's happened?'

'The old man . . . '

On each side of the barge, between its hull and the wall, there was less than a foot of clear water. This water, which came in torrents through the sluices, rushed down into those narrow channels then turned back on itself in a boiling mass.

Mistakes were made: for instance, when someone closed one sluice of the upper gate, which protested noisily and threatened to come off its hinges until the lock-keeper arrived to correct the error.

Only later was the inspector told that the whole lower stretch of canal could have been flooded and fifty barges damaged.

'Can you see him?'

'There's something dark. Down there!'

The barge was still rising, but more slowly now. Three sluices out of four had been closed. But the boat kept swinging, rubbing against the walls of the chamber and maybe crushing the carter.

'How deep is the water?'

'There's at least a metre under the boat.'

It was a horrible sight. In the faint light from the stable lamp, the bargee's wife could be seen running in all directions, holding a lifebuoy.

Visibly distressed, she was shouting:

'I don't think he can swim!'

Maigret heard a sober voice close by him say:

'Just as well! He won't have suffered as much . . .'

★　★　★

This went on for a quarter of an hour. Three times people thought they saw a body rising in the water. But boat hooks were directed to those places in the water, with no result.

The *Madeleine* moved slowly out of the lock, and one old carter muttered:

'I'll bet whatever you fancy that he's got caught under the tiller! I seen it happen once before, at Verdun.'

He was wrong. The barge had hardly come to a stop not fifty metres away before the men who were feeling all round the lower gates with a long pole shouted for help.

In the end, they had to use a dinghy. They could feel something in the water, about a metre down. And just as one man was about to dive in, while his tearful wife tried to stop him, a body suddenly burst on to the surface.

It was hauled out. A dozen hands grabbed for the badly torn corduroy jacket, which had been snagged on one of the gate's projecting bolts.

The rest unfolded like a nightmare. The telephone was heard ringing in the lock-keeper's house. A boy was despatched on a bicycle to fetch a doctor.

But it was no good. The body of the old carter was scarcely laid on the bank, motionless and seemingly lifeless, before a barge hand removed his jacket, knelt over the impressive chest of the drowned man and began applying traction to his tongue.

Someone had brought the lantern. The man's body seemed shorter, more thick-set than ever, and his face, dripping wet and streaked with sludge, had lost all colour.

'He moved! I tell you, he moved!'

There was no pushing or jostling. The silence was so intense that every word resounded as voices do in a cathedral. And underscoring it was the never-ending gush of water escaping through a badly closed sluice.

'How's he doing?' asked the lock-keeper as he returned.

'He moved. But not much.'

'Best get a mirror.'

The master of the *Madeleine* hurried away to get one from his boat. Sweat was pouring off the man applying artificial respiration, so someone else took over, and pulled even harder on the waterlogged man's tongue.

There was news that the doctor had arrived. He had come by car along a side road. By then, everyone could see old Jean's chest slowly rising and falling.

His jacket had been removed. His open shirt

revealed a chest as hairy as a wild animal's. Under the right nipple was a long scar, and Maigret thought he could make out a kind of tattoo on his shoulder.

'Next boat!' shouted the lock-keeper, cupping both hands to his mouth. 'Look lively, there's nothing more you can do here.'

One bargee drifted regretfully away, calling to his wife, who had joined some other women a little further off in their commiserations.

'I hope at least that you didn't stop the engine?'

The doctor told the spectators to stand well back and scowled as he felt the man's chest.

'He's alive, isn't he?' said the first life-saver proudly.

'Police Judiciaire!' broke in Maigret. 'Is it serious?'

'Most of his ribs are crushed. He's alive all right, but I'd be surprised if he stays alive for very long! Did he get caught between two boats?'

'Most probably between a boat and the lock.'

'Feel here!'

The doctor made the inspector feel the left arm, which was broken in two places.

'Is there a stretcher?'

The injured man moaned feebly.

'All the same, I'm going to give him an injection. But get that stretcher ready as quick as you can. The hospital is 500 metres away . . . '

There was a stretcher at the lock. It was regulations. But it was in the attic, where the flame of a candle was observed through a skylight moving to and fro.

The mistress of the *Providence* stood sobbing some distance from Maigret. She was staring at him reproachfully.

There were ten men ready to carry the carter, who gave another groan. Then a lantern moved off in the direction of the main road, catching the group in a halo of light. A motorized barge, bright with green and red navigation lights, gave three whistles and moved off on its way to tie up at a berth in the middle of town, so that she would be the first to leave next morning.

★　★　★

Ward 10. It was by chance that Maigret saw the number. There were only two patients in it, one of whom was crying like a baby.

The inspector spent most of the time walking up and down the white-flagged corridor, where nurses ran by him, passing on instruction in hushed voices.

Ward 8, exactly opposite, was full of women who were talking about the new patient and assessing his chances.

'If they're putting him in Ward 10 . . . '

The doctor was plump and wore horn-rimmed glasses. He walked by two or three times in a white coat, without speaking to Maigret.

It was almost eleven when he finally stopped to have a word.

'Do you want to see him?'

It was a disconcerting sight. The inspector hardly recognized old Jean. He had been shaved so that two gashes, one on his cheek and the other on his forehead, could be treated.

He lay there, looking very clean in a white bed in the neutral glare of a frosted-glass lamp.

The doctor lifted the sheet.

'Take a look at this for a carcass! He's built like a bear. I don't think I ever saw a skeletal frame like it. How did he get in this state?'

'He fell off the lock gate just as the sluices were being opened.'

'I see. He must have been caught between the wall and the barge. His chest is literally crushed in. The ribs just gave way.'

'And the rest?'

'My colleagues and I will examine him tomorrow, if he's still alive. We'll have to go carefully. One wrong move would kill him.'

'Has he regained consciousness?'

'No idea. That's perhaps the most surprising thing. A while back, as I was examining his cuts, I had the very clear impression that his eyes were half open and that he was watching me. But when I looked straight at him, he lowered his eyelids . . . He hasn't been delirious. All he does is groan from time to time.'

'His arm?'

'Not serious. The double fracture has already been reduced. But you can't put a whole chest back together the way you can a humerus. Where's he from?'

'I don't know.'

'I ask because he has some very strange tattoos. I've seen African Battalion tattoos, but they aren't like those. I'll show you tomorrow

273

after they've removed the strapping so we can examine him.'

A porter came to say that there were visitors outside who were insisting on seeing the patient. Maigret himself went down to the porter's lodge, where he found the skipper and his wife from the *Providence*. They were in their Sunday best.

'We can see him, can't we, inspector? It's all your fault, you know. You upset him with all your questions. Is he better?'

'He's better. The doctors will tell us more tomorrow.'

'Let me see him. Just a peep round the door. He was such a part of the boat.'

She didn't say 'of the family' but 'of the boat', and was that not perhaps even more touching?

Her husband brought up the rear, keeping out of the way, ill at ease in a blue serge suit, his scrawny neck poking out of a detachable celluloid collar.

'I advise you not to make any noise.'

They both looked in at him, from the corridor. From there all they could see was a vague shape under a sheet, an ivory oval instead of a face, a lock of white hair.

The skipper's wife looked as if she was about to burst in at any moment.

'Listen, if we offered to pay, would he get better treatment?'

She didn't dare open her handbag there and then but she kept fidgeting with it.

'There are hospitals, aren't there, where if you pay? . . . The other patients haven't got anything catching, I hope?'

'Are you staying at Vitry?'

'We're not going home without him that's for sure! Blow the cargo! What time can we come tomorrow morning?'

'Ten o'clock!' broke in the doctor, who had been listening impatiently.

'Is there anything we can bring for him? A bottle of champagne? Spanish grapes?'

'We'll see he gets everything he needs.'

The doctor directed them towards the porter's lodge. When she got there, the skipper's wife, who had a good heart, reached furtively into her handbag and pulled out a ten-franc note and slipped it into the hand of the porter, who looked at her in astonishment.

Maigret got to bed at midnight, after telegraphing Dizy with instructions to forward whatever communications might be sent to him there.

At the last moment, he'd learned that the *Southern Cross*, by overtaking most of the barges, had reached Vitry-le-François and was moored at the end of the queue of waiting boats.

The inspector had found a room at the Hotel de la Marne in town. It was a fair way from the canal. There he was free of the atmosphere he had lived in for the last few days.

A number of guests, all commercial travellers, sat playing cards.

One of them, who had arrived after the others, said:

'Seems like someone got drowned in the lock.'

'Want to make a fourth? Lamperrière's losing hand over fist. The man's dead, is he?'

'Don't know.'

And that was all. The landlady dozed by the till. The waiter scattered sawdust on the floor and, last thing, banked up the stove for the night.

There was a bathroom, just one. The bath had lost areas of its enamel. Even so, next morning at eight, Maigret used it, and then sent the waiter out to buy him a new shirt and collar.

But as the time wore on, he grew impatient. He was anxious to get back to the canal. Hearing a boat hooting, he asked:

'Was that for the lock?'

'No, the lift-bridge. There are three in town.'

The sky was overcast. The wind had got up. He could not find the way back to the hospital and had to ask several people, because all roads invariably led him back to the market square.

The hospital porter recognized him. As he walked out to meet him, he said:

'Who'd have believed it? I ask you!'

'What? Is he alive? Dead?'

'What? You haven't heard? The super's just phoned your hotel . . . '

'Out with it!'

'Gone! Flown the coop! The doctor reckons it's not possible, says he can't have gone a hundred metres in the state he was in . . . Maybe, but the fact is he's not here!'

The inspector heard voices coming from the garden at the rear of the building and hurried off towards the sound.

There he found an old man he had never seen before. It was the hospital superintendent, and he was speaking sternly to the doctor from the previous evening and a nurse with ginger hair.

'I swear! . . . ' the doctor said several times. 'You know as well as I do what it's like . . . When I say ten broken ribs that's very likely an underestimate . . . And that's leaving aside the effects of submersion, concussion . . . '

'How did he get out?' asked Maigret.

He was shown a window almost two metres above ground level. In the soil underneath it were the prints of two bare feet and a large scuff mark which suggested that the carter had fallen flat on the ground as he landed.

'There! The nurse, Mademoiselle Berthe, spent all night on the duty desk, as usual. She didn't hear anything. Around three o'clock she had to attend to a patient in Ward 8 and looked in on Ward 10. All the lights were out. It was all quiet. She can't say whether the man was still in his bed.'

'How about the other two patients?'

'There's one who's got to be trepanned. It's urgent. We're waiting now for the surgeon. The other one slept through.'

Maigret's eyes followed the trail, which led to a flower-bed where a small rose bush had been flattened.

'Do the front gates stay open at night?'

'This isn't a prison!' snapped the superintendent. 'How are we supposed to know if a patient is going to jump out of the window? Only the main door to the building was locked, as it always is.'

There was no point in looking for footprints or any other tracks. For the area was paved. In the gap between two houses, the double row of trees lining the canal was visible.

'To be perfectly frank,' added the doctor, 'I was pretty sure we'd find him dead this morning. Once it was clear there was nothing more we could try . . . that's when I decided to put him in Ward 10.'

He was belligerent now, for the criticisms the superintendent had directed at him still rankled.

For a while, Maigret circled the garden, like a circus horse, then suddenly, signalling his departure by tugging the brim of his bowler, he strode away in the direction of the lock.

The *Southern Cross* was just entering the chamber. Vladimir, with the skill of an experienced sailor, looped a mooring rope over a bollard with one throw and stopped the boat dead.

Meanwhile, the colonel, wearing a long oilskin coat and his white cap, stood impassively at the small wheel.

'Ready the gates!' cried the lock-keeper.

There were now no more than twenty boats to be got through.

Maigret pointed to the yacht and asked: 'Is it their turn?'

'It is and it isn't. If you class her as a motorboat, then she has right of way over horse-drawn boats. But as she's a pleasure boat . . . Truth is, so few of them pass this way that we don't go much by the regulations. Still, since they saw the bargees right . . . '

The bargees in question were now operating the sluices.

'And the *Providence*?'

'She was holding everything up. This morning she went and moored a hundred metres further along, at the bend this side of the second bridge. Any news of the old feller? This business could set me back a pretty penny. But I'd like to see you try it! Officially, I'm supposed to lock them all myself. If I did that, there'd be a hundred of them queuing up every day. Four gates! Sixteen sluices! And do you know how much I get paid?'

He was called away briefly when Vladimir came to him with his papers and the tip.

Maigret made the most of the interruption to set off along the canal bank. At the bend he saw the *Providence*, which by now he could have picked out from any distance among a hundred barges.

A few curls of smoke rose from the chimney. There was no one about on deck. All hatches and doors were closed.

He almost walked up the aft plank which gave access to the crew's quarters.

But he changed his mind and instead went on board by the wide gangway which was used for taking the horses on and off.

One of the wooden panels over the stable had been slid open. The head of one of the horses showed above it, sniffing the wind.

Maigret looked down through it and made out a dark shape lying on straw. And close by, the skipper's wife was crouching with a bowl of coffee in one hand.

Her manner was motherly and oddly gentle. She murmured:

'Come on, Jean! Drink it up while it's hot. It'll do you good, silly old fool! Want me to raise your head up?'

But the man lying by her side did not move. He was looking up at the sky.

And against the sky Maigret's head stood out. The man must have seen him.

The inspector had the impression that on that face latticed with strips of sticking plaster there lurked a contented, ironic, even pugnacious smile.

The old carter tried to raise one hand to push away the cup which the woman was holding close to his lips. But it fell back again weakly, gnarled, calloused, spotted with small blue dots which must have been the vestiges of old tattoos.

9

The Doctor

'See? He's come back to his burrow. Dragged himself, like an injured dog.'

Did the skipper's wife realize how seriously ill the man was?

Either way, she did not seem to be unduly concerned. She was as calm as if she were caring for a child with 'flu.

'Coffee won't do him any harm, will it? But he won't take anything. It must have been four in the morning when me and my husband were woken up by a lot of noise on board . . . I got the revolver and told him to follow me with the lantern.

'Believe it or not, it was Jean, more or less the way he is now . . . He must have fallen down in here from the deck . . . It's almost two metres.

'At first, we couldn't see very well. For a moment, I thought he was dead.

'My husband wanted to call the neighbours, to help us carry him and lie him down on a bed. But Jean twigged. He started gripping my hand, and did he squeeze! It was like he was hanging on to me for dear life!

'And I saw he was starting to, well, whimper.

'I knew what he was saying. Because he's been with us for eight years, you know. He can't speak. But I think he understands what I say to him. Isn't that right, Jean? Does it hurt?'

It was difficult to know whether the injured man's eyes were bright with intelligence or fever.

She removed a wisp of straw which was touching the man's ear.

'My life, you know, is my home, my pots and pans, my sticks of furniture. I think that if they gave me a palace to live in, I'd be as miserable as sin living in it.

'Jean's life is his stable . . . and his horses! Of course, there's always days, you know, when we don't move because we're unloading. Jean don't have any part in that. So he could go off to some bar.

'But no! He comes back and lies down, just here. He makes sure that the sun can get in . . . '

In his mind, Maigret imagined himself stretched out where the carter was lying, saw the pitch-covered wall on his right, the whip hanging from one twisted nail, the tin cup on another, a patch of sky through the hatch overhead and, to the right, the well-muscled hindquarters of the horses.

The whole place exuded animal warmth, a dense, many-layered vitality which caught the throat like the sharp-tasting wines produced by certain slopes.

'Will it be all right to leave him here, do you think?'

She motioned the inspector to join her outside. The lock was working at the same rate as the evening before. All around were the streets of the town, which were filled with a bustle that was alien to the canal.

'He's going to die, though, isn't he? What's he done? You can tell me. I couldn't say anything before, could I? For a start I don't know anything. Once, just once, my husband saw him with his shirt off when he wasn't looking. He saw the tattoos. They weren't like the ones some sailors have done. We thought the same thing as you would have . . .

'I think it made me even fonder of him for it. I told myself he couldn't be what he seemed, that he was on the run . . .

'I wouldn't have asked him about it for all the money in the world. You surely don't think it was him that killed that woman? If you do, listen: if he did do it, I'd say she asked for it!

'Jean is . . . '

She searched for the word that expressed her thought. It did not come.

'Right! I can hear my husband getting up. I packed him off back to bed. He's always had a weak chest. Do you think that if I made him some strong broth . . . '

'The doctors will be on their way. Meanwhile, maybe it would be best to . . . '

'Do they really have to come? They'll hurt him and spoil his last moments, which . . . '

'It cannot be avoided.'

'But he's so comfortable here with us! Can I leave you here for a minute? You won't bother him again, will you?'

Maigret gave a reassuring nod of his head, went back inside the stable and from his pocket took a small tin. It contained a pad impregnated with viscous black ink.

He still could not tell if the carter was fully conscious. His eyes were half open. The look in them was blank, calm.

But when the inspector lifted his right hand and pressed each finger one after the other against the pad, he had a split-second impression that the shadow of a smile flickered over his face.

He took the fingerprints on a sheet of paper, watched the dying man for a moment, as though he were expecting something to happen, looked one last time at the wooden walls and the rumps of the horses which were growing restive and impatient, then went outside.

Near the tiller, the bargee and his wife were drinking their morning *café au lait* fortified with dunked bread. They were looking his way. The *Southern Cross* was moored less than five metres from the *Providence*. There was no one on deck.

The previous evening, Maigret had left his bicycle at the lock. It was still there. Ten minutes later he was at the police station. He despatched an officer on a motorcycle to Épernay with instructions to transmit the fingerprints to Paris by belinograph.

When he was back on board the *Providence*, he had with him two doctors from the hospital with whom he had a difference of opinion.

The medics wanted their patient back. The skipper's wife was alarmed and looked pleadingly at Maigret.

'Do you think you can pull him through?'

'No. His chest has been crushed. One rib has pierced his right lung.'

'How long will he live for?'

'Most people would be dead already! An hour, maybe five . . . '

'Then let him be!'

The old man had not moved, had not even winced. As Maigret passed in front of the wife of the skipper, she touched his hand, shyly, her way of showing her gratitude.

The doctors walked down the gangplank, looking very unhappy.

'Leaving him to die in a stable!' grumbled one.

'Yes, but they also let him live in one . . . '

Even so, the inspector posted a uniformed officer near the barge and the yacht, with orders to inform him if anything happened.

From the lock he phoned the Café de la Marine at Dizy, where he was told that Inspector Lucas had just passed through and that he had hired a car at Épernay to drive him to Vitry-le-François.

Then there was a good hour when nothing happened. The master of the *Providence* used the time to apply a coat of tar to the dinghy he towed behind the barge. Vladimir polished the brasses on the *Southern Cross*.

Meanwhile the skipper's wife was constantly on deck, toing and froing between the galley and the stable. Once, she was observed carrying a dazzlingly white pillow. Another time it was a bowl of steaming liquid, doubtless the broth which she had insisted on making.

Around eleven, Lucas arrived at the Hotel de la Marne, where Maigret was waiting for him.

'How's things, Lucas?'

'Good. You look tired, sir.'

'What did you find out?'

'Not a lot. At Meaux, I learned nothing except that the yacht caused a bit of a rumpus. The barge men couldn't sleep for all the music and singing and they were talking of smashing the yacht up.'

'Was the *Providence* there?'

'It loaded not twenty metres from the *Southern Cross*. But nobody noticed anything unusual.'

'And in Paris?'

'I saw the two girls again. They admitted it wasn't Mary Lampson who gave them the necklace but Willy Marco. I had it confirmed in the hotel, where they recognized his photo, but no one had seen Mary Lampson. I'm not sure but I think Lia Lauwenstein was closer to Willy than she's letting on and that she'd already been helping him in Nice.'

'And Moulins?'

'Not a thing. I went to see the baker's wife. She really is the only Marie Dupin in the whole area. A nice woman, straight as a die. She doesn't understand what's been happening and is worried that this business is not going to do her any good. The copy of the birth certificate was issued eight years ago. There's been a new clerk in the registry for the last three years, and the previous one died last year. They trawled through the archives but didn't come up with anything involving this particular document.'

After a silence, Lucas asked:

'How about you?'

'I don't know yet. Maybe nothing, maybe the

jackpot. It could go one way or the other at any time. What are they saying at Dizy?'

'They reckon that if the *Southern Cross* hadn't been a yacht it wouldn't have been allowed to leave. There's also talk that the colonel has been married before.'

Saying nothing, Maigret led Lucas through the streets of the small town to the telegraph office.

'Give me Criminal Records in Paris.'

The belinogram with the carter's fingerprints should have reached the Prefecture two hours ago. After that, it was a matter of luck. Among 80,000 other sets, a match might be found straightaway, or it might take many hours.

'Listen with the earpiece, Lucas . . . Hello? . . . Who is this? . . . Is that you, Benoît? . . . Maigret here . . . Did you get the telephotograph I sent? . . . What's that? . . . You did the search yourself? . . . Just a moment.'

He left the call-booth and went up to the Post Office counter.

'I may need to stay on the line for quite some time. So please make absolutely sure I'm not cut off.'

When he picked up the receiver again, there was a gleam in his eye.

'Sit down, Benoît. You're going to give me everything in the files. Lucas is standing here next to me. He'll take notes. Go ahead . . . '

In his mind's eye, he could see his informant as clearly as if he had been standing next to him, for he was familiar with the offices located high in the attics of the Palais de Justice, where metal cabinets hold files on all the convicted felons in

287

France and a good number of foreign-born gangsters.

'First, what's his name?'

'Jean-Évariste Darchambaux, born Boulogne, now aged fifty-five.'

Automatically Maigret tried to recall a case featuring the name, but already Benoît, pronouncing every syllable distinctly, had resumed, and Lucas was busy scribbling.

'Doctor of medicine. Married a Céline Mornet, at Étampes. Moved to Toulouse, where he'd been a student. Then he moved around a lot . . . Still there, inspector?'

'Still here. Carry on . . . '

'I've got the complete file, for the record card doesn't say much . . . The couple are soon up to their eyes in debt. Two years after he married, at twenty-seven, Darchambaux is accused of poisoning his aunt, Julia Darchambaux, who had come to live with them in Toulouse and disapproved of the kind of life he led. The aunt was pretty well off. The Darchambaux were her sole heirs.

'Inquiries lasted eight months, for no formal proof of guilt was ever found. Or at least the accused claimed — and some experts agreed with him — that the drugs prescribed for the old woman were not themselves harmful and that their use was an ambitious if extreme form of treatment.

'There was a lot of controversy . . . You don't want me to read out the reports, do you?

'The trial was stormy, and the judge had to clear the court several times. Most people thought he should be acquitted, especially after the doctor's wife had given evidence. She stood up and swore that her husband was innocent and that if he was sent to a penal settlement in the colonies, she would follow him there.'

'Was he found guilty?'

'Sentenced to fifteen years' hard labour . . . Now, don't hang up! That's everything in our files. But I sent an officer on a bike round to the Ministry of the Interior . . . He's just got back.'

He could be heard speaking to someone standing behind him, and then there was a sound of papers being shuffled.

'Here we are! But it doesn't amount to much. The governor of Saint-Laurent-du-Maroni in French Guiana wanted to give Darchambaux a job in one of the hospitals in the colony . . . He turned it down . . . good record . . . 'docile' prisoner . . . just one attempt to escape with fifteen others who had talked him into it.

'Five years later, a new governor undertook what he called the 'rehabilitation' of Darchambaux. But almost immediately he noted in the margin of his report that there was nothing about the man he had interviewed to connect him with the professional man he once had been nor even to a man with a certain level of education.

'Right! Has that got your attention?

'He was given a job as an orderly at Saint-Laurent but he applied to be sent back to the colony.

'He was quiet, stubborn and spoke little. One of the medical staff took an interest in his case.

He examined him from a mental health point of view but was unable to come up with a diagnosis.

' 'There is,' he wrote, underlining the words in red ink, 'a kind of progressive loss of intellectual function proceeding in parallel with a hypertrophy of physical capacity.'

'Darchambaux stole twice. Both times he stole food. On the second occasion he stole from another prisoner on the chain gang, who stabbed him in the chest with a sharpened flint.

'Journalists passing through advised him to apply for a pardon, but he never did,

'When his fifteen years were up, he stayed in the place to which he had been transported and found a manual job in a saw mill, where he looked after the horses.

'He was forty-five and had done his time. Thereafter, there is no trace of him.'

'Is that everything?'

'I can send you the file. I've only given you a summary.'

'Anything on his wife? You said she was born at Étampes, didn't you? Anyway, thanks for all that, Benoît. No need to send the details. What you've told me is enough.'

When, followed by Lucas, he stepped out of the phone box, he was perspiring profusely.

'I want you to phone the town hall at Étampes. If Céline Mornet is dead, you'll know, or at least you will if she died under that name. Also check with Moulins if Marie Dupin had any family living at Étampes.'

He walked through the town, looking neither

to left nor right, hands deep in his pockets. He had to wait for five minutes at the canal because the lift-bridge was up, and a heavily laden barge was barely moving, its flat hull scouring the mud on the canal bed which rose to the surface in a mass of bubbles.

When he reached the *Providence*, he had a word with the uniformed man he had posted on the towpath.

'You can stand down . . . '

He saw the colonel pacing up and down on the deck of his yacht.

The skipper's wife hurried towards him looking more agitated than she had been earlier that morning. There were damp streaks on her cheeks.

'Oh, inspector, it's terrible!'

Maigret went pale, and his face turned grim.

'Is he dead?' he asked.

'No! Don't say such things! Just now I was with him, by myself. Because I should explain that though he liked my husband, he liked me better.

'I'm a lot younger than him. But despite that, he thought of me sort of as a mother.

'We'd go weeks without speaking. All the same . . . I'll give you an example. Most of the time my husband forgets my birthday, Saint Hortense's Day. Well, for the last eight years, Jean never went once without giving me flowers. Sometimes, we'd be travelling through the middle of open fields, and I'd wonder where he'd managed to get hold of flowers there.

'And on those days he'd always put rosettes on

the horses' blinkers.

'Anyhow, I was sat by him, thinking it was probably his last hours. My husband wanted to let the horses out. They're not used to being cooped up for so long.

'I said no. Because I was sure it meant a lot to Jean to have them there too.

'I held his big hand.'

She was weeping now. But not sobbing. She went on talking through the large tears which rolled down her mottled cheeks.

'I don't know how things came to be like that . . . I never had children myself. Though we'd always said we'd adopt when we reached the legal age.

'I told him it was nothing, that he'd get better, that we'd try to get a load for Alsace, where the countryside's a picture in summer.

'I felt his fingers squeezing mine. I couldn't tell him he was hurting me.

'It was then he started to talk.

'Can you understand it? A man like that who only yesterday was as strong as his horses. He opened his mouth, straining so much that the veins on the sides of his head went all purple and swelled up.

'I heard this growly sound, like an animal's cry it was.

'I told him to stay quiet. But he wouldn't listen. He sat up on the straw, how I'll never know. And he still kept opening his mouth.

'Blood came out of it and dribbled down his chin.

'I wanted to call my husband, but Jean was

still holding me tight. He was frightening me.

'You can't imagine what it was like. I tried to understand. I asked: 'You want something to drink? No? Want me to fetch somebody?'

'He was so frustrated that he couldn't say anything! I should have guessed what he meant. I did try.

'What do you reckon? What was he trying to ask me? And then it was as if something in his throat had burst, though it's no good asking me what. But he had a haemorrhage. In the end he lay down again, his mouth closed now, and on his broken arm too. It must have hurt like the very devil, but you wouldn't have thought he could feel anything.

'He just stared straight in front of him.

'I'd give anything to know what would make him happy before . . . before it's too late.'

Maigret walked to the stable in silence. He looked in through the open panel.

It was a sight as arresting, as unforgiving as watching the death of an animal with which there is no means of communicating.

The carter had curled up. He had partly torn away the strapping which the night doctor had placed around his torso.

Maigret could hear the faint, infrequent whispers of his breathing.

One of the horses had caught a hoof in its tether, but it stood absolutely still, as if it sensed that something grave was happening.

Maigret also hesitated. He thought of the dead woman buried under the straw of the stable at Dizy, then of Willy's corpse floating in the canal and the men, in the cold of early morning, trying to haul him in with a boat hook.

One hand played with the Yacht Club de France badge in his pocket.

He also recalled the way the colonel had bowed to the examining magistrate and requested permission to go on his way in a toneless, cool voice.

In the mortuary at Épernay, in an icy room lined with metal drawers, like the vaults of a bank, two bodies lay waiting, each in a numbered box.

And in Paris, two young women with badly applied make-up wandered from bar to bar, dogged by their gnawing fears.

Then Lucas appeared.

'Well?' cried Maigret, when he was still some way off.

'There has been no sign of life from Céline Mornet at Étampes since the day she requested the papers she needed for her marriage to Darchambaux.'

The inspector gave Lucas an odd look.

'What's up?' said Lucas.

'Sh!'

Lucas looked all round him. He saw no one, nothing that might give cause for alarm.

Then Maigret led him to the open stable hatch and pointed to the prone figure on the straw.

The skipper's wife wondered what they were going to do. From a motorized vessel chugging past, a cheerful voice shouted:

'Everything all right? Broken down?'

She started crying again, though she couldn't

have said why. Her husband clambered back on board, carrying the tar bucket in one hand and a brush in the other, and called from the stern:

'There's something burning on the stove!'

She went back to the galley in a daze. Maigret said to Lucas, almost reluctantly:

'Let's go in.'

One of the horses snickered quietly. The carter did not move.

The inspector had taken the photo of the dead woman from his wallet, but he did not look at it.

10

The Two Husbands

'Listen, Darchambaux.'

Maigret was standing over the carter of the *Providence* when he spoke the words, his eyes never leaving the man's face. His mind elsewhere, he had taken his pipe out of his pocket but made no attempt to fill it.

Had he got the reaction he had expected? Whether it was or not, he sat down heavily on the bench fixed to the stable wall, leaned forward, cupped his chin in both hands and went on in a different voice.

'Listen. No need to get upset. I know you can't talk.'

A shadow appearing unexpectedly on the straw made him look up. He saw the colonel standing on the deck of the barge, by the open hatch.

The Englishman did not move. He went on watching what was happening from above, his feet higher than the heads of all three men below.

Lucas stood to one side in so far as he could, given the restricted size of the stable. Maigret, more on edge now, went on:

'Nobody's going to take you away from here. Have you got that, Darchambaux? In a few moments, I shall leave. Madame Hortense will be here instead.'

It was a painful moment, though no one could have said exactly why. Without intending to, Maigret was speaking almost as gently as the skipper's wife.

'But first you have to answer a few questions. You can answer by blinking. Several people might be charged and arrested at any time now. That's not what you want, is it? So I need you to confirm the facts.'

While he spoke, the inspector did not take his eyes off the man, wondering who it was he had before him, the erstwhile doctor, the dour convict, the slow-witted carter or the brutal murderer of Mary Lampson.

The cast of face was rough, and the features coarse. But wasn't there a new expression in those eyes which excluded any hint of irony?

A look of infinite sadness.

Twice Jean tried to speak. And twice there was a sound like an animal moan and beads of pink saliva appeared on the dying man's lips.

Maigret could still see the shadow of the colonel's legs.

'When you were sent out to the penal settlement, all that time ago, you believed your wife would keep her promise and follow you there . . . It was her you killed at Dizy!'

Not a flicker! Nothing! The face acquired a greyish tinge.

'She didn't come . . . and you lost heart. You tried to forget everything, even who and what you were!'

Maigret was speaking more quickly now, driven by his impatience. He wanted it to be

297

over. And above all he was afraid of seeing Jean slip away from him before this sickening interview was finished.

'You came across her by chance. By then you had become someone else. It happened at Meaux. Didn't it?'

He had to wait a good few moments before the carter, unresisting now, said yes by closing his eyes.

The shadow of the legs shifted. The whole barge rocked gently as a motor vessel passed by.

'And she hadn't changed, had she? Pretty, a flirt, liked a good time! They were dancing on the deck of the yacht. At first you didn't think about killing her. Otherwise, you wouldn't have needed to move her to Dizy.'

Was it certain the dying man could still hear? Since he was lying on his back, he must surely be able to see the colonel just above his head? But there was no expression in his eyes. Or at least nothing anyone could make sense of.

'She had sworn she would follow you anywhere. You'd seen the inside of a penal settlement. You were living in a stable. And then you suddenly had the idea of taking her back, just as she was, with her jewels, her painted face and her pale-coloured dress, and making her share your straw mattress. That's how it was, Darchambaux, wasn't it?'

His eyes did not blink. But his chest heaved. There was another moan. In his corner, Lucas, who was finding it unbearable, changed position.

'That's it! I can feel it!' said Maigret, the words now coming faster, as if he was being rushed along by them. Face to face with the woman who had been his wife, Jean the carter, who had virtually forgotten Doctor Darchambaux, had begun to remember, and mists of the past rose to meet him. And a strange plan had started to take shape. Was it vengeance? Not really. More an obscure desire to bring down to his level the woman who had promised to be his for the rest of their lives.

'So Mary Lampson lived for three days, hidden on this horse-boat, almost of her own free will.

'Because she was afraid. Afraid of this spectre from her past, who she felt was capable of anything, who told her she had to go with him!

'And even more scared because she was aware of how badly she had behaved.

'So she came of her own volition. And you, Jean, you brought her corned beef and cheap red wine. You went to her two nights in a row, after two interminable days of driving the boat along the Marne.

'When you got to Dizy . . . '

Again the dying man tried to stir. But his strength was gone, and he fell back, limp, drained.

' . . . she must have rebelled. She could not endure that kind of life any more. In a moment of madness, you strangled her rather than allow her to let you down a second time. You dumped her body in the stable. Is that what happened?'

He had to repeat the question five times until finally the eyelids flickered.

'Yes,' they said with indifference.

There was a faint scuffle on deck. It was the colonel holding back the skipper's wife, who was trying to get closer. She did not resist, for she was cowed by his solemn manner.

'So it was back to the towpath, back again to your life on the canal. But you were worried. You were scared. For you were afraid of dying, Jean. Afraid of being transported again. Afraid of being sent back to the colonies. Afraid, unbearably afraid of having to leave your horses, the stable, the straw, the one small corner which had become your entire universe. So one night, you took the lock-keeper's bike. I asked you about it. You guessed I had my suspicions.

'You rode back to Dizy intending to do something, anything, that would put me off the scent.

'Is that right?'

Jean was now so absolutely still that he might well have been dead. The expression on his face was a complete blank. But his eyelids closed once again.

'When you got there, there were no lights on the *Southern Cross*. You could safely assume that everyone on board was asleep. On deck an American cap was drying. You took it. You went into the stable, to hide it under the straw. It was the best way of changing the whole course of the investigation and switching the focus to the people on the yacht.

'You weren't to know that Willy Marco was outside, alone. He saw you take the cap and followed you. He was waiting for you by the stable door, where he lost a cufflink.

300

'He was curious. So he followed you when you started back to the stone bridge, where you had left the bike.

'Did he say something? Or did you hear a noise behind you?

'There was a fight. You killed him with those strong hands, the same hands that strangled Mary Lampson. You dragged the body to the canal . . .

'Then you must have walked on, head down. On the towpath, you saw something shining, the YCF badge. You thought that since the badge belonged to someone you'd seen around, maybe you'd noticed it on the colonel's lapel, you left it at the spot where the fight had taken place. Answer me, Darchambaux. That was how it happened, wasn't it?'

'Ahoy, *Providence*! Got a problem?' called another barge captain, whose boat passed so close that his head could be seen gliding past level with the hatch.

But then something strange and troubling happened. Jean's eyes filled with tears. Then he blinked, very fast, as though he was confessing to everything, to get it over and done with once and for all. He heard the skipper's wife answering from the stern, where she was waiting:

'It's Jean! He's hurt himself!'

As Maigret got to his feet, he said:

'Last night, when I examined your boots, you knew that I would sooner or later get to the truth. You tried to kill yourself by jumping into the lock.'

But the carter was now so far gone and his

breathing so laborious that the inspector did not even wait for a response. He nodded to Lucas and cast one last look around him.

A diagonal shaft of sunlight entered the stable, striking the carter's left ear and the hoof of one of the horses.

Just as the two men were leaving, not finding anything else to say, Jean tried again to speak, urgently, disregarding the pain. Wild-eyed, he half sat up on his straw.

Maigret paid no attention to the colonel, not immediately. He crooked one finger and beckoned the woman, who was watching him from the stern.

'Well? How is he?' she asked.

'Stay by him.'

'Can I? And no one will come and . . . '

She did not dare finish. She had gone rigid when she heard the muffled cries uttered by Jean, who seemed frightened that he would be left to die alone.

Suddenly, she ran to the stable.

★ ★ ★

Vladimir sat on the yacht's capstan, a cigarette between his lips, wearing his white cap slantwise, splicing two rope ends.

A policeman in uniform was standing on the canal bank. From the barge Maigret called:

'What is it?'

'We've had the reply from Moulins.'

He handed over an envelope with a brief note which said:

Marie Dupin, wife of the baker, has confirmed that she had a distant cousin at Étampes named Céline Mornet.

Maigret stared hard at the colonel, sizing him up. He was wearing his white yachting cap with the large crest. His eyes were just starting to acquire the faintest blue-green tinge, which doubtless meant that he had consumed a relatively small quantity of whisky.

'You had suspicions about the *Providence?*' Maigret asked him point blank.

It was so obvious! Wouldn't Maigret also have concentrated on the barge if his suspicions had not been diverted momentarily to the people on the yacht?

'Why didn't you say anything?'

The reply was well up to the standard of Sir Walter's interview with the examining magistrate at Dizy.

'Because I wanted to take care of the matter myself.'

It was more than enough to express the contempt the colonel felt for the police.

'And my wife?' he added almost immediately.

'As you said yourself, and as Willy Marco also said, she was a charming lady.'

Maigret spoke without irony. But in fact he was more interested in the sounds coming from the stable than in this conversation.

Just audible was the faint murmur of a single voice. It belonged to the skipper's wife, who sounded as if she were comforting a sick child.

'When she married Darchambaux, she already

had a taste for the finer things of life. It seems very likely that it was on her account that the struggling doctor he then was did away with his aunt. I'm not saying she aided and abetted him. I'm saying that he did it for her. And she knew it, which explains why she stood up in court and swore that she would follow him and be with him.

'A charming lady. Though that's not the same thing as saying she was a heroine.

'She loved life too much. I'm sure you can understand that, colonel.'

The mixture of sun, wind and threatening clouds suggested a shower could break out at any moment. The light was shifting constantly.

'Not many people return from those penal settlements. She was pretty. All of life's pleasures were hers for the taking. There was only her name to hold her back. So when she got to the Côte d'Azur and met someone, her first admirer, who was ready to marry her, she got the idea of sending to Moulins for the birth certificate of a distant cousin she remembered.

'It's so easy to do! So easy that there's talk now of taking the fingerprints of newborn babies and adding them to the official registers of births.

'She got a divorce and then became your wife.

'A charming lady. No real harm in her, I'm sure. But she liked a good time, didn't she? She was in love with youth and love and the good things in life.

'And maybe sometimes the embers would be fanned and she'd feel the unaccountable need to go off and cut loose . . .

'Know what I think? I believe she went off with Jean not so much because of his threats but because she needed to be forgiven.

'The first day, hiding in the stable on board this boat, among the horsey smells, she must have derived some sort of satisfaction from the thought that she was atoning.

'It was the same thing as the time she vowed to the jury she would follow her husband to Guiana.

'Such charming creatures! Their first impulses are generous, if theatrical. They are so full of good intentions.

'It's just that life, with its betrayals, compromises and its overriding demands, is stronger.'

Maigret had spoken rather bitterly but had not stopped listening for sounds coming from the stable while simultaneously keeping a constant eye on the movement of boats entering and leaving the lock.

The colonel had been standing in front of him with his head bowed. When he looked up now it was with obviously warmer sentiments, even a touch of muted affection.

'Do you want a drink?' he said and pointed to his yacht.

Lucas had been standing slightly to one side.

'You'll keep me informed?' said the inspector, turning to him.

Between them, there was no need for explanations. Lucas had understood and began to prowl silently round the stable.

The *Southern Cross* was as ship-shape as if

nothing had happened. There was not a speck of dust on the mahogany walls of the cabin.

In the middle of the table was a bottle of whisky, a siphon and glasses.

'Stay outside, Vladimir!'

Maigret looked round him with new eyes. He was not there now pursuing some fine sliver of truth. He was more relaxed, less curt.

And the colonel treated him as he had treated Monsieur Clairfontaine de Lagny.

'He's going to die, isn't he?'

'He could go at any time. He's known since yesterday.'

The sparkling soda water spurted from the siphon. Sir Walter said sombrely:

'Your good health!'

Maigret drank as greedily as his host.

'Why did he run away from the hospital?'

The rhythm of their conversation had slowed. Before answering, the inspector looked round him carefully, taking in every detail of the cabin.

'Because . . . '

As he felt for his words his host was already refilling their glasses.

' . . . a man with no ties, a man who has severed all links with his past, with the kind of man he used to be . . . a man like that has to have something to cling to! He had his stable . . . the smell of it . . . the horses . . . the coffee he drank scalding hot at three in the morning ahead of a day spent slogging along the towpath until it was evening . . . It was his burrow, if you like, his very own corner, a place filled with animal warmth.'

Maigret looked the colonel in the eye. He saw him turn his head away. Reaching for his glass he added:

'There are all kinds of bolt-holes. Some have the smell of whisky, eau de Cologne, a woman and the sounds of gramophone records . . . '

He stopped and drank. When he looked up again, his host had had time to empty a third glass.

Sir Walter watched him with his large, bleary eyes and held out the bottle.

'No thanks,' protested Maigret.

'Yes for me! I need it.'

Was there not a hint of affection in the look he gave the inspector?

'My wife . . . Willy . . . '

At that moment, a thought sharp as an arrow struck the inspector. Was not Sir Walter as alone, just as lost, as Jean, who was busy dying in his stable?

And at least the carter had his horses by him and his motherly Madame Hortense.

'Drink up! That's right! I'd like to ask . . . You're a gentleman . . . '

He spoke almost pleadingly. He held out his bottle rather shamefacedly. Vladimir could be heard moving about up on deck.

Maigret held out his glass. But there was a knock at the door. Through it came Lucas's voice:

'Inspector?'

And through the crack in the door he added: 'It's over.'

The colonel did not move. He watched grimly

as the two policemen walked away.

When Maigret turned round, he saw him drink the glass he had just filled for his guest in one swallow. Then he heard him sing out:

'Vladimir!'

A number of people had gathered by the *Providence* because from the bank they had heard the sound of sobbing.

It was Hortense Canelle, the wife of the master, on her knees by Jean's side. She was talking to him even though he had been dead for several minutes.

Her husband was on deck, waiting for the inspector to come. He hurried towards him with little skipping steps, thin as a wraith, visibly flustered, and said in a desperate voice:

'What shall I do? He's dead! My wife . . . '

An image which Maigret would never forget: the stable, seen from above, the two horses almost filling it, a body curled up with half its head buried in straw. And the fair hair of the skipper's wife catching all the sun's rays while she gently moaned and at intervals repeated:

'Oh Jean! Poor Jean!'

Exactly as if Jean had been a child and not this granite-hard old man, with a carcass like a gorilla, who had cheated all the doctors!

11

Right of Way

No one noticed, except Maigret.

Two hours after Jean died, while the body was being stretchered to a waiting vehicle, the colonel, his eyes bloodshot but as dignified as ever, asked:

'Do you think now they can issue the burial permit?'

'You'll get it tomorrow.'

Five minutes later, Vladimir, with his customary neat movements, cast off.

Two boats making towards Dizy were waiting to descend through the Vitry lock.

The first was already being poled towards the chamber when the yacht skimmed past it, skirted its rounded bow, and slipped ahead of it into the open lock.

There were shouts of protest. The skipper yelled to the lock-keeper, telling him it was his turn, that he'd be making a complaint and much more of the same.

But the colonel, wearing his white cap and officer's uniform, did not even turn round.

He was standing at the brass wheel, expressionless, looking dead ahead.

When the lock gates were closed, Vladimir jumped on to the lock-side, showed his papers and offered the traditional tip.

'For God's sake!' grumbled a carter. 'These yachts get away with anything. All it takes is ten francs at every lock . . . '

The stretch of canal below the Vitry-le-François lock was congested. It hardly seemed possible that anything could pole a way through all the boats waiting for their turn.

But the gates had barely opened when the water started churning around the propeller, and the colonel, with a perfunctory movement of his hand, let in the clutch.

The *Southern Cross* got up to full speed in a twinkling and flitted past the heavily laden barges despite the shouts and protests but did not so much as graze any of them.

Two minutes later, it vanished round the bend, and Maigret turned to Lucas, who was walking at his side:

'They're both dead drunk.'

No one had guessed. The colonel was a respectable gentleman with a large gold insignia on the front of his cap.

Vladimir, in his striped jersey, with his forage cap perched on his head, had not made one clumsy movement.

But if Sir Walter's apoplectic neck showed reddish-purple, his face was sickly pale, there were large bags under his eyes and his lips had no colour.

The smallest jolt would have knocked the Russian off balance, for he was asleep standing up.

On board the *Providence* everything was shut up, silent. Both horses were tethered to a tree a hundred metres from the barge.

The skipper and his wife had gone into town, to buy clothes for the funeral.

We do hope that you have enjoyed reading
this large print book.

Did you know that all of our titles
are available for purchase?

We publish a wide range of high quality
large print books including:
**Romances, Mysteries, Classics
General Fiction
Non Fiction and Westerns**

Special interest titles available in
large print are:
**The Little Oxford Dictionary
Music Book
Song Book
Hymn Book
Service Book**

Also available from us courtesy of
Oxford University Press:
**Young Readers' Dictionary
(large print edition)
Young Readers' Thesaurus
(large print edition)**

For further information or a free
brochure, please contact us at:
**Ulverscroft Large Print Books Ltd.,
The Green, Bradgate Road, Anstey,
Leicester, LE7 7FU, England.
Tel:** (00 44) 0116 236 4325
Fax: (00 44) 0116 234 0205

Other titles published by Ulverscroft:

CRIME IN HOLLAND & THE GRAND BANKS CAFE,

Georges Simenon

When a French professor visiting the Dutch town of Delfzijl is accused of murder, Detective Chief Inspector Maigret is sent to investigate. The community seem happy to blame an unknown outsider, but there are culprits closer to home, including the dissatisfied daughter of a local farmer, the sister-in-law of the deceased, and a notorious crook. And in *The Grand Banks Cafe*, Maigret investigates the murder of a captain soon after his ship returns from three months of fishing off the Newfoundland coast. The ship's wireless operator has been arrested for the murder — but the sailors all blame the Evil Eye . . .

THE YELLOW DOG & NIGHT AT THE CROSSROADS

Georges Simenon

In the windswept seaside town of Concarneau, a local wine dealer is shot. Someone is out to kill all the influential men, and the town is soon sent into a panic. For Inspector Maigret, the answers lie with the downtrodden waitress Emma, and a strange yellow dog lurking in the shadows . . . And in *Night At The Crossroads*, Maigret has been interrogating Carl Andersen for hours without a confession. Why was the body of a diamond merchant found at his mansion? Why is his sister always shut in her room? And why does everyone at Three Widows Crossroads have something to hide?

PIETR THE LATVIAN & THE LATE MONSIEUR GALLET

Georges Simenon

Who is Pietr the Latvian? Is he a gentleman thief? A Russian drinking absinthe in a grimy bar? A married Norwegian sea captain? A twisted corpse in a train bathroom? Or is he all of these men? Inspector Jules Maigret tracks a mysterious adversary along a trail of bodies . . . The circumstances surrounding a murdered man's death all seem fake: the name the deceased was travelling under, his presumed profession — and, more worryingly, his family's reaction. Maigret must tease out the strands of truth from the tangle before him in order to construct an accurate portrait of the late Monsieur Gallet . . .